SLAM

CHINA

AS RED TERROR APPROACHES

WAYNE T HAALAND

SLAM
CHINA

AS RED TERROR APPROACHES

WAYNE T. HAALAND

508 West 26th Street KEARNEY, NE 68848
402-819-3224
info@medialiteraryexcellence.com

CONTENTS

Chapter 1
Chapter 2
Chapter 3
Chapter 4
Chapter 5
Chapter 6
Chapter 7
Chapter 8
Chapter 9
Chapter 10
Chapter 11
Chapter 12
Chapter 13
Chapter 14
Chapter 15
Chapter 16
Chapter 17
Chapter 18
Chapter 19
Chapter 20
Chapter 21
Chapter 22
Chapter 23
Chapter 24
Chapter 25
Chapter 26
Chapter 27
Chapter 28
Chapter 29
Chapter 30
Chapter 31
Chapter 32
Chapter 33
Chapter 34
Chapter 35
Chapter 36
Chapter 37
Chapter 38
Chapter 39
Chapter 40
Chapter 41
Chapter 42
Chapter 43
Chapter 44
Chapter 45
Chapter 46
Chapter 47
Chapter 48
Chapter 49
Chapter 50
Chapter 51
Chapter 52
Chapter 53
Chapter 54
Chapter 55
Chapter 56
Chapter 57
Chapter 58
Chapter 59
Chapter 60
Chapter 61
Chapter 62
Chapter 63
Chapter 64
Chapter 65
Chapter 66
Chapter 67
Chapter 68
Chapter 69
Chapter 70
Postscript

A JACK FLASHHARDT NOVEL

I would like to dedicate this novel to my favorite editor– my wife, Susan Nelson Haaland, who, because she was a very successful actress and model in Hollywood, and later spent decades teaching our nation's youth, is able to bring focus, drama and clarity to the obscure elements in my novel.

CHAPTER 1

Tijuana, Mexico

Mexicano Teniente Rodriegas called the phone number that had been given to him as he studied the young face of Jack FlashHardt on his computer screen. NSA Assistant Director Vance Hollin answered and Rodriegas reported, "The American deserter, Flashhardt, you requested tracking, has landed at Tijuana Airport. Do you want us to detain him?"

"If you would be so kind, I will send an escort to pick him up at your facility in Tijuana."

Rodriegas said goodbye and then ordered the American deserter to be held.

The subject of the Mexican official's careful observation, Jack Flashhardt, looked longingly at his US passport as he walked across the terminal–it was still slightly useful because it could get him across the US border from Mexico but in the end really useless for it would not get him past Border Guard facial recognition equipment that probably was already waiting for him at the US border in Imperial Beach, the southernmost city in California.

Facial recognition employed by the US Border Patrol would be watching for him because of his being branded a deserter officer from the U S Marine Corps.

He looked at his picture inside the passport critically: square Nordic face and jaw, wide set blue eyes, hairline a little low on the forehead at the ripe old age of the late twenties, but time would take care of that. He threw the passport with his innocent looking picture that was free of the scars and the hard knocks of the war in Afghanistan, back in his backpack and slid the straps over his arms as he exited the terminal. He waved at an approaching taxi but as the vehicle swerved towards the curb where Jack was waiting, a black van aggressively cut it off and skidded to a stop next to Jack. A small Hispanic man with eyes that were very close together jumped out of the vehicle, opened the side rear door and shouted, "Get in, Gringo!" He held a black semi auto pistol next to his chest, but pointed at Jack. It was obvious that he was ready to shoot, so Jack reluctantly complied and the man slammed the door shut. The driver, an overweight Hispanic with a scraggly beard and a very red complexion, was aiming

1

a pistol at Jack while the first man entered the van. There was trash and empty bottles littering the floor. Both men were wearing military style fatigues with no insignia or patches.

"What the hell is going on?" Jack exclaimed.

"You are being turned over to Autoridades Militares Estadounidenses," the driver said. "We are taking you to Immigration headquarters."

Jack slumped back and pasted a neutral expression on his face. He sized up the two men and started to develop a plan.

The driver turned his attention to the road and rapidly pulled out into the four lane street. The first man continued to cover Jack and the driver looked over his shoulder and said with a hateful tone, "Desertor Militar!" as he passed through the gate of a chain link fenced area that was opened by a man in military fatigues. The driver turned his attention to his driving and passed between two metal one story buildings.

The passenger guard relaxed and Jack struck. He grabbed the smaller man by his hair, knocked the gun out of his hand, lifted him and threw him to bash his head into the driver's head who squawked and crashed into a second building wall. Jack struck the small man's head against the other again as hard as he could and when both slumped to the van floor, Jack vaulted over the driver's body, opened the door, jumped free and ran farther into the complex of windowless metal buildings.

Past a similar one story third building about fifty feet long he hung a right and ran around the building and saw a perimeter fence. He jumped as high as he could, grabbed the chain link barrier and scrambled over the fence.

As he dropped to the ground, he ran along an alley until he reached the four lane street. He realized the first building he encountered was a large bar.

He ducked through the open doors and slowed as he walked along the bar. About halfway into the establishment he sat down on a stool and ordered a beer from the bartender who approached him.

As he tried to calm himself, he put a five dollar bill down when the Pacifico Beer arrived. He took a drink from the frosty bottle and glanced at the front and back entrances to the bar. They were empty but as he glanced back and forth, he saw faces and then he saw men approaching from both ends.

He realized they were the two men that had originally detained him. The smaller was faster and drew near. Jack threw his bottle at the man's head and charged. The man fired the pistol in his hand but the bottle struck at the same time and his shot went wide.

Jack crashed into the man, knocking him over and vaulted the collapsing body on the floor. As he ran, he knocked barstools over to delay his other pursuer. He reached the front entrance, turned right and ran down the sidewalk past two stores and dove into the third. It was a clothing store.

He halted at a rack of t-shirts and picked one up. A female clerk approached the American and said, "No, Senor, you need a larger shirt. She pulled another shirt off the end of the rack and held it up to his frame.

"I'll take it," he said. He grabbed the shirt and walked towards the cash register as he pulled it over his head and the T-shirt he was wearing. As he walked by a hat rack, he grabbed a straw sombrero. At the register, he took a pair of sunglasses off a stand and tried them on and when he saw that they fit, he put them on the counter.

The trailing clerk, a very pretty young teenage girl, asked, "Would you like to add some huaraches? Some sandals?"

"Yes, please, and then how much do I owe?" Jack asked.

She punched a few keys and said, "Vente— I mean twenty dollars. And for the sandals, nineteen dollars."

Jack paid her, then shifted his attention to the street and noticed two police cars pass by slowly. He pulled the sandals on, threw his shoes in a trash can, straightened the T shirt on his body, and then donned the straw hat and glasses. He casually strolled out of the store.

On the street again he hailed a passing taxi and told the driver to take him to his original destination before the cops had interrupted him–the La Fonda Hotel south of town. The driver grinned with delight at the long trip of about forty kilometers.

An hour later, he recognized La Fonda when he saw the two story brown stucco building and after checking into a room decorated with pictures of pretty Mexican senoritas on the walls, he changed clothes, then left the hotel room and carefully locked the door.

Jack was now wearing blue cotton shorts and a camo t-shirt which he had donned when he was getting ready for his run. He checked his watch and decided to go to the hotel bar and hydrate with a beer and then go for the run on the Baja California beach in front of the La Fonda Hotel. When he had first visited the resort years ago as a college student it was alone on the cliff, but now it was flanked by many ugly commercial buildings.

His half-brother, Billy Howling Dog, the son of Jack's father and a Sioux Indian housekeeper that his dad had hired after Jack's mother abandoned the father and son and their Montana ranch for the bright lights of Chicago, was typically late for their meeting. Billy, an ex-Marine, was driving down from LA so it was hard to predict his arrival, especially since he was still a crystal meth addict and only reliable when he was straight or if there was the threat of imminent combat.

After ordering and downing a Tres Equis Beer in the busy hotel bar, he paid his tab to a tall and extremely attractive Mexican barmaid. She had what was probably a very beautiful smile but it was hidden because she was wearing a white mask. Poised on her long blonde hair was a cute miniature Mexican straw sombrero and around her trim waist was a large hand tooled leather belt with a silver metal buckle that said OLE'!

The wide leather belt was holding up white short shorts. She looked at him with a very intent smiling gaze that unsettled him mainly because from what he could see, she was over the top gorgeous.

"Are you ready for another beer?" She asked in an accent-free and lovely voice.

"No, I'm gonna run this one off on the beach before I add a few more pounds," he responded. "My shorts are too tight now."

He finished his beer, then reluctantly left the barmaid's inviting smile, the seaside, cliff top hotel, and picked his way down a dirt trail to the late afternoon beach. As he walked, he imagined what would happen if he tried to cross the border at the control point.

After he was recognized by the computers, he would be asked to step aside, then he would be escorted to an office where he would be asked for his passport and then he would be held until a military representative could arrive. And then arrest him for desertion. No thanks would be offered for his service in Afghanistan.

Now on the beach, Jack kicked off his new leather huarache sandals, looked up at the cliff top hotel and remembered the fun college boy times he and his friends had there. Too much tequila, too much beer, extremely loud horns blaring in their ears, Mexican crooners screaming unintelligible lyrics at them— too much innocent fun... *Magna Tempora,* he thought. Great times.

He turned north towards San Diego and ran in the soft sand above the surf line and below the sandy cliffs that rimmed the Baja California coast, and as he ran, he enjoyed his temporary freedom.

After about a mile, avoiding the crashing surf as it surged onto the empty beach, he stopped to catch his breath next to a pile of washed up seaweed.

The vibrant and clear blue sky and beautiful white surf, not to mention the tangy salt breeze, cheered him up and he resolved to stay that way, if possible. So he flushed his fear of imminent arrest when he noticed a flat rock sitting in the water. It looked high enough to escape wave action. He waded knee deep about ten feet in the cool sea water and climbed on the rock as waves surged around it. He sat down and watched the waves form and crash against the beach. He wondered whether the waves knew their force was being spent on the land. His mind drifted and he wondered what his Afghan babe and their little baby boy were doing right now. He wished he could–suddenly, a large wave surged over the rock, drenching him in the waters of the California current as it flowed south from Alaska, and knocked him into the ocean.

Jack quickly retreated to the beach and headed back towards the hotel and as he ran, he thought again of the several times he and his fellow Stanford University law school classmates had stayed at the favored college resort hangout.

His mind unfortunately flashed to his time spent in Fort Leavenworth Prison where he had been serving a sentence of twenty years for stealing a military aircraft. He and his brother had been transferred out of the prison after being beaten badly by other inmates who had mistakenly thought they were traitors. They had to be evacuated to a military hospital in Maryland. They then later escaped with their father's help.

A voice interrupted his bad memories, "Senor! Senor Flashhardt! Don't forget your huaraches."

He stopped and saw a lone figure on the beach next to him that he immediately recognized as the gorgeous bartender from the hotel. She was tall and slender, almost as tall as he was at six feet. The short white shorts showed beautiful, shapely legs and a blue halter top revealed an attractive bare midriff below large breasts with skin that glowed golden brown. She was pointing at his sandals.

Like Penelope of Asia, mother of his little boy, she was a long haired blonde.

"Hello, you're right. I don't want to go shoeless." he answered her as he returned to her side. He could not have continued on for the world and luckily she was standing by his discarded sandals.

"Buenas dias, Senor Jack, You're all wet! Did you swim? The water is warm at our beach." She responded with probably another hidden smile with hazel eyes that glinted above the mask she wore. "Did you swim? Are you waiting for someone?"

"You speak English. You know my name. And you are right. I'm all wet."

Her beautiful voice was as remarkable as her masked appearance and it sang in his mind. She was way too beautiful to be a barmaid.

"'Of course," She added with a laugh. Her laughter sounded as musical as temple bells. "As you know, I work at the hotel. You are a guest."

"Why wear a mask on the beach?" He asked. "Getting ready to rob someone? Want to practice by robbing me?"

"Why are you all wet? Are you waiting to meet someone?" She asked again, ignoring his question and lame joke.

"Yes, my brother and his girl are driving down from L. A." Jack sat down on the warm sand and patted the ground next to him. "And I got mugged by a wave," he said as he put on his leather huaraches.

"My name is Margarita Valentino," she said.

"I'll wager you are very beautiful behind that mask, Margarita Valentino.

Do you taste as good as the famous Mexican drink, the Margarita?"

She sat down on the sand and did not answer his second attempt at a joke. She had bright white sandals on her feet and her toenails were painted a vibrant red. "You are not driving. You came by taxi," Margarita stated.

"I flew into Tijuana from Mexico City and then came here." Suddenly suspicious, Jack observed, "You seem to notice a lot around the hotel."

"That is because I am not just a bartender. I also work as a Relaciones invitada, that is to say Guest Relations for La Fonda Hotel."

Relieved, he smiled and reached a hand to remove her mask. She deflected it and said, "I don't want to get a sunburn."

He looked at her brown skin. "Fat chance," he said

"You are right, but you had better wear sun tan lotion during the day. You are very tanned, but as a blonde haired man with light eyes, you could still get easily sunburned as many gringos do."

"You are very blonde yourself for a Mexican woman," Jack remarked, "Blonde since birth," Margarita responded proudly.

"I guess I'll go to the shaded patio. ``Do you want to join me for a drink?" "I cannot drink with a guest, but I'll walk you up,"she replied. "Say, why didn't you fly into Los Angeles? Tijuana is a strange destination for an American."

Suspicion aroused again, he suddenly stood and said, "Well if you won't join me for a drink, let's go up."

She nodded assent, looked at him and was still very attracted to him, but she remained silent as she walked next to him and she wondered if he could overcome the scarred ugliness covered by her mask.

They walked up the hill and climbed to the patio in front of the hotel, which had a great view of the massive seascape below.

The patio floor was covered with large handmade reddish tiles. A short adobe brick wall separated the patio from the cliff. She led him to a table and just as he sat down at a small, circular table with a large palapa umbrella that was made of brown and very dead palm leaves, he spotted his brother, Billy and Billy's girlfriend, Zhang, walk onto the patio, "Over here," he called.

Jack told a hovering waiter to bring a trio of Corona beers and three glasses. Margarita quietly and reluctantly said adios and left the table. Jack thought about asking her to stay, but he did not because he needed to talk to Billy about his coming attempt at an illegal border crossing.

Billy Howling Dog and his Chinese girlfriend, Zhang Poon T'ang, who was now going by the stage name of Xu in Hollywood, Jack recalled, was a former or maybe not former Communist Chinese spy of some sort before her illegal entry to the US. They crossed the patio arm in arm.

Jack embraced his brother and then lightly hugged Zhang. She was a tall, beautiful Asian woman with some black features indicating an unusual mixed racial background. Feeling her body heat, he immediately thought of the last time she had hugged him in the motel back in the state of Washington but he said nothing as he broke off this embrace.

Billy flashed a wide smile that was bright against the brown skin he had inherited from his Sioux Indian mother, Little Willow. Despite his dark coloring he had blue eyes from Jack's side of the family.

Zhang also smiled at Jack. She was dazzling, as usual.

"Thanks for coming to Mexico. Did you bring the cash?" Jack sat down as the couple took their seats.

"Of course," Billy said. "It was more than I had on hand but Dad transferred money from the ranch bank account to mine."

He placed a brown paper bag on the table then stroked the black braids he had grown since leaving the Marine Corps.

"All here?" Jack asked.

"Twenty K in cash," Billy retorted. "What's your next move?"

"I've got to get across the border and get home to the Flying Eagle Ranch somehow," Jack replied.

"You're right. Being AWOL and then branded a deserter, they'd surely grab you at the border crossing. You've got to try some other way."

"How is Penelope?" Zhang asked.

When Jack thought of the beautiful blonde, Penelope, he suddenly recalled a conversation he had with Billy when they were flying from Singapore last year: Billy had said, "Hey, get your eyes off that stew, you've got a pregnant girl, Penelope, back in Shangri-la. You can't mess around."

Jack had responded, "Yeah. But now she's a power-mad queen of a two-bit tribe in the mountains of Afghanistan. Definitely crazy! And she wanted to keep me in her playpen by force." Jack grimaced at the memory. "Nothing has changed. She's back in her homeland and now has had our baby son, Willy. She won't leave Asia."

"So you going UA to try to get her to come back to America was all for nothing," Billy observed. He stroked his braids again. His black hair had grown long since he had become a freed civilian.

"I couldn't convince her to come back to America and I couldn't stay a deserter to the Marines in that Stone Age country, even for my baby son. I hope coming here will force her hand and change her mind."

"From what little I've seen of Penelope, she is quite Her Way," Zhang said. "How long since you've seen her?" She looked closely at Jack and as usual liked what she saw.

Jack felt her bare foot suggestively rub his lower leg under the table. He did his best to ignore it. "You're right," Jack said. "She's been a princess all her life and now with her Dad killed by Islamic ragheads, she's queen of that isolated paradise."

"Are you sure you can't cross legally in TJ? After all, you are a legitimate war hero. Billy has told me you have a Silver Cross or star or whatever it is, and a Purple star or heart, not to mention that medal you got from the President of Pakistan after you escaped from the Taliban!" Zhang asked as she rubbed his leg again.

"I reached my buddy, Charlie Davis. He said, don't try. He's a Marine. I got his status as a deserter changed and he now works for General Harmbruster who has retired and now runs a private company that works for the government. He said the military is watching for me at every border."

"After all we've done for those military assholes!" Billy snarled.

"You're wrong. The Military has rules. I didn't follow the rules," Jack said. "But at least we got out of prison and after we worked for General Harmbruster in Towelhead Land, you got your prison time in Fort Leavenworth waived by him. You're clean and free. Not like me," he added bitterly. "I've still got nineteen years of hard time to do on my sentence. I'll be an old geezer when I get out!"

"That conviction was bullshit!" Billy said. "We stole that airplane to complete our mission against the Taliban! I think that bastard Colonel Farley set it up so he would have leverage on us."

The small Mexican waiter arrived with three beers and poured them into three tall glasses.

"Here's to freedom," Zhang said. She chugged the glass and the brothers did the same. Jack waved at the departing waiter and ordered a round of margaritas.

"Who was the blonde babe with you when we got here?" Billy asked. "A gorgeous girl who works for the hotel," Jack responded.

"Great figure on that babe," Billy observed, which drew a dirty look from Zhang.

The three continued idle conversation about their experiences in Afghanistan, where both the brothers had met Zhang when she had worked as some kind of drum dancer and as an undercover Chinese operative for China's Second Department, a version of the CIA, before she illegally immigrated to the US.

They continued to talk through another round of margaritas and a dinner composed of black beans, Spanish rice and great fish tacos. After completing the meal, Jack said good night and retired to his room. Billy and Zhang got a key for the room Jack had reserved for them.

On the way Jack thought about Zhang's actions under the table. He knew what she meant when she rubbed his leg under the table but he wanted nothing to do with her because Billy would react like a wounded Montana mama grizzly bear whose cubs were being threatened.

As he walked, Jack tried to flush the anger over his deserter status and he was especially mad that he had to break the law to sneak into America, but there was no option. He would not be able to overturn his sentence unless he was free and physically in the U.S. where he could talk to his dad's buddy, the Montana Senator that Billy and he had saved from Islamic terrorists. The guy owed him. And Jack intended to remind him.

Glancing at his watch, Jack noted it was just after 2100 hours as he opened his hotel room door and when he hit the switch the light did not turn on.

The room was very dark as he closed and locked the door, then walked to the bedside lamp. But it was also not working and he mumbled a curse as he shed his clothes and money belt on the floor and fumbled onto the bed.

As he put one knee on the bed, suddenly he felt two hands grasp his shoulders and, unbalanced, he tipped face first onto a person in the bed. He swung a fist and an elbow, and elicited a small yelp and a feminine gasp.

"What the hell?" He grabbed a woman's hands and pinned them to the bed.

Suddenly two naked legs wrapped around his waist. "It is me-- Margarita Valentino!"

She rolled her muscular legs and he was twisted to his side. "What...what are you doing?"

"Is that not clear? I want you. You have left your woman in Asia. You are alone. As am I."

"How do--?"

"I put you at a table that has a listening device, Mr. Deserter! I know all about you."

He suddenly was aware of the heat of her muscular body and he semi- relaxed for a moment. Then he stopped resisting altogether when she kissed him with luscious, encompassing lips.

Later, when Margarita turned on the bedside lamp, Jack said. "The light-- it works now."

"It works better when the light bulb is screwed in," Margarita said with a smile.

"And as I also work better after being wonderfully screwed," Jack responded with a big smile.

He looked at her and immediately saw the three horrible scars on her face. His jaw dropped. One scar was a long, ragged cut below her nose that stretched completely across her face and the scars on her cheeks were jagged and terrible looking. They stretched from the corners of her eyes just below the cheekbones to her jawline under her lips.

She said, "Now you know why I wear a mask." I thought because of Corona--"

"No. I know I am very ugly." "I did not want to scare you away until you knew me better."

"You're not ugly, you are over the top beautiful!, But you are horribly disfigured. What happened? The scars can't be an accident." Her scars were still red, indicating that they were recent.

"No! Not an accident! The Cartel did it."

"What did you do to them?" Jack asked. "What's your game?"

"I don't want to talk about that. I heard you need to sneak across the border. So do I. And I want you to take me," Margarita stroked his arm. "I will take you to the Cartel smugglers and then the border. And I will make it a pleasurable trip. I promise."

"You ever thought of asking?" Jack leaned back against his pillow. Margarita smiled, "You do not like my way of asking?"

"No! No!. You are very persuasive. You would win a debate or even Sioux Indian leg wrestling every time! But from what I have heard it is a very dangerous trip."

"You are right. I could not make it alone. Nor could you. You have to pay the smugglers or you will be killed if you try."

"And you work for a Cartel."

"Yes, I do now," she said as she got out of bed. "I can take you to the Sinaloa Narcotraficante Cartel that will get you across the American border."

Looking at her fabulous body made him momentarily forget her horribly scarred face, then he said, "You know, plastic surgery could fix those scars."

"On a barmaid's salary?" Margarita laughed bitterly.

Jack leaned forward and kissed the girl. He shut his eyes and she turned very beautiful in his mind.

CHAPTER 2

In the morning, when Jack awoke, he saw that Margarita had put her mask back on her face. After going to the bathroom, he returned and realized she was awake. He told her that he would be back in a few minutes after checking on his brother. He pulled on his shorts and a white t-shirt, picked up his khaki money belt, entered the hallway and knocked on Billy's door. Wearing only a white hotel towel, Billy answered. Jack handed him his money belt containing the twenty thousand dollars.

"Keep this for me," he directed.

Rubbing the sleep out of his eyes, Billy asked, "Where you going?:

"I am going to arrange an illegal crossing to the US," Jack responded. "But I don't dare take this cash with me now. The cartel could pick me off like a wounded duck."

"When will you be back?" Zhang joined Billy at the door, wearing only a short, man's white t-shirt. Her naked muscular rear end was curved, tight, and beautiful. Jack felt a tingle of desire when he looked at her.

"If I'm not back today, I'm in trouble," Jack responded. "The girl you saw yesterday is taking me. She works here as a bartender. Her name is Margarita. She is taking me to a Cartel headquarters to set it up. I'll be back tonight."

"I got room service coffee," Billy offered. "Sure, I could use a cup."

"You look like you had a rough night," Zhang observed. Smiling, Jack responded, "I had pleasurable dreams."

Zhang stared at him, with a judging look on her face. He said no more.

After sharing Mexican hot, black coffee, Jack turned and went back to his room. Margarita was fully dressed in different clothes than she wore the day before, with white pants and a new blue top. Her hair was wet from a shower and her mask was back on, covering her scars.

Jack asked, "Let's go meet your people. I'm ready for an express trip to The Promised Land."

They walked out of the hotel and Margarita directed Jack to a Ford F-150 brown pickup that was parked in front of the hotel. It had a white sign for The La Fonda Hotel on the door. A young, slender Mexican man was behind the wheel. Jack climbed in the back seat which was clean except for a couple of AAA road maps of Baja California.

"He knows where we're going?" Jack asked.

"Yes," Margarita smiled. She looked over the front seat. "He works for the Cartel."

"As do you."

"That's a correct assumption. And I get a commission for finding you." "How do you speak such correct English?" Jack wondered.

She smiled, "I lived in Texas for ten years. I graduated from the University of Texas. I was in graduate school at SMU and my daughter was a US citizen when I got sent back to Mexico," Margarita frowned as she spoke.

As the driver started the truck, Jack asked, "Then why are you here?" "It's a long story."

"How far to the Cartel?" "About an hour."

"Then we have time, spill your– that is to say, tell me," Jack ordered. He looked at the driver.

Margarita glanced at the driver who was pulling onto the highway, and said, "He does not speak English." Then she said, "I was a DACA kid. That is, I was brought to the US illegally as a young girl. So was the young man who got me pregnant. I later married him. Then he joined the Marine Corps in order to qualify for citizenship. But he was killed in the Iraq war. After that tragedy I was deported despite my DACA status. But I was able to leave my daughter, Ava, who now lives in Boulder, Colorado, with my tia– my aunt. I have tried to get back to the US but I have been caught at the border and sent back to Mexico three times."

"If you were DACA, why did they send you back? Isn't your child an anchor baby?"

Margarita hit her thigh with a fist. "The Immigration man said I had to sleep with him. When I refused, he had me deported to Mexico. I was so stupid! And now I cannot get back across the border! I get caught every time and turned away!"

The pickup turned onto a dirt road off the four lane blacktop highway and bumped along as it led into the coastal hills. The sun burned off the morning coastal clouds and it got warmer.

"What's the deal with the scars?" Jack asked.

Margarita touched her face, then slowly responded, "When I got sent back to Mexico, I went to work for a maid service. In Cabo San Lucas," Margarita tossed her hair. "The casa fabuloso I went to was a beautiful estate on a peninsula that juts into the Sea of Cortez. But the second time I went to work there, the owner saw me. He must have called the service to complain because they fired me and told me to go fix what I had done wrong."

Margarita tossed her head again. "I had done nothing wrong but I went to the estate. A man took me from the servant's entrance to an office I had not seen before. There three men held me down while the owner ripped my clothes off and raped me. Then they locked me in a wine cellar. The three men all took turns on me. It was dark and I had no food, no water and my clothes were in tatters. Finally, late at night, I broke a bottle of wine and drank for my thirst."

"This is an incredible story." Jack stared at the beautiful scarred woman, "How did you escape?"

Margarita stared at Jack. "I didn't." "What happened?"

The next day they fed me tortillas and beans. And gave me a sheet to cover myself Then they took me back to the office and I was held and raped again by this same old man. The owner, I guess."

"Again!" Jack asked, "How did you escape?"

"The third time I went through this horrible nightmare, I pretended to be pleased."

"You're kidding!" Jack exclaimed. He glanced at the driver who paid no attention to the incredible tale and drove through a cactus as they moved along.

"I told you," Margarita said. "He does not speak English." She tossed her long hair again. "The next time, I told the men to let me go. I embraced the old man and gave groans of pleasure."

Jack stared at this incredible woman but said nothing.

"The next time they brought me to the office, the old man asked his men to search me and then told them to leave. Again, I cooperated enthusiastically."

"By this time I was getting better food and a somewhat dressing makeover. I was given a sack like dress and sandals'' She looked at Jack. "I was now ready to act."

Jack took a sip of water from a plastic water bottle. He offered it to Margarita. "What did you do?" he asked.

"I broke another bottle of wine and selected a piece of glass with a sharp point. I made a handle out of rags from my old dress. Then I took another rag, tied it around my upper leg and attached my makeshift knife.

"The next time a man came to fetch me to the old man, I smiled and when my escort left the office, I held out my arm in greeting to the old man and when he mounted me, I again gave moans of pleasure.

He smiled at me and I continued to behave as though he was pleasuring me as I carefully grasped my makeshift knife.. He smiled and said, "Cara mia," And then I stabbed him in the spine at the base of the neck. It paralyzed him! He could not even cry out. He stared at me with a horrified expression. I shoved him off me, then I held up the glass knife, and slowly cut his testiculos off. I held them up for him to see. Then I sliced his pene off and shoved the bloody mess into his silently screaming mouth. Finally I cut his throat."

"My God!" What did his men do to you when they found you?"

"When his men returned, they saw the old man's body lying in a pool of blood where I had shoved him. His penis, his testiculos in his mouth. They shouted and beat me and kicked me and finally threw me back into the cellar."

Jack gulped the water again and offered it to Margarita. She drank and finished the tale.

"No food, no water until the next day when men came. I was taken to a new leader, I guess he was."

"I expected to die but this younger man laughed when he saw me. I am sure I was a mess in a ripped up dress. He was dressed in a fine looking suit. I had broken another wine bottle and washed the blood off me, but the black eyes, bruises. I was a sight."

"What did he do?"

"He said, "You have killed our Jefe." He gave me an evil smile. "You have done me a great favor. I now lead our pandilla. Thank you. I am going to reward you. But I am not stupid. You are a dangerous woman so I am going to take away your best weapon.' He nodded to his two men and they held my arms. He pulled a knife and gave me these scars."

Jack listened as Margarita finished her story. He could not respond.

CHAPTER 3

"Crossing is not hard," Margarita said. "But they will charge you ten thousand dollars because you are a gringo, an American. I will tell them. I will suggest I go as far as the border as an interpreter. Go alone and not with the Cartel and you will be killed because you are a gringo in the badlands. That is if you could even survive crossing the desert on foot."

"Hey! I ran the Boston Marathon in college. I could outrun these characters."

"Try outrunning a bullet," Margarita said.

The truck continued to bump through the cactus and brush covered hills of the Baja Desert. Jack noted Barrel cactus, green Chollo bushes and an occasional unfamiliar cactus looking like a giant upside down carrot with long thorns as the truck advanced into the more and more remote hills.

Jack asked what the strange looking cactus was called. Margarita glanced and said, "It's called Boojum Cactus."

"Makes me hungry," Jack responded.

The hotel truck crested a hill and was waved to a stop by a guard standing next to the dirt road. He was holding a small rifle.

Margarita spoke quickly in Spanish and the guard, after speaking into a walkie talkie, waved them forward.

The truck stopped in front of a sprawling one story adobe house topped by a rough red tile roof. Jack looked at the tiles and remembered a story he had heard that the tiles got their rounded shape because when workers made them long ago they had shaped wet clay on their thighs.

The June sun beat down on them as they approached the front door. The house had brown shutters covering the windows. A large solar ground mount system was on one side of the house and there was no landscaping around the house, just bare sand.

The driver remained in the truck but Margarita led Jack through the front gate, across a dusty stone covered patio and into the main house. Inside, the house was cool, with an AC running, evidently powered by the solar system. A huge, fat Mexican in the large living room took one look at Jack, cursed and pulled a pistol, then pointed it at Jack. "You Americano!" He shouted. "DEA?"

"No, Jefe!" Margarita jumped in front of Jack. "He is American soldier! He needs to sneak across the border. Not DEA-- he is a military deserter. Going home. He pay!"

The fat Mexican relaxed and lowered the pistol. "So, you said earlier. I had to confirm. And, my Americano compadre, you want to go to the US border. We can help you. Pero, tienes mucho dinero?"

Jack eyed the revolver the man was holding. "What will you charge?" "We do not negotiate." The Mexican ran his fingers through his graying but full head of hair. His thick mustache was gray as well "It will cost you, a gringo, ten thousand dolares. Double what anyone else pays, I admit. But there it is. Take it or leave it." The Mexican cocked his head and gave Jack a calculating look. "Unless you carry meth or fentanyl for us across the border."

"Done," Jack said. "But no extra stuff. No drugs. When can we go?" He swallowed immediate rage that he had to consort with criminals to get home. *A home, an America I fought and almost died for. Now I have to sneak back home. No welcoming crowds! No red carpets!*

"Do you have cash now?"

"No, but I can go to my hotel and get it."

"You will start manana at seis.. er.. Six in the morning, mucho early. You will have a driver for our truck, and a guide. They will take you to the border. Then it is up to you to cross."

"Do they speak English?" "No Ingles."

"I can go and interpret, I have done so before," Margarita broke in. She held her breath.

The fat Mexican looked at her, then he studied Jack. "Si, do so."

CHAPTER 4

It was early evening when the Mexican F-150 stopped back in front of the very attractive Rosarito Beach hotel, La Fonda.

"I need beer like a thirsty steer needs a waterhole," Jack said. He added, "Sum siccus!"

Margarita looked at him and said, "You are thirsty. And you speak Latin." He and Margarita got out and went to the bar.

"I thought you couldn't drink with guests," he said as she sat down at a palapa covered table.

Margarita tossed her head, "I don't care! I am quitting here. Let us eat. I am starving."

Jack called his brother on his cell. "I'm back at La Fonda. In the restaurant bar."

Margarita ordered food for both of them while Jack was on his cell. A waiter brought two frosty bottles of beer. He exchanged words with Margarita in Spanish. Jack drained his beer.

He studied her masked face as she talked to the waiter. Now she did not look self-conscious about her covered scars. But he knew they were horrible under her mask, and even so she was a beautiful young Mexican woman when she wore the mask. Her large, wide set eyes sparkled.

The meal, consisting of rice, beans, fried fish and a large side of avocado, fried onions, and jalapeno peppers, was excellent.

As they ate, Billy and Zhang joined them. They both were dressed in shorts, wore huarache sandals that they had purchased in the hotel store and they each wore one of Billy's military t-shirts. One glance at Zhang and Jack could tell she was not wearing a bra over her impressive breasts. Margarita touched her mask and adjusted it whenever she drank or ate.

Billy looked at the plates and said, "Order the same for us." He stroked his black braids as he sat down. Then he placed Jack's money belt on the table. Jack clinched it around his waist below his t-shirt. Zhang sat across from Jack and suddenly he felt her bare foot rubbing his leg.

Not startled, Jack appraised the Asian woman. She was very beautiful and a very exotic looking Asian woman. Now as she rubbed Jack's leg, she was staring at Margarita. Her foot was so far up his leg, he wondered if she could count the change in his pocket.

"Margarita, this is my brother Billy and this is his girl, Zhang."
Margarita smiled. "Good evening," she said.

Billy muttered a hello under his breath and Zhang said nothing.

Jack noticed that Billy was in a bad mood, so he hummed a few
bars from the Gary Owen and Billy immediately started the refrain.
Jack joined and together they belted out a version of 'The Gary Owen'
which startled and disrupted the other guests:

We'll beat the bailiffs and demand more wine,
We'll make the ladies feel real fine,
Our demands are great,
We'll keep the ladies out late,
Wherever we go we'll raise such cane,
No matter what we'll get such fame,
We're Gary Owen in glory!

"Here's to Fallujah!" Billy exclaimed. "What is Fallujah?"
Margarita asked.

"It was a battle during the war in Iraq," Billy responded.

Just then a loud Mexican band broke into the bar blowing on
trumpets and strumming on guitars while they walked from table to
table of the guests.

"Do they sing because they are afraid you'll shout another verse?"
Zhang laughed as she spoke over the loud band.

Jack also laughed and said, "I wouldn't dare. We might get
arrested." The music was very loud.

A waiter brought two plates of food for Billy and Zhang. Another
brought a large pitcher of beer.

Margarita and Jack sipped their new beers while the other two ate.

"So Margarita is taking me to the border," Jack said. Zhang rubbed
his leg again but he ignored her. She rubbed harder.

Jack stood up, breaking contact with Zhang and said, "Margarita
has an errand to run and she has to get her stuff. I'll see you guys later."

He looked at Billy, then Zhang, and as he walked to his room, he
remembered what Zhang, the Chinese SD operative had said and done
to him the year before in the dark motel room next to the Juan De Fuca
Strait in the state of Washington:

"Don't move, Jack. I don't want to shoot you," she had said. He
did not recognize her Asian accented voice and he mistakenly thought
she was Mara Bhutto, the Pakistani spy and Chinese employed assassin
who was chasing him. He could not see more than a dim figure in the
dark motel room but he saw the glint of a pistol aimed at him.

Then she had tossed the plastic zip ties at his chest. They fell to the
bed. "Tie your wrists to the bedposts... Don't worry, it's just a safety

precaution. I don't want to shoot you." Her high pitched voice growled, "I won't shoot you, but I must secure you so I can question you. Now do it or I will kill you!"

At first terrified because Mara Bhutto had a reputation as a stone cold killer, Jack, seeing no options, had reluctantly and with difficulty restrained himself. When she spoke again with a softer tone, Jack's mind had raced. It wasn't Mara the Pakistani, as he had suspected, it was the Chinese woman, Zhang Poon T'ang. He questioned, "Zhang?"

She responded with a peal of laughter.

CHAPTER 5

Mara Bhutto walked out of the warehouse in the City of Ensenada and squinted in the hot Mexican sunlight. The weather reminded her of Singapore but it was less humid here in Ensenada which sat on the Baja California coast. The Sinaloa Narcotraficante warehouse was on a street one block off the waterfront of the city's harbor.

A policeman on the corner noted the striking woman coming out of the warehouse. He wondered what she was doing as she did not look like a common worker. Beautiful, if a little severe looking. Mara pushed her thick black hair out of her face. She was wearing tight jeans and a bulky gray sweater.

She had met the Chinese government assistants and their overseer, Yur Whang 'er, who had delivered a second one thousand kilos of fentanyl to the Cartel methadone pill manufacturer and the Fentanyl would be added to the ten milligram crystal methadone pills being manufactured by the cartel in the countryside just east of the city.

This was the second time the Chinese government had supplied fentanyl to the Sinaloa Cartel and that was why Mara was being utilized to supervise the delivery made by a small freighter that had originally sailed from Hong Kong. And like the first shipment, this fentanyl was much stronger than labeled and would cause many drug overdose deaths in America. The first shipment, Mara had heard, resulted in over 100,000 deaths of drug overdose in the prior year. Mara hoped this shipment would cause even more havoc in hated America.

The instructions said to use one milligram per dose but the net result would be to actually add the equivalent of two milligrams per dose.

Mara had flown commercially to Mexico City and then by the Mexican airline, Aeroflot, to Ensenada, quite near the US border, which was where the final destination of the cartel's' new drug combination was to be created.

She was tired but happy that all had gone smoothly, and she was looking forward to a side trip to Los Angeles to see her associate, Zhang Poon T'ang, now that she had overseen the delivery.

This was a valuable comeback after the disastrous events on the west coast of America last year and the horrible failure in Montana while trying to destroy Jack Flashhardt. And it was another effort made by China to enhance the rapidly growing drug deaths caused by fentanyl in the US. Of course, the Mexican Cartel did not know that the fentanyl purity was mislabeled and the additions to the methadone would result in many more user deaths in America. If the cartel later complained, the excuse would be mistaken labeling.

CHAPTER 6

$\mathbf{T}$he next morning, Margarita met Jack in the hotel lobby. She was wearing jeans, a blue jean shirt and a pair of sturdy boots and he was wearing military khaki pants, boots, and a green cammo shirt. She handed him a small canvas bag and kept a second bag. He dropped his back pack and looked inside the small bag. He saw a pistol in the bag, and two prepaid cell phones. He looked around, saw no one so he pulled the pistol out and looked closely: it was a black Hi Point 9mm lugar. A plastic bag contained ten bullets. He checked, the clip was full and there was a round in the chamber.

"Six hundred dollars for everything," Margarita added.

"Good work, Margarita," Jack said. "I prefer a .45 MI1911. But what the hell." He looked fondly at her. "I thought you might check on me last night."

She smiled, said nothing, but wished she had visited him when she remembered his hard, chiseled body, he was unlike anyone she had ever experienced. And when he smiled, his hard looks softened into a visage of youthful innocence and happiness.

They walked out to the waiting truck and climbed in, whereupon the Mexican driver, Jose, retraced his route to the adobe headquarters.

In the back seat, Jack took the pistol apart on a towel from the floor, and checked the firing pin and the workings of the weapon. Satisfied, he put it back together and put it in a thigh side pocket. Eventually they arrived at the headquarters. Jose stayed in the truck. Inside, they were greeted by the fat Mexican who was accompanied by two young Mexican men. Both men were small and dark.

"These are your escorts, Senor," the leader said. He held out his hand. Jack pulled a large packet of bills out of his cargo pocket and handed it over.

The Mexican turned and sat at a nearby wooden table. He started counting the one hundred dollar bills until he was satisfied there were one hundred of them. He looked up with a broad smile, said something in Spanish to his two men, and then said, "Te deseo un buen viaje."

"He wishes you a safe trip," Margarita interpreted.

"Thank you, Senor," Jack responded. "When I get to the American side safely, I will pay another five thousand dollars."

The fat Mexican grinned, "You are a wise man."

They followed the two Mexicans to a new truck and the men got in the back seat with Margarita, Jack got in the front passenger seat with Jose and the black Chevy Z 71 truck started to roll.

A cruising seagull squawked as it flew over the house, then it wheeled and headed for the coast as the truck turned east.

CHAPTER 7

After driving the rest of the day on a somewhat pretense of a road, the loaded truck crested a dusty hill and they saw a large ranch house constructed out of adobe bricks. A distance away was a large barn, a windmill, and a big metal silo along with accompanying corrals next to a long shed. The sun was setting to their rear.

"We have an arrangement with the ranch owner," Margarita said. "We stay here tonight."

"Nice pad," Jack exclaimed. "I figured we'd be slumming under a barrel cactus."

"Not the big house," Margarita said. "We sleep in that shed."

"Oh, well, I guess it's not a Hilton but it is better than a cattle barn. At least we won't have to shovel manure out of our beds."

When they drove down to the expanse between the ranch house and barn, a white man holding a pitchfork waved as they pulled to a stop next to a corral which contained four pinto mustangs.

Margarita leaned her head out the window and said in English, "Hello, we stay here tonight. We are sent by Sinoaloa Narcotraficante."

The man frowned, and said, "Park over there." He pointed at the door to the long shed. Like the ranch house, it was made of adobe bricks and had a red tile roof, but it had no windows..

After the group dropped their gear on a wood plank floor in the shed, Jack and Margarita walked outside and joined the white man who was leaning on the corral. He was an older man, in his sixties, with gray hair and a lined face, but he was erect and looked fit. His jeans and white shirt were faded but looked clean. Jack noticed that the truck turned and drove out of the valley with the two Cartel guys in the back seat.

"You are an American?" The man asked. "Yes," Jack responded.

"What are you doing?"

"I am trying to cross the border illegally." "The question is why?"

Jack looked at Margarita and added, "I'm helping this DACA girl reunite with her American family."

"It would be easier to put her in a car trunk. They would not search you, an American."

"They might but beyond that, I am on a list. I would be detained because of facial recognition."

"So it is more than the girl," the man accused. "Yes," Jack admitted.

"Do you feel confident in your ability to get her into the US?" Jack looked at Margarita. "Yes, or I would not try."

"I need to send my son to Salt Lake City. Will you take him with you?" "Why?" Jack felt a pang of regret as he was reminded of his young baby son, Willy, back in Shangri-La with his mom, Penelope.

The man shuffled his feet, then looked Jack in the eye. "He was taken by the cartel and sexually abused. He was in serious danger. I gave up this ranch to get him back. We had owned the ranch since the Mormon Retreat of the last century. I need to send him to my family in Salt Lake City for safety reasons and for re-education."

"I'm sorry to hear about your troubles. It must have been terrible for the young boy. We will be glad to help

"The worst! And he has been sampling drugs. I have to get him out of here!"

"How old is he?" "Sixteen."

Jack glanced at Margarita. She was shaking her head side to side. "Let's meet him," he said anyway.

The man turned, beckoned and yelled at a figure on the opposite side of the corral.

When the young man approached, Jack was surprised to notice that the boy was an albino and that he was larger than most Mexicans. His skin was dead white and his eyes were pale pink. He had light whitish hair, cut very short. The father said, "This is Pete. Or Pedro as he is known in Mexico."

Jack stuck his hand out to shake and said, "Hello." The young man responded with a limp handshake and a faint smile.

"Where did our escorts go?" Jack asked Margarita.

"They have a separate delivery," she responded. "They'll be back tonight."

Jack turned to the old man and his son. "We will leave early. But one question. You work for the cartel. Why…?"

'You think it is our desire?" The man responded. "They force us. Another reason why I have to get my son out of here!" He looked into Jack's eyes. "Why is it so important for you to sneak into America?"

"I love and miss my country. And I want to clear my name with the military," Jack responded.

The old man added in a quieter voice, "You can have breakfast before you go."

"Fine," Jack said. "See you in the AM."

Jack pointed at the shed and followed Margarita as she entered. Inside, he asked, "So when will the Cartel guys come back?"

Margarita walked past a row of bunks and sat down on the last bunk. A window on the back side of the shed threw a little light on the interior.

"They are taking meth to a contact that will smuggle the drug across the border. They should be back before midnight."

"Holy Shit! That stuff is dangerous!" Jack exclaimed. "It has a high risk for addiction. I've heard it can cause death."

Later that evening, Jack awoke when he heard someone enter the shed. Margarita, sleeping in the next cot, woke up when Jack poked her, then arose and went to the person. They conversed very excitedly and spoke very rapidly. Soon, Margarita returned to Jack. "Our Cartel men are missing," she said. "They left Jose, the driver, near the border but did not return. He waited three hours. He thinks they were captured by the US Border Patrol or they were killed by bandits! By robbers on this side of the border."

Mystified by this new event, Jack got out of bed. LIke Margarita, he was fully dressed. "What should we do?"

"We could return to La Fonda, or we could try to cross on our own," Margarita tossed her head. "We'll wait and see if they come back later."

"How are they getting back if their ride is here?"

"That is their problemo, I'm tired," Margarita said. She returned to her cot and lay down.

An hour later Jack awoke when Margarita crept into his bed.

"I want you, "she said. She wrapped her arms around his mostly naked person and pressed against his hard body.

Jack's mind flashed to Penel back in Afghanistan, "I don' think--"
"Stop thinking," Margarita slowly rubbed his crotch.

"But I have--"

She drew back and said, "It's my ugly scars, isn't it?" "No, Margarita, that's not it. I have a woman--"

Margarita grasped him again. "Are you talking about some mythical girl in a mythical country across the sea called Shangri-la?" She slowly fondled him. "I am here. It is dark. You cannot see my scars. And I can lead you to a real paradise."

CHAPTER 8

Jack woke in the morning and looked up at a now fully dressed Margarita who was holding out a large mug of black coffee. She had her mask on and her beautiful eyes smiled over it as he took the cup.

"Thanks."

"It's black as you like it. Thank you for making me feel so good last night," Margarita said with a hidden smile that made her lovely eyes look beautiful.

"You were wonderful!" He reflected on their romp and smiled broadly, then asked, "Did our missing smugglers show up?"

"No," she said with a serious glance at the door. "How long do we have to wait?"

"We are not waiting," Margarita responded. "We will leave after we eat.

Jose is ready and the boy--"

"Yesterday you did not want to take him."

"We did not have room in the truck," Margarita tossed her hair, "And we will be saving the boy." She tossed her hair again. "Let's go. Time is wasting."

Jack hurriedly dressed and followed her to the main house, where food was already on platters on a large plank table awaiting them. It had long benches for seats and looked like it could seat over a dozen people. A Mexican lady, short and rotund, served huevos rancheros, toast, which she called pan, and more coffee and fresh orange juice.

Jack and Margarita ate with gusto and were enjoying a last cup of coffee when the owner and his son entered the large kitchen.

"Hello, Pete," Jack said. "Are you ready to travel?" "Of course he is ready," the father exclaimed.

"I would rather hear it from Pete,'" Jack said.

"Yes, sir," Pete said in a low voice. He picked up a backpack he had carried into the kitchen.

"Margarita, why don't you collect Jose, the driver, and let's hit the road," Jack directed.

Margarita left and walked outside. A minute later, Jack heard her scream. He ran out to the truck and saw her standing next to the vehicle with her hands on her face. She was staring inside the truck and wailing,

Jack ran to the truck and saw Jose's body half on the seat and half on the floor. He pulled the young man out and put him on the ground. The boy's body was drenched in sweat and pale green vomit was dribbling out of his mouth. He was not visibly breathing. Jack checked his pulse. There was none. He cleared his mouth with one hand while he thumped the boy's chest with the other. Then he checked the pulse again.

He was sure Jose was dead. Jack and Margarita carried the limp body to the shed they had slept in and put it on a bunk bed.

Pete came out of the house, entered the shed and said, "I told him not to take it."

"Take what?" Jack asked as he walked outside. "What did he take?"

"The two guides," Pete said to Jack's disappearing back. "When he asked where they were going last night, they told him they were delivering meth capsules to a border guard. They had broken open the pack and he asked for a sample and they gave Jose two meth pills as they were getting ready to leave."

"I have seen this .. He took fentanyl. But he is not dead. I am sure of it!" Margarita exclaimed to Pete. "See the bright green vomit? That means fentanyl. He is in a coma!!"

Within fifteen minutes they had left the passed out boy, were loaded and departed the ranch. The father had hugged his son with tears in his eyes and now was waving goodbye. Jack was reminded again of his son, Willy. He wondered again when he would see his chubby, blue eyed, blonde, and baby boy. The kid could laugh and laugh.

Jack, driving now, navigated over the still mythical trace of a road and once they went over the crest of a cactus covered hill, the ranch disappeared and Jack looked fondly at Margarita, thinking of the night before. But then the fear of the unknown crept over his thoughts and he tried to think of the home ranch in Montana, hoping that would favorably color his negative thoughts.

"You are smiling," Margarita said. "What are you thinking of? How can you smile after what has happened?""

"Last night," Jack said. "You were wonderful."

"My thought, exactly." She gazed at the handsome American and wondered if he would dump her after they reached America.

Pedro spoke in Spanish.

Margarita's eyes widened and she beamed. She finally leaned back and said, "The Trump fence shuts us out of Tecate and Mexicali but Pedro says he knows another way. He has heard there is a new tunnel in Mexicali."

"A tunnel under the border?"

"There have been a lot of tunnels discovered by the U S Border patrol.

But this one is new."

"I think it's about one hundred miles to Mexicali."

Margarita nodded her head. "You are right. About 180 kilometers. If you go by Carretera Veinte. That is, Highway Twenty."

"But do we dare take the highway?"

"No one will stop us on the road but we have to get there," Jack responded by turning north towards the US.

CHAPTER 9

As the trio crested a desert hill, they saw the highway in the distance. It was late in the afternoon, and Margarita pointed at a young girl huddled next to a fallen body. She told Pete who was driving now to stop and he pulled up next to the figures. It was a young teenage girl sitting next to a body on the ground. Just before they reached the girl and huddled body, Pete tried to slam on the brakes when he saw an eroded ditch but he failed and the truck nosedived into the four foot ditch. It slalomed to a stop but luckily everybody had their seat belts on and were saved from going through the windshield. The airbags exploded.

When the dust settled down, Jack crawled out of the truck and when he saw the body of the vehicle was sitting on a ledge, he realized it would probably need a tow truck at the very least.

"I'm sorry," Pete said. "I just did not see the hollow until it was too late." "I understand. But what a mess!" Jack exclaimed.

Margarita got out and headed for the girl and the body. She had to jump down the bank and crawl up the other side.

When the girl had noticed the truck she had tried to hide behind a Chollo bush. Margarita called out in Spanish and the girl crept into view. They talked and Margarita said, "The girl says her mother lying here is dead! The mother was raped and killed!"

"And the girl?" Jack was almost afraid to ask.

Margarita spoke to the girl again but the girl began crying and mumbled a few words.

"She was raped, as well, but they let her live. It just happened."

"Probably figured she would die of exposure anyway," Jack said with disgust in his voice. "It's not only hellishly hot, it's a horrible country! Mexico used to be a fun destination. It's been ruined by drug cartels. And criminals!"

Pete got out of the truck and got a bottle of water from a partially spilled box in the truck bed. He gave it to the girl and she drank all of it.

"We must take her with us!" Margarita exclaimed.

"We're not going anywhere in this truck!" Jack exclaimed.

"We can't leave her," Pete added. "She'll die!"

Jack nodded agreement. She appeared to be about twelve years old or so and very dirty while wearing ragged clothes. She looked like she had not had a bath in weeks.

Suddenly a large red RAM 3500 pickup filled with three men appeared at a bend on the road.

The young girl screamed, "Son Ellos!"

Margarita spoke to the girl and yelled, "She says they're coming back!"

The Ram truck skidded to a stop in back of the Chevy and three men jumped out of the cab.

"Trouble!" Jack mumbled under his breath.

One of the Mexicans had a revolver in his hand and the other two held machetes.

"Everybody get out of the truck and raise your hands," Jack instructed. "We can't just--" Margarita exclaimed.

"Just do it!"

As they all got out with raised hands, Jack got out last behind the others, with his pistol held against his leg, pulled it up and immediately shot the gun carrier who sprawled to the ground.

Because he had been behind Margarita, the gunshot terrified her and she leaped to the ground. Jack fired again and he hit a second machete wielder and his pistol jammed. He jumped over Margarita and attacked the last man in front of them. He backhanded the knife carrier and the man's knife went flying.

When the third man got up and attacked, he grabbed the man's wrist and jerked him until he fell to the ground. Jack kicked him in the head.

The guy fell to the ground but he picked up his machete. Jack stepped on the man's wrist and the long knife fell away. Jack kicked it and it flew about ten feet. He leaned over and hit the man in the head as hard as he could with the jammed pistol and the man stopped struggling. His aggressive attack stunned and silenced the Mexicans.

Jack glanced at his pistol and saw a spent shell casing was jammed in the receiver.

"Let's take their truck and get out of here," Jack ordered. As they climbed in the still running pickup, Margarita hugged the young girl they had rescued and said, ``Hurry!''

Jack floored the accelerator and skidded away to the east, leaving the road behind. He glanced back at the fallen men. "This country is insane. It's like existing in the Old West!"

"How far is it to Mexicali?" Pete asked.

"If we get on the highway, it should take about one hour," Margarita said. She looked at Jack and asked, "You killed the man with the gun! Did it--? The one with the gun?"

Jack exclaimed, "Hah! He was going to shoot us. I will not give it a second of remorse, or pity for him. The dumb bastard chose his fate. And I can add it to a long list!"

CHAPTER 10

Just as the sun was setting to their rear, Jack and the others and their stolen pickup entered the outskirts of Mexicali. Traffic was heavy. Most of the commercial buildings on both sides of the street were one story concrete block structures.

Jack, who was driving, turned to Pete and asked where to go.

"Head straight ahead until you get to Ave Reforma," Pete instructed. "It's the street that parallels the border. We can get a room in a hotel and I'll call my amigo about the tunnel."

On the street going to Reforma, Margarita told Jack to stop outside a clothing store. She asked him for money and he gave her four twenty dollar bills from his wallet. She grabbed the rescue girl and climbed out of the pickup and went inside the store. After fifteen minutes, they came out with two paper bags with new clothes. Five minutes later, Jack parked outside a nondescript, two story hotel on Reforma Street and he and Margarita went in and booked two rooms.

They put Pete and the rescue girl, who Margarita now introduced as Blanca, in one of the rooms but they discovered when Blanca started crying again, that she was afraid to stay in the room with Pete, so they took her into their room and Jack threw his pack on the fake leather sofa. Margarita took the still crying Blanca into the bathroom to clean her up.

Later, Jack took a shower, and then Margarita took one. The young girl, exhausted but clean, climbed into the only bed and immediately fell asleep.

Jack asked Margarita," Are you hungry?" "Yes," she responded. "I could eat a burro."

Jack looked at the Mexican girl but restrained a comment. The two collected Pete and walked down the street to a small restaurant, ate beef and bean burritos, Spanish rice and drank Dos Equis Beer.

Jack asked, "Did you have any luck about the tunnel?"

"There are two ways to cross." Pete responded. "One is still a tunnel but there is also a break in the fence at the golf course on the southwest side of town. The golf course parallels the border. Working women cross on a path to an American factory that makes clothes for Walmart. My amigo, Fidel–his wife Consuelo, works there. She crosses and the factory owner must have a deal with the Calexico police and the US Border Patrol because they allow the intrusions every day." Pete swallowed a last bit of burrito and added, "We can take the path or my friend will take us to the tunnel entrance. But he said you will have to pay to use it. Five hundred dollars should work. He will come to the hotel at midnight."

"I think I should go first to the tunnel and check it out," Jack said. "You all can wait at the hotel. If it's clear, we will all go tomorrow night."

Margarita wrapped up a last burrito for the lost girl. " Her name is Blanca," she reminded as they walked back to the hotel.

Jack sprawled on the sofa and Margarita lay down next to Blanca and they both slept until Pete and his friend knocked on the door at midnight. Jack, still dressed, answered and invited them into the room.

Pete introduced Fidel to Jack and Margarita. The Mexican was short and skinny. He wore overalls and a straw hat that made him look like a farm worker.

Jack gave Margarita two hundred dollars, kissed her and motioned for Fidel to go. As the two left, Fidel said, "We'll take my truck. It is only a couple of blocks from here to the tunnel."

They entered a gray Toyota mini truck.

"Is the tunnel safe?" Jack asked as he handed over five hundred dollars. "No, Senor Jack," Fidel made a sweeping gesture with a hand. "Nothing is safe in Mexicali or Calexico. All of Baja is, how do you gringos call it, 'Cowboy and Indian country'?"

"From what I've seen so far, I have to agree with you. I wish they had let Trump finish the wall. That would have cut down the migrant flow and the drug problem."

"Of course, Senor. But it would be easier if there was no border at all. Did you ever hear of the Bracero policy?"

"No," Jack answered. "What was that?"

"Under the program, Mexicans were allowed to work in the US for a period of time and then go home, where they wanted to live."

"Why was it stopped? It seems to make sense."

"The Democrats, I am told, stopped it because they said it hurt the US job market."

Jack thought about that for a moment but had no answer.

Fidel pulled into a dark commercial building's driveway and parked in its parking lot. They got out and Fidel led the American to a metal side door and opened it with a key. Then, with a flashlight he showed Jack the tunnel entrance cut into the concrete floor and gave him the flashlight. "Good luck, Senor," he said as Jack lifted the wooden trap door and took a wooden ladder down to the tunnel floor.

It was cooler in the tunnel, Jack noticed. He traveled north about 500 feet until he felt he was past the US border. The tunnel ended when he came to a canvas tarp covering the end of the tunnel. He pushed it aside and saw a hole had been cut into a concrete structure. Inside the now concrete tunnel, he saw English lettering and reading it, he realized an access to an American storm drain system had been cut and the drain was being used. He followed the five foot diameter drain, ducking to save his head. He sensed that the drain was paralleling the border fence and then he came to a drain cutting away and heading north. He turned and followed the new drain until he saw a shaft headed towards the surface.

CHAPTER 11

Where the American storm drain ended was a long handle that he turned until he realized it opened a cover. He climbed up metal steps and saw he was in an empty field next to a subdivision of condos or apartments. It was very dark and much cooler in the field. He could feel his heart beating rapidly. He paused and took a few deep breaths. As he climbed out of the drain, two figures approached him. He saw a knife blade shining from the reflections of the street lights in the condos. HIs heart began pounding again.

"Entrega tu dinero!" THe knife wielder exclaimed. "What?"Jack did not understand.

"Dinero. Give money!" The man shouted.

"Get screwed!"Jack shouted when he knew what the two men were after. He quickly advanced and kicked the man's knife carrying hand and punched the other man in the face with the flashlight. Disarmed and shocked by his aggressive actions, the two men retreated. Jack pulled his pistol and shot at the ground near the running men to speed them on their way. "This is America, you assholes!" He tried to fire another shot but the pistol failed to fire again. He checked the receiver with his free hand and felt the jammed empty casing in the slide.

A minute later, a police cruiser slammed to a stop on the street next to the vacant acreage and two cops jumped out and approached. One had a drawn pistol and the other aimed a shotgun at Jack. They both were wearing dark uniforms and white helmets.

"Put any weapons on the ground and raise your hands!" one cop yelled. Jack put the pistol and the flashlight down and complied with the order.

He felt his heart start to race again.

"Who did you shoot? We heard the gunfire," the shotgun cop asked.

"I didn't shoot anybody," Jack responded. "Two guys tried to hold me up and after one of them got my wallet, I disarmed one and they ran away. I shot into the ground to hurry them along." Jack pointed at the knife on the ground.

"What are you doing out here in the field? One cop asked. The other asked, "Do you have a permit for that pistol?" He bent over and picked it and the flashlight up and then collected the knife.

"It was not mine. I was just out for a walk," Jack answered lamely. "Not even my wallet, now."

"Nobody walks around here late at night!" The shotgun cop exclaimed. "What are you up to? Do you have any other weapons?."

The first cop holstered his pistol and frisked Jack. "Put your hands behind your back." He handcuffed Jack.

"Why the cuffs? I did nothing wrong." Jack exclaimed. "I was the victim."

"We're taking you to the station for questioning, sir. You can't be in the cruiser unless you are cuffed. I'll take them off when we get there."

The two policemen escorted Jack to their vehicle. He noticed that they both were overweight and short and looked Hispanic. They put him in the back seat with a metal screen separating him from the front seat. They drove to the main street of Calexico, turned left and soon turned into a fenced lot next to the police station. Once outside the car, one of the cops uncuffed Jack.

Terrified that they would discover his military status, Jack complained, "I'm a victim. Why are you treating me like a criminal?"

"Victims don't walk around a border town like Calexico after midnight." The shotgun cop pointed out. "Do you live here? I haven't seen your face around town."

"Where do you work?" The other asked.

"Not around here," Jack admitted. "I got off a ... I got lost and started walking." He realized how lame his responses were. He took a deep breath and tried to calm himself. He thought of his first imprisonment in Afghanistan:

'Take him away,' Ahmoud, the Afghan Taliban guy, had shouted. A giggling guard led Jack until he stumbled, fell. Another guard immediately started kicking him. Terrified, he pushed to his feet and staggered ahead. Shoved into a room--sprawled on a dirt floor. Door crashed shut.

Jack glanced around the police station parking lot. He noticed the two cops were close together between two cars. And neither had drawn weapons. Suddenly, he shoved one cop hard and knocked him into the other man and they both sprawled to the ground. He turned and dashed around parked vehicles and jumped on a small car's hood and then leapt over the five foot chain link fence next to the car. When he hit the ground he rolled head over heels, came up and ran. Without looking back he dashed in front of a commercial shop and turned left down an alley. The two policemen shouted for him to halt but did not chase him.

He ran to the end of a block, turned right and crossed a empty lot, then over another wood rail fence

With no idea where he was going, he ran, turning right and left at every opportunity in case his followers were coming. He soon realized the cops were not chasing him.

He slowed to a trot, trying to regain his wind. The eastern sky was just starting to lighten. *Luckily, I am in great shape*, he thought. Those cops looked like they had spent too much time in a donut shop. He jogged for another ten minutes and came upon the golf course.

As he moved along the first five fairways he reflected on his situation: *I've been turned into a common criminal. How did this happen? I was in Stanford Law School, then got activated from my Marine mountaineering Reserve Unit, sent to Afghanistan, trained and led men, got stranded in a crazy isolated valley when my parachute flew wildly from a huge updraft of wind--- a valley isolated when Russia left their occupation of Afghanistan and blew up the only tunnel road to the valley, met Penelope, a blonde, blue eyed descendant of Alexander the Great's long ago army deserters, got her pregnant. And now she has my son in that crazy isolated valley and I'm on the run with a nineteen year sentence at Leavenworth left to serve. Convicted for stealing an Afghan Aircraft which we used to transport us to fight terrorists. And it 's still hanging over my head even though General Harmbruster said it was fixable...*

He broke off his reminisces when he spotted a worn dirt trail coming from the border fence and crossing the sixth fairway. He followed the trail and saw the break in the chain link fence that served as a border wall at that part of town. As he reached the border fence, he paused and looked back at the US side. He immediately saw a Border Patrol SUV parked north of the golf course. As he looked he saw the glint of light from the rising sun on binoculars that were studying him. He stepped through the fence. *I guess the Border Patrol does not care if I sneak into Mexico*, he thought.

Now, he was back in Mexicali but, as he no longer had his one shot pistol, thanks to the Calexico cops, he was very nervous as he moved east back to the hotel on Avenida Reforma.

The streets were getting busy with people and vehicles as the sun grew higher and no one took notice of Jack as he moved along. When he got to the hotel he went to his room and knocked on the door. Margarita quickly answered and hugged Jack when she opened the door. "I was so worried!" She exclaimed. "How did it go?"

"Not good," Jack replied. "Let's go get some breakfast."

"The girl, Blanca, is still sleeping," Margarita said, "She was awake and crying in the night."

Jack looked at the bed and noticed the girl was sleeping with Pete's lap for a pillow. "She seems to be doing better."

Margarita grabbed her purse and they collected Pete and went to the small restaurant next door to the hotel. Margarita said, "Blanca and Pete seem to be getting along better. They had a long talk. But what happened to you?" Margarita had a look of concern on her face.

The small restaurant had only two men drinking coffee at a table. Jack and the other two sat down at an empty table that had dirty plates on it.

Jack patted her hand and said, "I'm alright. But the tunnel is a non-starter. When I came out, two banditos tried to rob me and then two Calexico cops arrested me."

"Arrested you!" Margarita grabbed his arm. "How did you get away? Did they let you go?"

"Doesn't matter. The point is we have to find another way across the border." He ordered coffee from a waitress as she cleaned their table. "Trump built the 20 to 30 foot high wall," Jack said. "How are we gonna get over that? We will have to make numerous side trips to find an opening. In a dangerous country."

"I know for sure where there is no wall," Pete said.

Jack and Margarita looked at Pete as he accepted a cup of coffee from the young waitress.

"Where?" Jack asked.

"The Colorado River. It comes from the US and dumps into the Sea of Cortez. There is no wall across the river."

"How far is it to the river?" Jack asked. "I seem to recall that it is about one hundred miles from El Centro-- just north of here to Yuma, on the Colorado River."

Margarita shook her head. "I have no idea."

"No," Pete said. "It's only about sixty miles to the river."

"And, at least on the road to Yuma, you pass through an area of massive sand dunes. Will the truck handle the dunes? They look like that's where they filmed Star Wars."

"There is a road from Mexicali all the way." Pete offered. "Do we dare take a highway?"

"How safe has it been across the desert?" Margarita asked. "You've got a good point," Jack concluded. "Let's do it!"

CHAPTER 12

NSA Assistant Director Van Hollin walked across the office of former General Farley, now the Director of the NSA. Hollin was a tall man and slightly overweight with a balding head and a white mustache. "How are you doing, General?"

He shook the short, chubby ex-military man's hand. Farley, who was dressed in a khaki uniform nodded a greeting as they shook, then said "We have to take action before that bastard Harmbruster gets his act together."

"And the reason for action?"

"Harmbruster wants his company to take out this Ransomware gang in Russia. I want to take the same gang out and I want the credit for accomplishing the mission." Farley looked up at Hollin, "Do you know this Ransomware gang has even penetrated the FBI's computers? This Chinese sponsored crowd is getting out of control and very dangerous to our country. The goddam Chinese want to destroy us!"

"I heard that the FBI has discovered more than one penetration. They have been keeping it secret. Embarrassed no doubt," Hollin pointed out.

"They should be. But it tells us these computer freaks can do anything. They must be stopped! I need a source of funds so I can equip and send a team to Russia that can terminate the freaks with prejudice. I want to show the Chinese pricks that we won't tolerate their bullshit! And," the General continued after a pause, "I need to outperform Harmbruster because he got me to have to retire from the army."

"Even if they get the gang, it sounds like a suicide mission. They'll never get out of Russia." Hollin wondered why Farley was in a uniform if he was out of the army.

"There is a way. The gang is headquartered in Min Vody, a city about one hundred miles from Georgia, the country. They can fly into Min Vody from Moscow, masquerading as a mountain climbing expedition, and after they take out the gang, they can grab a car or truck and drive to Georgia before anybody figures it out. And Georgia requires no visas from American citizens."

"Perfect," Hollin said. â€œHow much will we need? And how soon can we start?"

Farley regarded Hollins. "ASAP. I'll get back to you."

CHAPTER 13

Jabuli Jazreti hurried down the narrow street to his cousin, Telavi Pasanaui, who was waiting at his favorite coffee kiosk in all of Tbiliski. Georgia. Telavi had been so excited when he called, he had shouted over the telephone so loudly that Jabuli had to hold the receiver away from his ear.

When the narrow street designed for horse carts long ago curved to the left, he saw his cousin sitting at a small table with two cups of coffee in front of him. Telavi jumped up and embraced Jabuli. "We are going to be rich as the prophets of old!"

"That is wonderful news," Jabuli agreed as he disentangled from the brace of his shorter cousin. "How many infidels do we have to kill?"

Telavi stroked his short black beard as he sat back down. His black eyes twinkled as he added, "No one! We are going to be hired to guard a computer center in Min Vody. We will have to sign up ten more locals to help guard the installation.."

"Will we need weapons?" Jabui asked.

"Yes, but we will have to obtain some AKs in Min Vody. We can't travel on the train with guns," Telavi said,

"Who is threatening the center?"

"Who cares?" Telavi exclaimed. "The point is we have a job! And we will make a fortune. The Center is stealing from America. We will get a share!"

"Who will we be guarding against?"

"Nobody! That is the beauty of it! Russia does not care." "But we are Georgians."

"Awh! Russia still considers Georgia as a satellite. And we sons of Allah are two thousand kilos from Moscow." Tevali gulped his coffee. "And their targets are Americans and Europians anyway. Who cares?"

CHAPTER 14

"The sand dunes are as astonishing as I remember!" Jack commented as they sped along Highway 2 halfway between Mexicali and the Colorado River. They were still driving the truck they had taken from the Mexicans they had left in the desert.

The barren sand dunes were about fifty feet high and twice as broad. "You're right," Margarita responded, "I didn't know there were dunes like this in Mexico, they look just like in the movie, Star Wars, like you said." She looked back to check on the two teenagers. They had their heads together and were whispering in Spanish.

Jack was cruising at eighty miles an hour and the traffic was very light. The sky was cloudless. They stopped for an early lunch at a small town, Ejido Hermosillo. It had a few small stucco bungalows, a couple of plywood shacks, a very old gas station and an outdoor restaurant.

When a middle aged, chubby waitress came outside to take their order, Margarita ordered beef burritos, rice, beans, and sliced avocados with Cokes for drinks for everybody after they sat at the outdoor cafe shaded by a large canvas top spread over the table area.

"I've been checking my cell for the area around Rio San Luis, when I got a wifi signal from the waitress," Jack said after they had Cokes and were still waiting for their food. "It appears there is some joint US Border patrol and Mexican Federali activity up the road about five miles."

"What kind of activity?" Margarita asked.

"Drug intervention. Smuggling. We cannot get involved," Jack pointed out.

"But we don't have any drugs to worry about," Pete said.

"True, but we have to avoid the US Border guys for other reasons," Jack said. "Let's head into the dunes and drive around the intervention. It's on the highway up ahead."

After they finished their meal, Jack paid for it plus a twenty percent tip. Pete got behind the wheel of the truck and everybody else loaded. Jack sat in the front passenger seat. Pete left the restaurant parking lot, drove about a quarter mile down the road, then turned left towards the US and steered between two huge sand dunes completely uncluttered with vegetation of any kind.

As long as they stayed in the relatively flat areas between the monstrous dunes, Pete had no problem driving. After about two miles,

Jack directed him to turn east towards Yuma. But because there was limited vision due to the same sand dunes, it was nerve wracking.

They continued winding through the empty dunes and made slow progress. Several times they noticed military helicopters and airplanes flying over the area but luckily none seemed to take notice of the truck.

Jack finally directed Pete back to the highway. "It seemed too easy," Margarita observed.

"Maybe it wasn't," Jack responded. "Maybe they are tracking us."

He thought for a minute. "Here's what we're going to do -- we'll go to San Luis Rey. I found it on my google maps. It's a large city in Mexico, just south of Yuma. We'll check into a hotel with a parking garage. Then we'll abandon our stolen truck and sneak out of the hotel. And get away from anybody tracking us."

"What makes you think anybody's following us?" Pete asked. "And if they are, why not just arrest us?"

Jack looked at the young sixteen year old boy. "Maybe they want to wait and see who we are meeting."

Pete looked left and right as they pulled back on the highway. There was no traffic from the west where the road was interdicted but a couple of older cars were driving westward. "Let's get to San Luis Rey," Jack directed. "Muy pronto."

CHAPTER 15

A U S Border Patrol drone handler in a trailer in El Centro, California, checked the image of Jack against a series of photos on his computer, and after hundreds of rapidly flashing screens, he got a match. After reading Jack's federal bio he called a friendly contact, Ned Thomas, at the FBI.

When he got an answer, he said, "I've got a guy in Baja heading toward the border. He is on multiple BOLO lists including yours, Ned." He tapped the screen several times and said, "I'm sending you his info now."

Ned Thomas scanned his computer entries for the Marine, Jack Flashhardt. He found multiple entries from multiple sources. One was made by Howard Hucks, a former FBI agent, who had investigated Flashhardt's family during the Crow Nation lawsuit that had awarded the Flashhardt family ranch of twenty thousand acres to the Crow Indian Nation. The tribe had apparently sued over the original purchase and won their case due to a lack of documentation by the Flashhardt family. Another entry was from David Holland, another former agent noting that the Marine had received a special medal personally from the President of Pakistan honoring Flashhardt's escape from the Taliban. He also found DOD records showing Flashhardt had received a Silver Star medal for bravery under fire and a Purple Heart for wounds received in combat in the Marines. And he had been promoted to Captain. Then he found entries from Special Agent Tucson Luvabrest in the last year when, in a joint op with DHS, she had cooperated with Flashhardt and his brother against some Serbian Muslim terrorists in Washington, Oregon, and California and Montana. And finally, a huge surprise: that Flashhardt was now a deserter from the USMC.

Ned gazed at the entries and wondered what had happened to a guy who obviously had been an American hero of sorts and now was an outlaw. He reached for a hard line and called Tucson after searching a directory. He got a voicemail and left her a message to call back re Captain Flashhardt.

CHAPTER 16

$\mathbf{J}$ack's party soon entered the city, San Luis Rey, and drove until they saw a large hotel in the downtown part of the Mexican city. Like most northern Mexican cities, the streets were relatively clean and the commercial buildings looked a little worse for wear. Pete pulled into the under building parking garage and parked in a space. The group got out, carrying their gear and made their way past the lobby until they walked into a restaurant.

"I notice," Jack said, "that if we stayed in the hallway, it terminates in an alley. Let's order drinks and then head out to the hallway and exit to the alley. Go one at a time and we'll meet in the alley."

Jack was the last to leave the table. He threw down a twenty dollar bill and left.

Outside he saw the group standing around a bus stop bench. A shuttle bus was approaching in the alley. "Let's take it," he directed.

They climbed on the bus and the driver asked, "Cual aerolinea?" Jack shrugged and Margarita offered, "Aero Mexicana."

Fifteen minutes later, the hotel shuttle bus dropped Jack and his team off in front of the Aero Mexico sign at the airport terminal. The four exited the bus and Jack waved at a taxi parked on the curb. The driver nodded and they jumped into the cab and Jack directed the cab to Habitaciones Rino, a hotel he had found on his cell. "It's close to the Colorado River," he explained to the others.

The cab pulled out and drove through the city for almost a half hour, then, after crossing over a bridge, stopped at a nondescript, average looking hotel. Jack paid the driver and they got out. "It's not the Ritz but it is next to the river," he said. "And that bridge back there crossed the Colorado, If you looked, it had water about one hundred meters wide, but did not look big like I remember the Colorado River."

They entered the hotel and Jack signed up for two rooms. After they dropped Margarita and Blanca off at their room, Pete and Jack left the hotel and walked towards the river and as they moved along, Jack read from a note he had pulled up after searching on his phone during breakfast:

"The Morelos Dam near the American border, was opened on March 23, 2014, setting loose a huge volume of water into the Colorado River. As the water roared south, observers were amazed at the 100,000 acre feet of water flooding open the dry channels of the Colorado River: That's one hundred thousand acres covered with one foot of water or about thirty two and a half billion gallons of water, Wow!" He had put down his fork. "And they just did it again yesterday! Not as much, this time."

Once they got near the bridge, they realized how long it was. They looked down and saw a blue stream crossing under the concrete bridge. They saw several men standing next to a boat about a half mile downstream.

"Let's go down, check it out," Jack ordered. " See if we can rent that boat."

They walked down a faint dirt path and as they got closer, they saw a man tending to the runabout motor boat. As they got next to the boat, Jack saw it had an inboard engine, two rows of seating and an open cockpit where more passengers could sit. The Mexican washing the boat clean with buckets of river water, smiled and waved. "Hola," he called a greeting.

"Buenos Días," Pete answered. "?Podemos alquilar su barco por un dia?" "?Para que lo desea?"

"Do you speak English?" Jack asked.

"Un poco..Uh.. that is a little." The Mexican smiled.

"We just want to go for a ride on the river tomorrow,' Jack explained. "Like a picnic."

"?Como, no?" the man replied. He wore a woven straw hat with a wide brim and he smiled as he took it off. His smile revealed a missing front tooth. He looked about forty years old.

"How much to rent for a day?" Jack asked. "?Quiero. Do you want a driver, senior?" "Not necessary," Jack replied.

The Mexican thought for a minute, then said, "Two hundred fifty dollars, Americano, and a five hundred dollar deposit and a credit card."

"You got a deal, we will be here tomorrow at one o'clock. But we want it for two days and an extra one thousand dollars deposit but no credit card."

"?Como, no?"

As Jack and Pete walked back up to the bridge, Pete asked, "Why so late tomorrow?"

"Because we will want to cross into the US after dark."

CHAPTER 17

Jabuli Jazreti strapped his holstered Russian MP-443 Yarygin 9 mm pistol on his belt, donned his Russian army utility jacket and hurried to the Ransomware facility next door.

Telavi was fanatical about Jabuli's team standing guard at the appointed hour. Jabuli unslung his PPS 41 submachine gun and entered the huge mansion. Glancing at the old weapon, captured from Russian infantry troops when Russian troops had invaded Georgia, during the South Ossetia War, he wished he had an AK 74 instead of this relic, but the old 41s were the only weapons available and they did not have time to look around.

CHAPTER 18

The Border Patrol drone handler called Ned, his friendly contact at the FBI. When he got an answer, he said, "I've got the deserter guy, Flashhardt, in Baja heading toward the Colorado River. Looks like he'll try the river."

Ned said thanks, then disconnected and picked up his phone to call a pal at NSA, Brad Knowling. "The guy you wanted to hear about is going to try and sneak across the border at Yuma."

Are you going to round him up?"

"As soon as he tries. Even if we miss him, we got a call that was recorded.

To his father. The deserter is heading home."

Knowling, a recent entrant to the NSA, called a friend who was an aide to General Farley, the head of NSA. The two had gone through OCS (Officer Candidate School) together. Brad said to his pal, Joe Rogers, "Tell your boss. The Marine deserter he said to put on all BOLO lists, Flashhardt, is crossing into the US."

CHAPTER 19

The next morning, after a good sleep, Jack's group joined for breakfast in a small restaurant in the hotel with typical Mexican decor and planned their expedition.

"So, once we pick up the boat, we'll head north until we can see the border," Jack began.

"Won't we just cross then?" Margarita asked. "Why delay?"

"There'll probably be Border patrol boats to prevent any attempts," Jack guessed. "We'll have a better opportunity after dark."

"So when will we cross?" Pete asked.

"Later tonight." Jack responded. "When we have a great chance to escape detection. We'll find a sandbar and have a picnic while we wait."

Jack sat back, sipped a cup of coffee and thought about the Flying Eagle Ranch. He longed for the comfort and security of his home. But then his thoughts skipped to the battle he and his comrades had fought with the Muslim terrorist foes who had tried to take over the ranch the year before: Luckily they had defeated the bad guys but it had been close.

CHAPTER 20

Late in the afternoon, Jack and the others were sitting in the boat where it was beached on a treeless sandbar, he checked his watch as he observed the sun set over the sand dunes that engulfed the land to the west. He said, "Let's load up and take off as soon as it is dark."

Pete, Blanca, and Margarita climbed into the boat and waited as Jack untied the mooring line and climbed aboard. He had already started the two motors and climbed to midships and sat in the tan leather seat at the steering wheel. Margarita moved and sat in the seat next to him. Pete and Blanca sat in the bow area on the front side of the windshield.

"There are four life Jackets on the bottom. Put them on." He put his on then helped Margarita and after making sure it was snugged tightly, he checked Pete and Blanca. Jack turned the running lights off and advanced the throttle and steered into the middle of the river. "We are lucking out. There was a notice online that they are releasing more water tonight. Should make it easier to avoid sand bars." He looked at the others in the fading light, and remarked, "And the Border Patrol is pulling off the river during the release. It can't get any better for us."

"That is unbelievable!" Margarita exclaimed. "How could we be so lucky?"

"We deserve it after our run of bad luck," Jack added.

He turned the boat and headed upstream, to the north. Blanca and Pete sat in the bow area and intently stared up north,

As they slowly cruised farther into US waters, Jack noticed a large bridge as they passed under it. He knew it was Highway 8 and they were now deeper into America. He suddenly heard an engine sound over the throb of their engines. He turned the throttle down to idle and the sound upriver grew greater. He spotted a long rubber skiff approaching from the eastern shore. A man was operating the outboard motor and two men were in the bow of the skiff. When the boat was about fifty feet away, one of the men pointed a spotlight at Jack and the other raised a microphone and said, "Head to shore!"

Jack opened the throttle, turned towards shore, increased his speed and then did a quick one eighty spin and headed directly towards the boat. He hit the rubber craft in the middle at top speed. His action catapulted all the border patrolmen into the river as the two ends of the rubber boat bounced high in the air when Jack crashed into it.

Jack's motor revved to an even higher speed once they were over and past the capsized rubber skiff.

Jack aimed the boat up the river and they roared away. "What is that noise?" Margarita shouted.

Listening over the sound of his motors, he heard a huge rumbling sound up river. "It must be the water they are releasing!" he shouted.

"It sounds horrible!" Margarita explained.

Blanca began to cry and Pete put his arm around her.

Suddenly, in the dim light from the lightened sky of Yuma they saw a huge wall of water rushing towards them from upriver.

"Hang on!" Jack shouted. He grabbed Margarita's hand as the water hit the boat and flipped it end over end. Jack threw his arms around Margarita and lost all sense of direction. He was pushed down until he slammed into the bottom of the river. He kicked off the bottom and was tumbled down the stream until he finally broke the surface of the river. He looked for the two young Mexicans but did not see them. Margarita had also hit her head and was unconscious in his tightly clenched arms.

The boat was nowhere to be seen and the river was pushing Margarita and Jack downstream at a rapid rate. He angled across the rushing current but the tumbling water kept pushing them back towards Mexico.

Jack struggled but it was hard to make headway while holding Margarita's head above water. He could only use one arm to make advances but he kicked as hard as he could until finally he could touch bottom. Struggling against the current he finally reached shore and collapsed next to the still unconscious Margarita.

After a few moments, Margarita stirred, sat up, rubbed her bruised head and exclaimed, "Where are the children?"

"Nowhere to be found! "Jack exclaimed. "Probably somewhere in Mexico if they are alive."

"Can we go back for them?"

"They could be dead. They could be miles downstream. They are gone," Jack explained. "So is our boat! But the good news is we are still in the US." He grabbed his money belt. It was still secure around his waist. "At what cost!" Margarita said.

"Yes, it was a horrible accident. Who knew they were going to release such a huge volume of water," Jack responded.

CHAPTER 21

$\mathbf{J}$ack and Margarita waded across a swampy area and reached the river's shore.

"We must buy dry clothes: she exclaimed.

"You're right." He agreed. "We can't check into a hotel looking like this. We need some luggage as well."Where does your daughter live?" Jack asked Margarita as they walked through a shopping district not far from the river.

"She lives with my aunt in Erie, close to Boulder, Colorado." Margarita glanced at Jack. " Let's get some clothes at that Target Store, " She suggested. A half hour later, they emerged wearing new blue jeans and Carta Blanca t-shirts and carrying two small suitcases with their wet clothes inside. Jack was also carrying a new cell with 100 minutes prepaid on it. He set up an Uber app and used it to call for an Uber. When the car arrived minutes later, Jack directed the driver to take them to a hotel.

"Which one? There is a Hilton and a Radison." The Mexican-American driver asked in English.

"Nothing so fancy," Jack instructed.

The driver suggested something in Spanish and Margarita translated, "How about the Coronado Motor Hotel? It is old but clean."

"Perfecto!" Jack responded.

Within minutes they stopped in front of the hotel, an old Mexican hacienda with white stucco walls and a red tile roof.

"May as well be in Mexico," Margarita observed.

"Let's go," Jack ordered. "I want to get to our room and call my brother."

After they paid cash from Jack's money belt and got a room, they went to it and both collapsed on the king size bed. Jack called BIlly and when his brother picked up, he said, "I'm in the Coronado Motor Hotel in Yuma. Can you come and get me?"

"Great! You made it! Where do you want to go?" "The Flying Eagle Ranch, of course."

"How far is Yuma from LA?"

"Two hundred miles, maybe two fifty." Jack answered, "But it's an easy drive on the 10 Freeway."

"Should take about four, maybe five hours. Hang on." The phone went silent except Jack could hear muffled conversation, then Billy came back on and said, "We'll be there by lunch tomorrow."

"Wonderful! Then I guess Zhang is coming?" "Of course."

Jack felt the dread of another encounter with Zhang. She seemed to want to relive their motel encounter in the motel next to the Juan De Fuca Strait in the state of Washington the year before. *She's beautiful*, he thought. *But trouble. Billy would be over the top angry.* He recalled her harsh words again: "Jack, if you want to live. .."

It had been a terrifying and then an amazing experience and he envied Billy and what she was to his brother. But he wanted no trouble with Billy Howling Dog. They had patched up their childhood squabbles caused by the Indian/white man differences and were good now. And Zhang, with her easy but troublesome drug connections, kept Billy supplied with Meth.

Jack hung up and said, "Where does your daughter live?"

"I told you," Margarita said, "Erie, Colorado, with my aunt. Close to Boulder.."

"Well, Boulder is on the way to Montana so we can drop you off." "Perfecto!" Margarita exclaimed. But she wondered if she would ever see

Jack again after Erie.

"And maybe you should do a little research… find a good plastic surgeon in Boulder. As I recall, it's a university town. I'll bet they have some good ones. And I haven't forgotten. I owe you big time for all you have done for me."

Margarita thought and then said, "I'm tired, both physically and emotionally after losing the two kids. But tomorrow morning, I promise to give you a huge thank you."

"I feel exactly like you." he answered.

Jack and Margarita took off their clothes, got into bed, hugged each other and quickly fell asleep.

Jack woke at midnight and stared at the sleeping woman next to him. He thought of Penel back in Shangri-la and wished she and their one year old son were here with him. He wondered when he would be able to go back to Asia and solve that problem. He sadly thought of Pete and Blanca and hoped their life jackets had saved them from the flood that had capsized the boat and washed them away. Then his thoughts turned to Tucson, the FBI agent who had been such a big part of his life until she was kidnapped and gang raped by the Serbian terrorists and the White Supremacist in Big Bear last year. He wondered if she had recovered as much as possible from her horrible experience with the Muslim terrorists before Jack and the Army unit led by Mick Nakamura had rescued her. Tucson Luvabest had begged him to tell no one what had happened to her. She said that she would be stigmatized by FBI agents because of what horrors she had experienced. With that last regretful thought, he turned over and fell back asleep.

Jack awoke when a still naked Margarita rolled over on top of him. It was a glorious waking.

More than an hour later, Jack fell asleep and when he awoke again, Margarita was talking on the hotel telephone. They got up, dressed and in minutes were at a table looking at two Hispanic women making tortillas by hand in the hotel's kitchen. The restaurant had about a half dozen small tables and a large coffee dispenser was on a table in front of the kitchen. The Hispanic women took balls of dough, expertly formed the tortillas by hand, and fried them on a comal which, Margarita explained, was a metal platter that was commonly used to cook on in Mexico.

Margarita looked at Jack and wondered if she would ever have the chance to cook for Jack. She thought how wonderful that would be. Then one of the women shifted to another comal and put strips of red snapper on the tortillas, added bits of lettuce, onions, tomatoes, guacamole, and red salsa, expertly wrapped the ingredients into burritos and served them to Jack and Margarita.

CHAPTER 22

Both Margarita and Jack were sleepy after their big breakfast so they went back to their room and slept until Billy and Zhang knocked on their door, waking them.

Jack opened the door and greeted Billy and Zhang. Billy was dressed in a cammo t-shirt and tan shorts. Beautiful and exotic Zhang was wearing skin tight slacks and a white half t-shirt. She looked wonderful, as usual and, Jack noted, she had no bra on, as usual.

"Come on in," Jack greeted them. He looked at Billy's eyes. They were clear. No drugs were apparent.

They entered and Zhang went straight to the bathroom. Jack and Billy went to the outdoor patio and sat in black metal chairs.

"How was the drive?" Jack asked.

"Long and tedious," Billy responded. "And it did not put me in a mood to drive to Montana."

"I can't rent a car," Jack complained, "If I use a credit card, the feds will spot me."

"If you use mine, how will I get it back?" "That's why you need to drive us."

Zhang came out of the bathroom and joined them on the patio. "What's the verdict?"

Billy looked at Zhang, "He wants us to drive him to the ranch."

"I can't. I have an upcoming recording session in LA," Zhang said. "Use my credit card," Billy suggested.

"They might be watching you," Jack responded. "Use mine," Zhang suggested.

"Too close, as well," Jack said.

"I have a credit card in my trade name, XU, " Zhang offered. "I doubt the feds read the Hollywood gossip sheets. They'll never catch that name."

"Perfect!" Billy exclaimed.

Jack glanced at his watch. "Let's wake up Margarita and go to lunch." Billy asked. "How's the chow at the restaurant here?"

"Wonderful! We will meet you there in ten minutes." Jack said as he walked with them into the room. Margarita had gone to the bathroom. Jack walked the two to the door and said as they left, "See you in a few."

Ten minutes later, the brothers and the two women reunited in the hotel restaurant.

"This is quite charming," Zhang commented. She looked at the Mexican decor then at Margarita. Billy checked out Margarita's hip hugging jeans and bare midriff.

Margarita was wearing a mask to hide her scars. Jack had explained about the scars on Margarita before and Billy and Zhang made no comment on the issue, then Zhang said. "Let us see your face."

Margarita glanced at Jack and said, "I'd rather not."

Great food here!" Jack commented. He ordered four beers from the hovering waiter, an old Hispanic man with a pockmarked face.

The four ordered fish tacos and black bean and green olive tostadas. They watched as a middle aged and slightly overweight woman, who looked very Indian in her features, made fresh tortillas and proceeded to cook their food. "What do you hope to accomplish at the ranch?" Billy asked. "You can't hide forever."

"I'm hoping I can meet with Dad and his pal the Senator. I'm trusting they can pressure the Marines to lay off. We saved their butts from the Serbian terrorists last year at the ranch. So the Senator owes me."

"The Senator might blame you for attracting the Serbs," Zhang pointed out. "You were the targets, not the Senator."

"So what?" Jack responded. "They would've been toast if we hadn't shown up."

He thought back to moments in the battle at the Flying Eagle Ranch in Montana the year before:

Jack crawled around an armchair in the ranch house's darkened living room. A suppressing shot came from Billy who was in the hayloft of the barn aiming a 25 mm gun they had earlier taken from a terrorist hiding in the barn. The large fired bullet rang out and hit a picture on the living room wall. Jack bumped into a Serbian crawling in the opposite direction. The two struggled, Jack shot and missed with the last round in the Beretta, then cut the guy in the arm with his long knife . The Serbian scrambled away, Jack stabbed, pinned the man's lower leg to the floor. He arched up and another of Billy's 25mm rounds hit him in the chest, jerking him away like a rag doll on a string. Jack barely hung onto the knife.

A waiter, serving their food, interrupted his memory.

"Are you going with Jack to the Flying Eagle Ranch?" Zhang asked Margarita.

Margarita glanced at Jack and thought, *Wouldn't it be wonderful if we could pick up my daughter and continue to his ranch?*

When Jack did not respond, Margarita glanced at Jack and said, "No, he is dropping me off in Colorado. At my aunt's home, where my daughter is. I am so excited to see her. I talked to her on the phone in the room this morning."

"How old is she?" Zhang asked.

"Juanita is seven. And I have not seen her for four years," Margarita lamented.

"Why not?" Billy asked.

"I got deported and kept getting caught trying to sneak back to the US. But now I am here across the border, thanks to Jack!" Margarita slapped the table with a laugh of triumph. Then she hugged Jack and he spilled his fork full of veggies into his lap.

"Let me clean this up." Zhang, sitting next to Jack, said. She scraped the veggies onto a small plate and quickly also caressed Jack's groin under the table. She sat back down and took a bite of her taco with a smug look on her face that Billy did not notice.

Trying not to react to the careful but seductive caress and accompanying squeeze, Jack took a drink from his bottle of Corona Beer.

"So when do you want to take off?" Billy asked.

"We've got the room for another night," Jack said. "If we take off after lunch, you can stay in our room tonight if you want and head back to L A tomorrow."

After lunch, they climbed in Zhang's BMW convertible and after directions from the desk clerk, they drove to a car rental shop, just a mile away.

There, Zhang rented a Jeep wagoneer in her name after explaining the Xu stage name on her credit card to the clerk. Intimidated by her flashy beauty he quickly agreed, She drove the Jeep back to the hotel and gave the keys to Jack when they all arrived at the hotel.

Jack and Margarita got their bags from the room, and hugged Billy and Zhang. The latter managed to grope Jack as they parted. Jack and Margarita left after dialing in St George, Utah, on the Jeep's GPS system.

"What's with the Asian bitch?" Margarita asked. "I saw her paw you twice."

Jack shook his head. "We had a mistaken identity encounter in a hotel last year. Billy does not know about it. And he is quite possessive so I am trying to avoid her while she keeps trying to hook up."

"I can see why. She is very beautiful but she seems ruthless," Margarita added.

"You can say that again," Jack exclaimed. "I just want to stay away from her. And her hold on Billy is relentless. And I am sure she supplies his meth."

"She scares me," Margarita exclaimed. "I am glad she is in our rear view mirror."

"Me too for that," Jack agreed. "St George, here we come."

Two Hispanic men stepped out of a Honda sedan and walked in front of their rental car.

"This looks like trouble," Jack said.

One of the men. a fat Mexican-looking man snarled, "Hombre, no pagaste tu tarifa fronteriza."

Margarita translated, "He says you owe the cartel money." "They abandoned us!" Jack retorted.

"El cartel está en todas partes de las que no puedes escapar!" The fat man screamed as he drew a knife and moved towards Jack, who kicked the knife hand and punched the man in his huge stomach roll of fat. The man groaned and writhed in pain, clutching his belly.

Margarita screamed with panic in her voice, "Jack! Let's get out of here.

He says the cartel is everywhere. Not just Mexico!"

The second smaller man pulled a large, stainless steel switchblade and aimed the blade at Jack, who ripped his shirt off and wrapped it around his left arm as he lunged at the man. The knife-wielding man stabbed at Jack and sunk his knife into Jack's shirt. Jack kicked the man's arm and the knife went flying. He swung a fist at the man's nose. His fist smashed deeply. The man screamed as he sank to the ground.

Jack turned back to the first man as the other man scrambled to retrieve his weapon. When he bent over to pick up the knife, Jack turned and kicked him in the crotch from behind. The man also screamed in pain and fell to the ground.

CHAPTER 23

Jack and Margarita jumped in the Jeep and drove through the suburbs of Yuma and soon hit the freeway heading east. They quickly entered the same huge sand dune area they had encountered on the Mexican side of the border. After a while they were out of the empty of vegetation dunes and into the normal desert with the typical Joshua Tree cacti with their outstretched cactus branch arms and low to the ground Chollo bushes. Here and there mountains seemed to sprout out of the desert and rule the horizons. Every stream bed they crossed was bone dry.

Two hours later, they stopped at a gas station.

"You pump the gas," Jack instructed. He handed her three twenty dollar bills. "Pay inside," he added.

"Why do you want me to do this?" Margarita asked. "I'm a bartender, not a gas pumper."

I'm afraid they might have facial recognition software in their cameras." "Ohh, okay, I get it," Margarita said as she stepped out of the car. She entered the old looking station and handed the man attendant the money and said, " I want to fill it up."

A hundred miles later, they had wound down enough to talk about the latest Mexican attack.

"You were very strong!" Margarita exclaimed.

"Those two yokels were not much of a threat," Jack said. "But the knife!" Margarita pointed out.

"Knife fighting 101 says, Pick up your left foot, then put it down. Then pick up your right foot and put it down. Repeat until you have escaped."

Margarita burst out laughing. Then she said, "You ignored your knife fighting training."

Jack laughed as well and concluded, "I didn't have time to instruct you." Soon they crossed the massive Hoover Dam and saw the valley containing

Las Vegas spread before them. Massive Mt Charleston was in the north western background, overlooking the valley.

"Can we stop and eat?" Margarita asked. "We'll hit a drive thru," Jack said.

"Dare I ask? I've never been to Las Vegas. Can we visit a casino? They look so grand. I would love to see their insides."

"I'm sorry," Jack responded. He touched her leg. "Maybe next time. I'm too hot. I can't take a chance because of the same issue. The casinos all have facial recognition cameras. We're only two hours from St. George. Then, the next stop will be Boulder."

They stopped at a gas station and then a Jack in the Box restaurant near a racetrack on the east side of the city. After ordering burgers and fries and coffees, they continued on their way. Two hours later, they passed into St. George where Margarita got a room with cash at an older, slightly run down hotel on the east side of town. They *feasted on* beef tacos and Seven Ups from a drive thru Del Taco restaurant.

The six hour plus drive had worn them out and after a half hour of watching TV, they both fell asleep.

The next morning, they took a fast shower together, dressed and stopped for gas and breakfast at another wayside center, then hit the road for Denver. Margarita noticed that Jack made no romantic moves toward her. She was sorry she had not taken the initiative in the shower.

About an hour later, they turned off Highway 15 onto Highway 70 for the last leg to Denver. The scenery was spectacular and reminded Jack of the Bighorn mountains of Wyoming and northern Montana mountains,

They descended into a huge valley, covered with pine trees and rimmed by craggy mountains. By afternoon they were exhausted and decided to stop in Glenwood Springs. They found a small hotel constructed of timbers next to the rushing Colorado River which was only about sixty feet wide. Margarita filled the vehicle with gas at Jack's urging and bought sandwiches, chips and a six pack of Coors in a small store.

Margarita, after wearing her mask all day, ached to take it off but she did not want to reveal her scars to Jack. She could not help but notice that every time he saw her mask less face, his eyes went to the horrible scars.

Jack thought of the town of Aspen, just thirty miles to the south and all the good times he had spent skiing there. He wondered if he would ever see or ski Snowmass or Aspen Highlands again.

Their room's patio fronted on the Colorado River and it was pleasant to sit and watch the flowing water but as they watched they were reminded of the flood that had carried Pete and Blanca and the boat back to Mexico so they went inside, ate their meals and watched mindless comedy shows on the TV. Margarita kept quietly glancing at Jack, wondering how she could maintain a relationship with the handsome criminal. She wondered how long he would have to go to prison when they caught him. She wondered if this time she could stay in the United States and not be deported.

The next morning, she got up early, took a quick shower and after drying off, moved into the bed and carefully embraced Jack. He was slow to respond, but finally he awoke and responded to her advances with delayed but then fervent enthusiasm.

After a successful seduction, Margarita could not stop grinning all morning. As they shot down from Glenwood Springs to Denver, her excitement grew as her attention shifted from Jack and she began looking forward to reuniting with her daughter, Juanita.

When they finally entered Denver, Jack turned north on the 25 Freeway.

He, too, was smiling as he drove.

And in a fast hour, they headed into Erie. The small city lay at the foot of the magnificent Rocky Mountains and they stopped at a Shell gas station where Margarita purchased and pumped gas and then went back inside and got snacks for Jack's final journey. Then they continued and finally pulled to a stop after his GPS directed him to Margarita's Tia.

Margarita could not contain herself when she saw her aunt and Juanita standing on a lawn in front of a modest but clean looking house. She had her daughter on Jack's cell phone and she jumped out of the car and ran to her daughter and her aunt.

She returned after a moment with her daughter and introduced Jack. The young girl, about seven years old and dressed in a colorful short dress and white blouse, was as pretty as her mother and had a shy smile.

After Jack got out and shook hands with Juanita, he embraced Margarita and said, "Call me tonight."

Margarita replied, "Thank you for everything you have done for me. And the four thousand dollars."

"After you have met with your plastic surgeon, call me and we will take care of your surgical costs. I hope to see you soon" Jack climbed back in the Jeep and began his lonely odyssey to the Flying Eagle Ranch.

As Margarita waved goodbye, she prayed she would see Jack again.

CHAPTER 24

T ucson Luvabrest was operating out of the FBI field facility in Denver, Colorado. She received a message requesting to call Agent Jed Thomas regarding Captain Flashhardt. When she saw Jack's name, she got a horrible tremor throughout her body. She felt so ill, she almost threw up. She tried to stand and run to a hallway bathroom but her legs felt too weak to move. She glanced at the waste basket next to her desk but resolved not to vomit.

She took several calming deep breaths but it did not slow her racing heart. Finally after five minutes, she felt enough calm settle over her body and mind to enable her to call Jed Thomas.

"Thomas here," he answered the phone.

"This is Special Agent Tucson Luvabrest, I am returning your call." Thomas glanced at his notebook to refresh his memory. "Yes," he said.

"We have an order to arrest deserter Jack Flashhardt. He was observed crossing into the US at Yuma. I see here by my computer entries that you know him personally.":

"What do you mean by personally?" Tucson asked. "And he is a war hero! What do you mean by deserter?"

"I'm just reading an order to arrest." Thomas replied. "And the fact that you know him personally and worked with him for a brief time makes you the logical person to collect him." He paused, then added, "Is there some reason you cannot comply?"

Tucson took a deep breath and tried to respond promptly. "No reason," she finally said. After receiving more details, she hung up and shuddered at the thought of confronting Jack Flashhardt again.

CHAPTER 25

Jack's GPS took him to the Foothill Freeway and eventually he transitioned onto the 25 and would soon be crossing into Wyoming. He stopped for gas in a small and old fuel station south of Casper which did not look like it had cameras outdoors.

Finally, he got a room in a tattered motel in Buffalo, just south of the Montana border. The next morning, he was in Montana by sunrise. The blue sky was cloudless and the morning was magnificent. He reached Billings by lunchtime so he ate at a Hardee's restaurant drive thru as he was starving after not having any breakfast. He wolfed down a double burger and ate all the fries served.

Knowing now that he was only 100 miles from the ranch increased his excitement until he was pulled over by a Montana Sheriff's SUV just forty miles from the ranch.

Jack rolled down his window and called a greeting to the deputy that approached his Jeep. The man was tall and looked very fit. He wore a Canadian Mounty type hat.

Jack's heart was hammering and he took deep breaths as he watched the deputy approach.

"You in a hurry, young man? You were topping eighty five miles per hour."

Jack took a deep breath and said, 'You are right, officer. I am close to home. I've been gone for a while." *Please do not run my numbers,* he thought.

After Jack turned over his driver's license and the Jeep rental agreement, the officer asked, "Who's Xu? And where exactly are you headed with his rental vehicle?"

With mounting apprehension, Jack said, "Xu is my brother's girlfriend. She rented the Jeep for me. And I'm going to my family's ranch. The Flying Eagle Ranch."

The officer tapped Jack's license on his hand for a moment, then asked, "Isn't that where there was the big dustup last year?"

"Yes, Sir, the ranch was attacked by Muslim terrorists. I was there. We managed to defeat them."

"I'll be go to hell! That sounded like a huge brouhaha. And our Senator Jenson was rescued, I heard."

"That's right, deputy. The Marines and the Army were involved."

"Damned ragheads! You know, I served in Iraq!" the deputy exclaimed.

"You did fine work, I heard. You follow me and get on down to the Flying Eagle, son." He handed the papers and license back to Jack, saluted him and returned to his vehicle. Then he pulled ahead of Jack and escorted him the last forty miles at speeds topping eighty miles an hour. Finally he turned onto a private asphalted road about twenty feet wide and drove another five miles until he got to the huge entry sign spanning over the approach road stating Flying Eagle Ranch, whereupon he turned around and with a parting wave headed back towards Billings.

Jack, with mounting excitement, drove along the road to the ranch for about ten minutes, and when he finally turned a last curve and saw the huge barn, the windmill, the silo, the granary, and the sprawling ranch house, he felt overjoyed.

As he pulled to a stop and got out of the Jeep, his dog, Bullet, and a mate came bouncing out of the lavender hedges that surrounded the house and when they realized it was Jack arriving, the dogs went into a whirling frenzy of happiness as they spun around him. Bullet was a big, black, thick Rottweiler and his companion was a tan female Rhodiasn named Jennifer.

A moment later, his father, Bill Flashhardt, came out of the house and approached with wide spread arms and when he got close, he enveloped Jack in his embrace.

Bill, a tall, lean man, was dressed in typical western garb,, cowboy boots, weathered jeans, and a western style shirt with snap down buttons. His white hair was cut short.

He ran his fingers over his full head of white hair and then squeezed Jack tight. "How the hell are you, son? It's great to see you!"

"Hi, Dad. I love you! It's great to see you!"

"As always, son! Welcome home!"

As the father and son embraced, the dogs continued to leap with pleasure at Jack's homecoming. After a moment, all four companions went across the porch that spanned the entire front of the two story log house and walked through the new wooden carved front door. It had replaced the door Billy had shot out with the 25 caliber weapon during the terrorist siege last year. He had fired from the terrorist gun he had captured moments earlier in the hayloft of the barn. Jack paused and admired the large bull elk carved on the face of the door.

Sparkling new leather furniture was scattered throughout the living room as well. The floors were polished wood and two leather recliners flanked the lava rock surfaced fireplace. A huge elk antlered head was mounted over the fireplace. Jack had a sudden sense of bewilderment as he noted all the changes.

"Where did the elk head come from?" Jack asked.

"I shot it last season," Bill answered. "You must be tired," he commented.

"But I want to hear about your crazy travels."

Jack wondered if he would ever be able to hunt again after all the death he had experienced in Asia. He wondered about what aspect of his adventures he could share with his father, then said, "How about a cup of coffee?"

The two went into the kitchen and Jack saw a young boy sitting on a stool at the kitchen island. He was about ten years old and was a towhead.

"Who is this?" Jack asked.

"Bill patted the boy on the shoulder and said, "This is your cousin, Sammy. My sister Alicia's son. "Remember, she married an Australian and moved there years ago. She sent Sammy here for the summer."

The young boy smiled as Jack said, "Hello, Sammy. How do you like Montana?"

"I'm learning to ride a horse," Sammy said proudly.

"That's neat!" Jack responded. He went to the pantry and got two dog bone treats for the dogs while Bill poured two mugs of coffee and retrieved a plate of cinnamon rolls from the double, wood panel-faced refrigerator. The dogs went outside to eat their treats. Bill put the cups down on the countertop which was a single slab of polished wood. Then got milk out of the fridge and re-filled Sammy's glass.

"I want to thank you and Senator Jensen's efforts to exonerate me and get my sentence dismissed by the military." Jack said. "Do you think he can help me again?"

"You deserved it, son." Bill sipped his coffee after blowing on it. "You saved me, the Senator, and your Afghan girl from certain death."

"And then I screwed it up by following her back to Asia and trying to convince her to return to the US."

'She gave birth to your son. No one can blame you for wanting a family that you love."

"The Marines don't see it that way. Over thirty days UA and they flipped me over to deserter status."

"After all you've accomplished for them!" "You sound like Billy. He said the same thing."

"Well, you can't blame the military. You did not play by their rules. But more importantly, what are you going to do to fix it?" Bill got up and refilled their coffees.

Jack looked at his Dad. "Do you think Senator Jensen would try a do over?"

"I talked to him. He did not sound very sympathetic at all. I think you should meet with him, tell him your side of the story. Maybe you can change his mind." Bill sat up. "Say, you know who called me?" He answered his own question. "General Harmbruster of Eagle's Aerie."

"Why? Was he looking for me?"

"No, he was asking about our mountain-climbing expeditions. Specifically, he asked me details about our Mt. Elbrus climb."

"Just Elbrus? Our Russian climb? I wonder why?" Jack asked. "He didn't ask about any other climbs?" Jack sat down. "Climbing experience is what got me pulled out of law school. Changed my whole life. I'll never become a lawyer after all I've been through. I know that now."

"You mean when they activated you out of the Marine reserves and sent you to Asia to train Army troops?"

"Exactly! They said they needed trained mountaineers so they could look for their lost bio bomb in the Hindu Kush Mountains."

"And that's what got you into the lost valley and Penelope. How is my grandson and Penelope doing?"

"He's as cute as can be. And she is as beautiful as ever."

"I'd love to see him. And her. She saved my life with that medical water she gave me. So she's still in that remote valley?"

"Yes. The valley that I found when that updraft pushed my parachute over a ridge into what turned out to be a river of Islamic terrorist blood.."

"Stanford will let you go back and finish law school, you know. You've only got a year and half left and then the Bar exam."

"Do you think I can deal with torts and divorces and legal crap after all this? Never happen!"

"Well, I would rather you take over the ranch in a few years anyway. I am about ready to hang up my spurs. I'll put a call into the Senator, see when he'll be back in Montana."

"I guess I'll hang here for a while. Worst case, I can drive to DC and meet with him." Jack held up his Jeep keys. "But I need to return the rental Jeep to the rental shop in Billings."

"I'll have a couple of the hands caravan it this afternoon," Bill said. "Do you have any chores that need to be done?"

"We've got a missing cow and calf from the end of a roundup yesterday. Give you a chance to get back in the saddle."

"That would be great! " Jack looked at Sammy. "Hey, you want to ride out and look for a calf?"

"Sure!" Sammy answered. "I want to go!"

"We'll take the dogs with,`` Jack added, "One other thing, Dad, there's a girl who helped me get out of Mexico, big time. She had a very bad encounter with outlaws and needs medical attention. I want you to fund whatever she needs from my savings from the Emerald reward the Chinese government gave Billy and I for the ancient relics we returned to them."

Bill took the note about Margarita from Jack, then picked up a phone and said, "I'll have one of the hands saddle a mount for you. His name is Blaze."

"Can he jump a four rail corral fence?" Jack asked.

"You better believe it!" Bill exclaimed. "He's young and full of piss and vinegar."

Eager to get back on a horse, Jack went to the bathroom, then he and Sammy walked to a corral on the east side of the hay barn and Jack thanked an Indian worker for saddling a completely black horse with a white blaze on its face and an older gray mare for Sammy. He asked which way the cattle movement had come from. The man pointed north. The Indian, when asked, confirmed the horse's name was Blaze.

He, Sammy, and Bullet, who was shadowing Jack's every step, mounted up and headed out in the western direction from the corral. About an hour later, as they came over a hill, Jack was wondering why the General had asked about Mt Elbrus, in the Caucasus Mountains in the south of Russia, when they saw a Hereford calf standing knee deep in water on a small sandbar in the about ten meter wide stream with its mother standing nearby on the shore. On the other side of the water from the mother cow stood a large gray wolf. It was regarding the calf with hungry interest.

Bullet took off immediately. He was about 100 yards from the wolf and across the river. He jumped off a four foot bank and crashed into the water.

Jack pulled a saddle carbine out of its holster, levered a round. Aimed at the wolf, then shot at a rock next to the wolf. The bullet hit the rock and the wolf immediately turned and ran away. It and Bullet, trailing quite a ways behind because he had been held up by the river, disappeared over a hill.

Jack and Sammy urged their horses down to the stream. The calf was knee deep in mud on the sand bar and struggling.

Jack said, "Why don't you swim to the sandbar and rescue the calf?" Sammy said, as he dismounted, "I can't swim."

"You live in Australia and can't swim?" Jack said as he dismounted. He glanced at the river and added, "I learned to swim in this stream. Go for it!"

Sammy stood at the water's edge, frozen.

Jack picked the boy up and tossed him in the river.

Sammy splashed frantically at the water and despite himself made headway until he reached the sandbar. Jack took a lasso off a ring and tried to lasso the calf but missed. He tried again and missed again. The calf bleated and the mother spun around in frustration and fear.

Jack slowly twirled the rope again and dropped it over the calf's head. He backed the horse up and the calf heaved itself free with Jack's aid. Sammy grabbed the rope and was also pulled back to shore. He and the calf scrambled up the bank.

"I thought you said you can't swim." Jack said to the dripping wet boy. "I did it!" Sammy exclaimed.

As the mother joined the calf and Jack retrieved his lasso, Bullet trotted over the hill after giving up on the wolf. Despite his lack of success he had a big grin on his face showing he had enjoyed the romp after the wolf.

They slowly continued to the ranch headquarters, and the mother and calf joined the herd, while Jack took the saddles off the horses, released them to the corral after wiping them down with a towel. He hung the saddles next to others in a row on a long rail inside the barn.

That evening, after a dinner of pork chops and fried potatoes, Jack and his father and Sammy watched the depressing news about the state of the nation. When the on scene newscaster commented on illegals crossing in Texas, Jack related the highlights of his trip from the west coast of Baja to the Colorado River.

Bill was amazed and happy for Jack's successful crossing except for the lost boat and teenagers. But after listening to another of Jack's amazing adventures he wondered whether Jack could ever settle down and run the ranch.

Sammy, after telling his adventure in the water for the second time, listened to Jack tell how his dad had taught him how to swim using the same method, then went to bed.

Jack wondered for a moment whether the two kids had survived their washback to Mexico. He wondered if they, like Sammy, did not know how to swim. He was very happy he had put life jackets on them. He sent them an imaginary wish of luck. Then he said goodnight and went to his bedroom to sleep.

Everything looked as it had always done and he slept soundly until a roar of noise outside, early the next morning, roused him. His bedroom window looked out the back so he could not see the source. He quickly dressed and went to the living room and looked at the huge expanse between the house and the barn.

In the middle of the yard was a CH-47 military helicopter and a black Suburban Chevrolet parked side by side.

Jack heard voices in the kitchen so he turned and entered it whereupon he saw his old Afghanland flying buddy Charlie Davis, and FBI agent Tucson Luvabrest and one other man talking to his Dad.

When Charlie saw him enter the room, he exclaimed, "Jack! Old buddy! It's great to see you!" He came around the island and shook Jack's hand. Charlie, tall, with a strong build, had a huge smile with flashing white teeth and bulging muscles on his upper body. They had been friends since meeting in Afghanistan where Charlie, who had deserted service. was working for Afghan General Hammar, the Pakistani military man who had been involved in drug smuggling and had helped Jack defeat an Afghan Taliban force.

Tucson spun around when Charlie called out. She waited for Charlie to move out of the way and then embraced Jack with a big hug.

Jack pulled back and looked into Tucson's face. She looked very upset and her face was red. But not like the last time she saw him when she was recovering from multiple rapes and abduction by the Serbian Islamic terrorists who had later attacked the Flying Eagle Ranch. She re-embraced Jack and kissed him passionately. Jack was so happy to see her apparent recovery. Then he felt something hard pressing against his stomach. He glanced down and saw a pistol aiming at him.

"Jack Flashhardt, you are under arrest for desertion from the United States Marine Corps," she said in a flat voice. She tossed her flaming red hair and scowled.

CHAPTER 26

Charlie, upon hearing her, spun around, saw the pistol pointed at Jack and shouted, "You can't arrest--!"

"Special Agent Sloan (Tucson nodded at the man standing to one side of the kitchen) and I came for the purpose of arresting Jack. He is wanted for desertion from the Marine Corps." Tucson backed up to be clear of Jack's embrace. She continued to aim the pistol. "You are his buddy, Charlie. I couldn't count on you to help arrest Jack so I said nothing to you about our reason to arrive today. And I am an FBI agent, committed to enforcing the laws of the United States. Something you know, Jack has little regard for. I can't name a law Jack wouldn't break."

"Hey!" Bill protested, "Jack's no criminal. He wiped out the Serb terrorists last year in multiple encounters. He saved all our's and Senator Jensen's asses!"

Tucson looked at Bill, then added, "I admit his unorthodox ways get things accomplished, but there are rules to keep a society functioning, and Jack has no concept of that." She shook her head. "And, anyway, it's not up to me to decide. He'll have to answer to a court martial."

Bullet, feeling the tension in the air, brushed against Jack's leg and whined. Jack patted the dog. "Let's get it over with," he said. Then he crossed the kitchen, to his Dad and hugged Bill. "See you whenever." He bent over and patted Bullet's eagerly outstretched head. "I'm sorry I can't take you old buddy. You have always welcomed me home. You are a wonderful friend."

Charlie, Tucson, and Jack left the kitchen, walked outside and Charlie climbed into the cockpit to join the pilot who had never left the aircraft while Jack and Tucson got in the troop cabin in the back. The FBI agent climbed into the black SUV and drove away.

"You can put away the pistol," Jack said as he sat down on a web seat along the portside bulkhead of the chopper. Tucson put her gun away and sat next to him. Charlie turned lights on overhead as it was dark with the gun hatches closed. The only other light in the cabin was over the rear hatch. The helicopter lifted into the air.

"I'm sorry, Jack," Tucson said. "This was one of the hardest orders I ever carried out."

"How'd you get on to me?"

"I heard a DEA drone caught your image through a windshield in Mexico.

You've been tracked ever since."

"All my efforts to be sneaky!" Jack shook his head. "All for naught!" He glanced at Tucson. "So, you've recovered."

"And I repay your saving me by this," Tucson said ruefully.

"Well, you're right. I am guilty. But I had my reasons," Jack admitted. "What could be so important that you would just go AWOL?"

Jack thought of his little son and Penelope, and then his thoughts turned to the now dismal future. He thought of the romantic relationship he had with Tucson while they were chasing the terrorist gang, The Fist, and their terrorist leader, Mara Bhutto,, and decided not to speak of his baby son and Penelope back in Asia.

He thought of the American terrorists, Joshua Trumpet, and Bobby Ray Dawklings, who with the Serbians had repeatedly raped Tucson in Big Bear last year after they disarmed and kidnapped her.

The flight droned on for an hour and then the pilot, Joe Fresco, came back and sat on the starboard web seating across from Jack and Tucson. He was a young man, about late twenties in age, had a high and tight Marine Corps haircut with black hair, was about six feet tall and slender. He was wearing his Marine green utility uniform. "We are being diverted to Warren Air Force base in Cheyenne Wyoming," Joe said. "We'll land in about a half hour."

"We're supposed to go to Omaha!" Tucson protested.

"We would have to refuel anyway," Joe said. "We can refuel there."

When the CH-47 settled to the ground. Twp jeeps and four armed MPs were waiting to escort Jack and Tucson off the base to a nearby commercial center. The two got in the jeep and were driven to a large concrete block building. Charlie and Joe were transported in the other jeep. There were lines of grass landscaping outside the building. It had a red metal standing seam roof.

They were escorted into the building and into an office, where Jack was astonished to see General Harmbruster sitting behind a metal desk bare of any work papers. An Army Colonel in fatigues, was sitting in a chair in acorner of the office. He nodded but did not get up when the General introduced him as Colonel Weatherbee.

CHAPTER 27

The General stood and shook Jack's hand. "Welcome home, Captain Flashhard," he said with a welcoming smile. He turned to Charlie and the pilot and said, "Thank you for bringing Flashhardt."

"What is going on, General? I am taking Captain Flashhardt into custody for desertion," Tucson protested.

The General picked up a desk telephone and handed it to Tucson. "Speak to one of your bosses. He's waiting on the line to talk to you."

She looked at the General. He had a hard face and had a very grim look on it. She took the phone and said with a shaky voice, "This is Agent Tucson Luvabrest."

"Hello, Special Agent Luvabrest. This is FBI Executive Director, Counter terrorism, Agent Donald Johnson. Please stand down on your arrest and give the phone to the General of Eagle's Aerie and follow General Harmbruster's directions in every way." She handed the phone back to the General who hung it up.

"What's going on, General?" Jack asked.

"I want, no, Eagle's Aerie needs your help, Captain. You climbed a mountain in the Caucus Mountains of Russia a few years ago."

"Mt Elbrus, the highest mountain in Europe," Jack responded.

"That's right. And it's on the border of Georgia and Russia," the General added. "And more importantly, the city, Min Vody of Russia is only a little over one hundred miles away," the General added. "And one of the biggest, most successful Ransomware gangs in the world is based in Min Vody."

The General turned and sat down behind the desk. "We are facing a major problem in America. With China. They are basically at war with us. They use technologies including artificial intelligence., quantum computing, semiconductors, biotechnology, and other autonomous systems.

A study from Georgetown University's Center for Security and Emerging Technology (CSET) found that only 8% of the 273 companies that supply AI equipment to the PLA are on the Commerce Department's blacklist. According to the study, the remaining 92% of Chinese AI companies are free to purchase key U.S. technologies for use in their military."

He looked at all four people in front of him. "You are all too young to remember, but back in the 1960's, China was a low rent, mud road country whose major transportation was the bicycle. Then Richard Nixon sadly decided to bring China into the world of nations. There's an old saying "Don't wake China, the sleeping giant." The General sat down and waved at the four chairs set up in front of his desk. All sat down. "So Nixon woke up China and now we have to deal with it. Our government is cautious because they are afraid of China. We don't have that problem."

Jack said, "I thought we kicked their asses in Korea."

General Harmbruster sat back. "We did but they were no pushovers. It's too bad we did not listen to MacArthur when he wanted to cross the Yalu River and take the Reds out."

"Could we have done it?" Charlie asked.

The General looked out a window, then responded. "It's a damned big country but it might have been fun. At any rate now we are basically in a state of undeclared war with China. And most Americans don't even realize it. And like I said, major American companies do business with the Chinese to line their own pockets. And the Chinese control our movie industry. And they even own the Port of LA! The President called me and asked Eagle's Aerie to handle the situation."

"How did our leaders let this happen?" Jack asked.

"A lot of them are on the take. And the American businesses have shut down US factories and moved to China. Even most of our medicine is made in China. It's crazy!" The General rose and walked to an easel in the corner of the office. "Come over here," he said.

The group got up and gathered around the General. On the easel was a rough drawing of a country on a large piece of heavy paper. On it was marked the words, Tbilisi, Elbrus and Min Vody.

"The Chinese have started a cyber-war against us and we don't even realize it. And now they are stealing military secrets!"

"This is a map of Georgia," Jack said. "There's Mt Elbrus. Right across the border in Russia."

"General, what's that have to do with China?" Tucson asked.

"Basically this: the Chinese government is funding this gang of crooks! It is a ransomware crowd in Min Vody that is one of the first large cyber gangs successfully attacking America. I want to take them out as a message to China and others conducting these scams." The General pounded one fist into the other. "I want you to go to Georgia, climb into Russia under the guise of innocent mountaineering, then cross to Min Vody and eliminate that Ransomware gang." He pounded the desk with his fist. "They are raking in millions of dollars from American companies and institutions. People, innocent people, are dying because of these nutcases!" And worse than that, like I said, these creeps have invaded our DOD and are even selling technical secrets to Russia!"

The pilot, Joe Fresco said, "What's wrong with the government of Russia?

Why won't they shut it down?"

"Russian leaders are probably getting paid off, and their military is being paid with military secrets, and probably laughing at our pain and losses. I want to show Russia that they can't allow this nonsense to continue, as well."

"These gangs are bleeding American companies and institutions dry. They have even caused gas shortages. People are lining up for expensive, over the top gas like back in the 70's. People are even dying over this. It is absolutely crazy. And no one seems to notice or care!

So, as Jack here knows, through Elbrus is an easy way to Min Vody. Otherwise, it's a thousand miles from Moscow." The General stood up. "You could slip in, shut the gang down, and slip out with little fuss."

"If you call climbing the highest Mountain in Europe, easy." Jack exclaimed.

"You have done it before, You know the way."

"I'm under arrest for desertion! Slight complication." Jack pointed out with an ironic tone to his voice.

Tucson stirred and looked attentive.

The General waved a dismissive hand. "Take this mission on and I promise I will get the government off your back. All that will go away."

Jack felt excitement rising at the general's words. "You… you are very persuasive, General!" Jack exclaimed. "But there are only a couple of climbing months left. There is little time to organize, train a team."

"Can't you assemble some of your buddies? Put something together?

You're our best hope at stopping this drain on America."

Jack looked at Tucson. "Miss Luvabrest would be a great asset if she would join us. She is tough as they come and fearless."

Tucson looked at the General and said, "I'll tag along. I may have to arrest Jack at some point, anyway."

"Listen here, Agent," the General cautioned. "You heard your boss. You will not interfere with this mission."

Jack stepped up to resolve the conflict between the two. "The question is, will Charlie join us? My brother, Billy, of course. Except he's a civilian now."

Charlie and Tucson both nodded approval.

"Will your brother join you?" The General asked.

"Probably, but it would help to include some incentive. And we'll have to have some Russian cooperation. Which will cost."

"Eagle's Aerie will supply an ample mission budget. That should take care of any money issues. And I know how much China paid you for those gems. Money should not be an issue with you." He looked at his assistant, and added, "Colonel Weatherbe here will handle the details of the mission." Jack felt a huge burden drop off his mind. He could not believe his good fortune. "I'd say we will be on our way very soon. Thank you for the opportunity, General."

"I'm just thankful you can and will do it and have the necessary background to ensure success," General Harmbruster said. "This shutdown will resonate through their worldwide ranks. When we finally shut down a ransomware crowd in Russia, it will spread quakes throughout the world." He stuck out a hand to shake and Jack shook his hand, then turned, shook Charlie's and Joe's hand and then Tucson's. The General watched and smiled as the four turned and left his temporary office.

Then he called out, "Captain Flashhardt. A moment."

Jack turned around and came back to the General's desk and stood at attention. ""Yes, Sir," he said.

"I think it would be helpful if you write a report as to your recent activities, and your reason for going UA that revolved to Deserter status. Bring it with you when you report back to me."

"Yes, Sir," Jack said. He turned and left the office.

The General's assistant, Colonel Weatherbe said, "So he'll do it. Are you sure he is the man for the job at hand?"

"He is terrific! He escaped capture in Pakistan, fought his way to Afghanistan, then later turned a horde of terrorists into popsicles last year when he set off an avalanche in Asia. Then he returned to the US, killed a bunch of Serbs -- blonde, blue-eyed terrorists, including a bunch that attacked his ranch. That kid is amazing!"

"He's only in his twenties," the Colonel pointed out. "How can he be so experienced? So cool?"

The General pounded his desk. "He grew up on a ranch. He hunted and trapped, and lived outdoors a lot. It was grand training for combat."

"But there is one problem," Colonel Weatherbe added. "I think General Farley of the NSA has been informed that Jack has been arrested by the FBI and is being delivered to Omaha."

"How the hell did that fat little bastard get knowledge of Jack's return to the US so quickly?"

"Farley has tentacles everywhere."

The white tiger suddenly looked up. It could not describe the feeling, but it knew what it had to do: travel north and west. It had just killed and eaten a wild boar and it felt like a nap. But the surging feeling contained a longing. It tried drinking the southern waters of the Caspian Sea but it was salty everywhere it tried.

The blue-eyed tiger stood, stretched its long body of more than nine feet, dug its huge claws into the ground and started its journey of more than what would turn out to be four hundred miles.

A journey of reunification with a treasured friend.

CHAPTER 28

When General Farley learned that the FBI agent sent to arrest Jack had not arrived in Omaha with Flashhardt, he exploded. "How did that young punk jailbird bastard get around that arrest?"

"General Harmbruster of Eagle's Aerie interfered for some reason," His aide, Marcus Blofeld, answered.

Farley pounded his desk. "I thought we had him when he was spotted crossing the border. Find out what that deserter is up to. Eagle's Aerie got something to do with this!"

Blofeld backed out of the irate General's office thinking, *Did he call a former American General, Hamburger?*

Refueled, Charlie and the pilot, Joe Fresco, flew Jack and Tucson back to the ranch. Jack called his Dad with the great news as they traveled across the clear Wyoming skies.

Tucson was uncharacteristically silent. After Jack talked to his Dad, he turned to Tucson. "So what do you think, Tucson? Are you up for this adventure?"

"It is difficult keeping up with the changes," she said. "It was hard taking the assignment to arrest you. After you saved my life at your ranch last year and before that, at Big Bear Lake. I think I am almost in love with you. And then I had to take you into custody. Now to work with you. It's all spinning." She sat back and shut her eyes.

It was night by the time they got back to the ranch and Bill's cook had a dinner prepared for the four travelers. They enjoyed a meal of wonderful tasting roast beef, baked potatoes and sour cream, salads, and a loaf of homemade bread. Bill uncorked two bottles of red wine and poured liberally.

"This is great news!" Bill said for the third time. "This Ransomware issue is getting to be huge! And the shutdown of the Ransomware gang is really needed. They hijacked The Mayo Clinic in Minnesota and then the VA

Clinic in Denver last spring. I'll bet that's what got the government so exercised."

Jack said, "We have to climb Elbrus to get there. Are you sure we can hack it?"

"Remember, Jack, there are two peaks with a saddle in between. You can cross over the saddle and there is no need to summit. As I recall it's only 5300 meters. This Isn't a climb. This is a great way into Russia!"

Jack looked at Tucson. "You're right, Dad, But we'll still have to rope up. There were a lot of crevasses in that saddle as I remember. And 5300 meters is still 3000 feet higher than all the fourteeners in Colorado."

"What's a fourteener?" Tucson asked.

"A mountain higher than fourteen thousand feet in altitude," Jack responded. "There are about one hundred in the US. That Russian saddle would still be a tough climb."

"You're right. Hey, remember that body we found?" Bill added. "What was that all about?" Joe asked.

"Not really a body, " Jack recalled. "Just clothes and a wallet. Must've been really old. The money in the wallet, we later figured out, was from the 1930's." Jack shook his head at the memory. "Glacier must have spit out what was left of the guy's body when the sun melted some ice."

"Climbing a mountain sounds like serious business," Joe said. He rubbed the shaven side of his head.

Charlie observed. "And we owe it all to Jack, the expert mountaineer. But I've never climbed one of the Seven Summits."

"And we might say the most important one." Jack observed. "How so? It's not Everest," Joe remarked.

"You ever hear of the legend of Prometheus?" Bill asked.

When Joe shook his head, Jack began, "Prometheus was a Titan, and the Titan Gods predated the Greek Gods. But the God Zeus was the more powerful, the most powerful God and he chained Prometheus to a cliff on Mt. Elbrus. Then he sent an eagle to eat the Titan's liver every day."

"Why'd Zeus get so pissed off?" Fresco asked.

Charlie broke in and continued, "Zeus and Prometheus had argued because Prometheus wanted to give humans civilization and Zeus wanted to keep them down like animals. So Prometheus stole one of Zeus's lightning bolts and gave it to humans so they would have fire and that would jump start civilization. And not only that," Charlie continued, "he tricked Zeus by dressing up two offerings to the Gods: one was lard and bones, the other was prime cuts of beef. He made the lard look good and the beef look bad so Zeus gave the beef to humans and kept the lard and bones for the Gods. When Zeus took a bite of lard and discovered the deception, he was doubly pissed."

"Hopefully, things will have calmed down by the time you get there," Bill observed.

Jack glanced at Tucson, yawned and said, "It's been a horrible slash wonderful day. I'm going to hit the rack."

Bill stood. "I'll show everyone their bedrooms and there is wine and more in the bar off the family room."

Jack went to his childhood bedroom, smiled at some of the mementos on the walls from his younger age, like group photos of football and wrestling teams, boy scout groups and pictures of him and a prom date. He undressed and crawled into bed after turning off the lights. About fifteen minutes later, the door opened and Tucson slipped into the room. She came to the bed and said, "I can't have sex but can I sleep with you?"

"Remember that first time we made love in the Oregon woods?" Jack whispered. "It was magical!"

"How could I forget?" She climbed into bed and Jack put his arms around her, he felt her stiffen. "I'm sorry, Jack. Big Bear Lake, and Joshua Trumpet and Dawklings and the horrible Serbs," she whispered.

He withdrew his arm. "That's okay, Tucson. Let's go to sleep." But his mind went to the horrible tattoos the American terrorist, Bobby Ray Dawklings had all over his face and neck. He tried to block those images and memories, but could not:

Jack followed in trace behind the wave of Mick's attacking infantry team in the Big Bear Lake home of the domestic terrorist, Dawklings. After clearing each room, the men shouted "Clear!" He cautiously moved ahead to the last room. There was kidnapped Tucson! Tattoo Dawklings was standing in a corner, Tucson was held as a shield in front of him. Knife at her throat, he aimed a pistol at Jack, but as he fired, Tucson twisted, spoiling his aim.

Tucson stared at Jack with a pleading for help look of terror. Both eyes were swollen, blackened, her lips puffed and bloody. Jack shot and Dawklings fell to the floor.

CHAPTER 29

The next morning, when Jack woke up. He looked and saw Tucson lying next to him, staring at him. Her beautiful, wide set eyes were looking like she could see into his soul. Her thick mane of red hair cascaded across her white shoulders.

"Good morning, " he said.

"Hi," she said quietly. Her full lips formed the word. He wanted to kiss her but he restrained himself and said, " I had a strange dream last night."

"What was it about?"

I dreamt about Tigger." "Who's that?"

Jack took a deep breath, thought for a moment, then said, "I met this tiger. A white tiger when I was escaping from the Taliban in the Hindu Kush Mountains. He must have escaped from a zoo or he must have been in a show of some kind because he was partially tame."

"So he didn't try to eat you?" Tucson asked.

"Well… I thought he was trying to decide whether to eat me raw or first throw me into a fire to cook me."

Tucson laughed, then asked, "So what happened?"

I noticed he was limping. He was limping and I was sick. So we had a sorta common bond."

"What was wrong with you?"

"I was very hungry. I saw some wonderful looking mushrooms and I ate them the day before."

"You might have died!"

"Right," Jack took a deep breath and continued, "So I saw he had a bamboo shard piercing his front paw. I pulled it out and he musta been very grateful because he led me to a nearby village. A British SAS guy happened to be stationed as a trainer of some sort, and that guy, Robert Arses, saw I was sick and he fixed me up." Jack thought for a minute, then added, "And much later in a cave in the mountains, Tigger showed up and saved me again by attacking this Chinese guy who was trying to kill me."

"Some pet!"

"You can say that again," Jack concluded. "I'm taking a shower. Want to scrub my back?"

"'I'm not--" Tucson drew back.

"Come on, It'll be just a shower, I promise. The water will wake you up." He grabbed her wrist and pulled her out of the bed and into the bathroom. They stepped into the shower enclosure and Jack turned the water on and adjusted the temp. Then he directed the flow over himself and Tucson's superb body. With no fooling around, he soaped her down and then himself, then rinsed them both off, climbed out of the shower, handed her a towel and took one himself. While he shaved, she dressed in the bedroom.

When he rejoined her, Tucson said, "Thanks for understanding." She adjusted her denim blouse and tucked it into her jeans. "Every time I think about sex, I see that horrible gang who "

"What do you think, Tucson? Do you want to go with us to Russia? The last time you hooked up with us it nearly got you killed and left you mentally damaged from those multiple rapes in Big Bear Lake. Things are different in my world from your FBI. You can't apply FBI standards out here. It will be dangerous, but–," Jack paused and looked at her, "it should be a grand adventure." He stared at her breasts.

She hit him with a pillow.

"I'm sorry but I can still see your breasts."

"That's because I'm not wearing a bra. I don't need one. "That makes you a bra-gert."

"Bra-gert?

"One who brags about her breasts," Jack said as he dodged another swing of the pillow.

She looked intently at Jack then said, "All right, I'm in. But it's not an adventure. Let's fix these Russian jerks who are ripping off America! Then come home."

The two went to the kitchen where Charlie and Joe were eating scrambled eggs and toast, which Bill was serving. They smiled and nodded hello but kept eating. Bill quickly put eggs and toast on two plates for Jack and Tucson.

After breakfast, Jack called Billy on his cell. When Billy answered, Jack said, "I made it." He left the kitchen and walked into the living room.

"How's Dad?"

"Dad is good. He is completely recovered from his gunshot wound to the belly." Jack shook his head. "Penelope brought those containers of mineral water from Shangri-la when she came to the ranch to tell me she was pregnant. They have electrolytes that seem to cure anything. He completely and rapidly recovered after she gave him some of that mineral water. You remember, she called it Tarn water."

"Great news!" Billy exclaimed. "Say, did you turn in the rental?"
"Yes, and, you are going to be shocked by this--"

"What's that?"

The General wants me to lead an expedition into Russia." "What now? Is he declaring war on the Ruskies?"

"He wants me and I want you to join me, " Jack held his breath.

"We gotta kick Russia's ass to keep you outta prison? Seems a bit much!" "No," Jack laughed. "Not quite that bad. It's about some Ransomware crowd of criminals. Come on to the ranch and I'll tell you what it's all about."

Let me talk to Zhang and I'll call you back later."

Jack hung up and mentally crossed his fingers. If they had any chance of success, he would need fearless Billy. His half-brother, the half breed Indian, and the son of Little Willow was tough as nails. He went looking for Charlie and found him and Joe, the pilot, pre-flighting the CH-47. Then he went to his Dad's office and spent an hour of research and emails on the ranch computer. He was interrupted by Charlie and Joe.

"We're heading back to Warren, Jack, but guess what?" Charlie said. "Joe here, wants to join us."

Jack looked at the pilot. "Do you have any combat experience?

"I served in the infantry in Iraq. Then I went to flight school and got my wings and bars at Pensacola. So I would be good to go. And it sounds like it will be fun!"

"Invading Russia?"

"Yeah, but it's a long way from Moscow," Joe said.

"I just checked it out," Jack said. "So we'll fly to Georgia then hike to Elbrus. We won't need a visa in Georgia just to go hiking and we won't ask for one from Russia. We'll fly to Tbilisi, the main airport in Georgia and then charter a flight to Mestia in north Georgia near the Russian border, which is only about 25 miles across to Elbrus." He turned to Joe, "Are you jet rated?"

"Yes, I am," Joe responded. "Rotary as well."

"So I suggest you arrange our flight to Tbilisi. Talk to Charlie about that, right?" He looked at Charlie who nodded his head in agreement. "By the way, how the hell do you pronounce it?"

"Tib ah lise ee," Charlie tried and they all laughed.

No one had an answer and his cell rang. Jack saw it was from Billy. "Hello," he said.

"Zhang has a show try out and won't go. So I can't." Billy, I need you to do this.," Jack pleaded.

"Sorry, brother, Zhang rules my roost. I have to go now," Billy hung up.

84

CHAPTER 30

Zhang Poon Tang called her contact at the Chinese embassy in Washington DC. When an operator answered, she asked to be put in contact with a former agent with Second Division she had worked with in Afghanistan, a man called Wu Ting . She was told to leave a callback number. She did and waited patiently for a callback. When her cell finally rang she answered and found she was speaking to Wu. She said she needed to speak to Mara Bhutto in the Foreign Ministry. She was given a number to call and when she did, she was told to meet a person called Hung Tu Muc at theTranquility Bamboo Hotel in LA at 4 PM. It was who she expected to be put in contact with as he was in charge of Fentanyl exports from China to Mexico. She had met him a month ago when he had overseen the second Fentanyl shipment to Sinaloa Trafficante in Ensenada.

She checked her watch and saw she only had an hour to get to ChinaTown so she left her condo in Beverly Hills after an Uber arrived at her address to transport her.

At the hotel, Zhang entered the lobby and sat on a white leather sofa near a large window. Precisely at four PM, a Chinese looking man entered the lobby, spotted her and approached. He was tall for a Chinaman and looked very physical with wide set shoulders. He was wearing a gray suit.

"Hello, Hung," Zhnag said when he stopped in front of her. "Sit down." She patted the sofa next to her.

"What is the need for this meeting?" Hung said with an irritated tone to his question as he sat next to her. "You know, you are still not greeted favorably by the Second Division."

"Please listen," Zhang replied. "That is why I am contacting them. I have information that will restore my standing with the Second Division." She took a deep breath and said, "The Americans are planning an attack against a Ransomware operation in Russia."

"Why should we care about an American attack on criminals in Russia?" "Perhaps you are not aware of the fact that The Republic of China created

and supports that Ransomware unit and a similar Ransomware unit in   Hue   City,   Vietnam.'"

"Again, who cares what happens in Russia or Viet Nam?" Hung asked. "Why are you wasting my time with irrelevant things? You need to focus on future Fentanyl shipments."

"Our country benefits greatly from that operation. You are obviously not exposed to the intricacies of the Ransomware movement. It is growing like an octopus and the money and data is huge." She sat back then added, "And we have started another Ransomware unit in Hong Kong."

"You are right, I do not know of these issues, " Hung admitted. "How have you found this out?"

"I have a Pakistani friend who also works for the Second Division. She was the instigating force for the Ransomware unit. And coincidentally, I have a relationship with the brother of the leader of this anti-ransomware crowd." Zhang grabbed Hung's arm. "If the Americans are successful, they will naturally be sent against the Chinese team in Hong Kong," Zhang concluded. "You must carry the issue to Mara Bhutto in Peking. Our country must be prepared." She sat back and added, "The leader of the Americans is extremely capable. And they are attacking very soon."

Hung Tu Muc appraised Zhang and said, "You are right to be concerned. I will pass this information along."

Zhang Poon T'ang stood up to leave and as she did she asked, "Do you get much jokes about your name?"

Hung Tu Muc looked curious but did not respond.

As Zhang walked away she regretted ratting out Jack Flashhardt, but her duty to herself came first. With this action, she might be able to turn around hostile forces against her in the Chinese government. She thought of Mara Bhutto and shivered. Mara had threatened her one time in Afghanistan while trying to make Zhang talk during a mistaken interrogation:

"We will cut off your hands and your feet. We will cut out your tongue and of course blind you. Then we will release you onto the streets of Kabul as a beggar unless you cooperate at once."

Terrified, Zhang had talked as fast as she could.

She tried to dismiss that thought with a better one: She thought of the time she had tricked Jack into making love to her when he thought she was the same Mara Bhutto. She thought of his rock hard body that was such a turn on and wanted more but now that was not to be. It seemed that she, Mara, and Jack were in an eternal dance of death with no outcome. But she had to do something to end it all. She went to her bathroom and took out the fentanyl laced meth supplied by the Chinese government in the first shipment, with the intent of giving it to Billy.

Tu Muc, as soon as he was separated from Zhang, called his superiors and then Mara Bhutto. "You were right," he said. " You will have to lead this expedition as you originally established the operation, and I have been told that Zhang Poon T'ang will take over your responsibilities for the Fentanal shipments to hated America.

CHAPTER 31

$\mathbf{J}$ack and Bill and Tucson rose the next morning, ate a good breakfast of pancakes, bananas and coffee, then set out on a rapid paced hike that covered five miles through the hills surrounding the ranch central compound. The sky was cloudless and the sun was bright. Bullet happily tagged along. Jack took note that Bill and Tucson had no trouble keeping the pace he set. And he spotted two men who trailed them by about two hundred yards.

When they got back to the ranch, Tucson and Jack went to his bedroom suite and each took a shower. Afterwards, a fully dressed Tucson joined Jack on a sofa across the room from his bed.

"What do you think our chances are?" She asked.

"Of getting together, getting it on?" He paused and half laughed. "Oh, you mean If we make it over the mountain? Well, then there will be a pretty good chance of accomplishing the mission."

"And after?"

"Of getting together, getting it on? Oh, you still mean the mission. We'll give it our best shot. But I'm not as confident about our chances of getting away," Jack said. He looked at her and added, "Or getting it on."

"How many missions has the General sent you on?" Tucson rose and got a bottle of water from a small electric cooler. She held it up and Jack nodded his head so she got him one as well.

Jack thought for a minute but could not recall the exact number so he said, "About a half dozen."

"And you survived every one of them. So I'd say our chances are pretty good," Tucson concluded. She emptied her bottle in one long draft.

"Of getting–" he stopped when Tucson gave him an exasperated look.

"I have friends in Min Vody I have already contacted," Jack said. "From when I climbed before. One is a young Russian lady who was the assistant guide for the expedition that climbed with us, the other one was our lead guide when we climbed Elbrus. The guide is a wheeler dealer type of guy. He sells Russian timber to Western countries. For the right price, he'll help us." Jack finished his water and set the bottle down. "He knows who the Ransomware gang is.

They are not Russians. They are Muslims from Georgia and Chinese guys. So he will help us. Especially when the General makes him and the girl rich."

"So things are looking good," Tucson concluded. "Except we need more team members," Jack observed. "How are you going to find more men?"

"My Dad has a couple of Indians who sound like they would like an adventure. They were the two men trailing us earlier."

"Do you know them?"

"They served in Afghanistan. In the army. So they are not greenhorns when it comes to battle. They'll be joining us for lunch."

"Will they work with a woman?" Tucson, used to male prejudice, asked. "Ask them at lunch," Jack directed. "If they ask me, I'll tell them you are hard as nails." Jack touched Tucson's arm. "Well you used to be, I don't have much up to date knowledge, " he added with a slight smile.

"I'm sorry, Jack." Tucson smiled ruefully. "I have issues to deal with. The Serbians…"

"I understand, Tucson."

When Bill's maid announced lunch, they joined Bill and the two young men in their early twenties. They were sitting at the kitchen table, and were the ones who had followed them earlier on their hike.

As they sat down, Bill introduced one young man as Dakota and the other as Anakan. The young Indian men smiled. They both had short black hair and deeply dark brown faces. Anakab had a flat-looking face and Dakota, in contrast, had a face so sharp it could have been used to chop firewood for a campfire.

Anakan said, "I have heard about you, Jack, you have made many climbs."

"And we have heard that you are a fierce warrior," Dakota added. "My Dad has told you what we have to do. And you are up for it?"

Anakan glanced at Dakota and then back at Jack. "It sounds like a grand adventure. And very lucrative."

"Yes," Dakota agreed. It sounds like a lot of fun. And the money Charlie mentioned…"

"It could be dangerous, " Jack added.

Anakan pointed at Tucson. "Would you bring this lady if it was very dangerous?"

Jack patted Tucson on the shoulder. "She is a trained FBI agent. "She is very deadly."

"Good to know," Anakan responded. "We are in."

Relieved, Jack smiled at Bill and said, "You brought two good men to our team."

Just then he noted his cell phone ringing and saw it was Billy calling. He crossed his fingers for luck and answered the call. "Tell me you have changed your mind?" Jack asked.

"Don't yell, 'cause Zhang has been screaming at me for hours!" Billy exclaimed.

"I really need you on this, Bro," Jack said.

"You don't understand what you are asking. Zhang says if I go, don't come back. You are asking me to break up with her." He looked at Zhang and she nodded her head.

"I'm asking for your help, I need it," Jack tried to keep a pleading tone out of his voice. He did not succeed.

Billy said nothing and Jack listened to dead air for at least a minute, then Billy said, "I'll be in Billings tomorrow. You'll need to gear me up."

After Billy hung up he packed a backpack and he double checked the six meth tablets Zhang had given him. She had received them from Hung when they had met in Ensenada the night before. Hung had given Zhang assurance that a couple of them already contained fentanyl.

The next morning, when Jack played a message that Billy had left for Billings for some ranch business, he called his father and told him Billy was arriving on a Western Airlines flight at noon.

Bill responded that he would wait in town and pick up Billy at the airport.

That same late morning, when Billy debarked he found his father waiting at the gate. The two hugged and shook hands.

Bill hugged Billy again and said, "I haven't had a real chance to thank you for last year when you and Jack saved the Senator, Penelope, and me."

"I'm glad we could. It was real tight, real touch and go for a while."

Bill laughed and said, "Of course I haven't sent you a bill for the front door you demolished with that cannon you had in the barn hayloft."

Billy laughed as well, then said, "I gotta admit, as I was gunning down the front door of your ranch house, I could almost hear my mom, Little Willow, cheering me on."

"Speaking of your mom. Can we talk about our past history?" Bill asked.

"We never have," Billy retorted." I never knew about you and Jack until Mom died and Talking Dog told me you were my Dad and Jack was my half-brother." Billy rubbed his hands together. "I had graduated from high school and Grandpa was taking me to Billings to fly to MCRD for basic training."

"He wanted you to know who you were in case he died before you got back."

"Mom had always refused to tell me who my father was."

"Well, now you know and I want to say I am very proud of you and I am sorry for our troubled past." Bill looked at his son, "I can't tell you how much I regret what happened when she quit her job as my housekeeper and went back to the Reservation. And never told me she was pregnant. But hopefully we can move forward as a united family after we solve Jack's new problems." He stopped and hugged Billy. He looked into Billy's eyes, They were clear and alert. Jack had warned Bill about Billy's meth addiction.

"You and Jack are quite rich as a result of the China reward. And as my son, you stand to inherit half the ranch."

BIlly thought about his new wealth but did not know how to respond. "When are we leaving for Russia?" He asked.

"Jack wants to embark on the mission tomorrow, Friday the 13th," Bill said.

"Bad luck day," Billy commented.

"He is in a rush to get this done," Bill concluded.

Later that day, back at the ranch, Billy was pleasantly surprised to discover that Dakpta and Anarkan were part of the team. They met and relived childhood experiences from their friendship days on the Reservation.

While they were getting reacquainted, Jack sat down in Bill's office and wrote:

I was activated from my Reserve officer status in the Marine Corps while attending law School at Stanford University and ordered to report to active duty in the Far East.

When I arrived in Islamabad, I was ordered to start a mountaineering training mission with an Army unit and we flew into northern Pakistan where we were to train in the foothills of the Hindu Kush Mountains. But a vicious updraft hit me after I and the unit parachuted. It carried me and my low level static line chute up and up and over the highest ridgeline and deposited me on the west side of the ridge. The same updraft killed a soldier when he crashed into a sheer cliff.

I secured my landing spot, then released my parachute and slid down a very steep mountain side and eventually landed in a tarn water pool below a short waterfall.

There I met two native women of a Afghan tribe that lived in this isolated valley.

It was isolated because when the Soviet Union withdrew from Afghanistan, it blew up the tunnel that the inhabitants had used for access to the outside world.

The women took me to their village and I left their valley the next day, climbed over the highest ridge and eventually reached Islamabad thanks to a Lift from Pakistani Army forces.

I was subsequently attached to the United Nations and later returned to duty with US Forces. I was sent to the isolated valley by you and while there I unknowingly impregnated the native girl I had met on my first accidental arrival.

She came to the US to find me and tell me the happy news that she was pregnant. She went to my family's ranch and was there when the Moslem terrorists attacked the ranch.

After we took back the ranch, she felt threatened by the violent events and returned to her isolated valley. I went UA to convince her to come back to the States. I failed. By the time I returned, I had been reclassified from UA status to Deserter. I snuck across the US border and came to Montana to try and get help and influence from Senator Jensen to get my deserter status lifted. I was apprehended almost immediately by the FBI.

CHAPTER 32

Wu Ting, a tall and very physical senior agent with Red China's Second Division, the entity that was comparable to America's CIA, looked at the legendary assassin, Mara Bhutto. She was beautiful with thick black hair, cut very short. She had blue eyes as many Pakistani and Afghan women did. Her jaw was firm and she did not look like a hardened killer but her reputation was solid. She was widely known in the Far East as the Black Orchid Assassin. With a degree from Quad e-Azam University and an advanced degree from Cairo University she was a highly educated woman which was unusual in a Moslem country. And with her subversive warfare training at Hainan Island in China, she was an expert at mayhem.

"So, we go to Russia," he said in Chinese to her and the nine Chinese Operatives behind her. He pointed at Mara. "She established this outpost and she will lead us to it. When we get there we will defend it against some hated American criminals."

CHAPTER 33

Joe Fresco reduced engine power as he prepared to land at Billings Airport.

The Gulfstream C-20G he was flying, rounded up by General Harmbruster 's aide, former Colonel Weatherbe, who had borrowed it from the US DEA seizures at Denver Airport, had a range, depending on cargo and passengers, of up to 5000 miles. It could carry a crew of five and up to 26 passengers.

It's more than what we need to get to Tbilisi, Georgia, he thought. *And it has civilian labels and logos on the wings and main body. Ostensibly, it is a Gulfstream civilian aircraft, not a military one.*

Charlie Davis, who was also jet certified, sat in the engineer's seat in the cockpit and watched Joe and the co-pilot, Harry Lakken, as they flew and landed and taxied the jet to the terminal. Joe turned the engines off and watched Jack, Billy, Tucson, and two other men, who were all on the ground waiting for Charlie and Joe, grab their large duffle bags and approach the aircraft. He pushed a button and the steps dropped to the ground.

As Jack watched the Gulfstream jet roll to a stop, he felt optimistic about the mission and his perhaps freedom from Leavenworth Prison. He wondered what General Farley would think or do when he heard that Jack was working for Harmbruster. He wondered again why Farley hated Jack and Billy. He glanced at the calendar on his watch. It was the 19th of June. It had been maddening to wait for days while the General got them a jet to fly to Georgia but now it was done.

Charlie Davis and Joe Fresco looked on as the team climbed the jet steps.

As they took their seats, Charlie handed out AK 74s rifles to each member, they all inspected the rifles except Tucson, who held up her M17 9mm Sig Sauer pistol and said, "This is all I want or need."

Charlie held up his M27 rifle. "This is what I'll use.The M27's parent rifle is a German-designed Heckler & Koch 416, which was famously used to take down Osama bin Laden during the Seal Team Six raid in Abbottabad, Pakistan."

"It's bigger," Tucson said.

Charlie said, "The M27 benefits from a 16.5-inch free-floating barrel and a short-stroke piston action that give the M27 accuracy, range, and reliability improvements over both the legacy M16 rifle and M4 carbine."

"What do you think, Charlie? Is this going to work?" Joe asked as Charlie returned to the cockpit.

"I've never seen anyone like Jack," Charlie responded. "Action seems to flow to him and he is always successful. You should have been there when Jack and this other prisoner, General Hammar, escaped from that prison in a leper colony by building a catapult and catapulting themselves over the prison wall and into a river! It was amazing!"

"Good to know," Joe responded as he pictured Jack flying through the air. He waited for the team to get settled in their seats, then took off for Bamgor, Maine for a refueling stop before heading for Georgia. After refueling at Bangor, and after Charlie paid for the fuel with a credit card supplied by General Harmbruster's aide, they all ate box lunches Tucson had picked up in the terminal and then all went to sleep as the jet crossed the Atlantic. After a long flight, with Harry spelling Joe, they refueled in Dresden, picked up some sandwiches and soft drinks in the terminal, and continued on to Mestia, Georgia's Queen Tamar Airport.

As they were on final approach, Joe went back to the cabin and sat down with the team. "So the surprise is, we can land in Mestia without going to Tbilisi," he said. " We'll land in five minutes. And we will only be about fifteen miles from Elbrus. So we can't announce our plan to cross into Russia, but once across the border there will be no one to stop us. And there is no-Trump wall on the border." Everybody listened intently.

Jack said "And we don't need visas to get into Georgia and we won't ask for a Russian visa," Jack continued, " So we can hire a taxi to Ushba on the border and then just cross illegally."

"Let's do it," Charlie said as the jet touched down. "Hey, look at that terminal!"

They all went to the windows and saw a very modern looking building shaped like an L laying down with a glass circular Control Tower on the top.

"Totally weird!" Tucson exclaimed. "And look at the buildings. The two story buildings in the village have no windows on the first floor!"

"Looks like maybe because there are a lot of bandits around here," Billy said.

The jet stopped at the parking area for airplanes where Joe had been told to park. He chocked the wheels and tied down the wings with

Charlie's help, Jack led everybody out of the plane and then he walked around the side of the terminal to the street and hired two 4 wheel drive SUV cabs to transport them to Upper Sventeli. While he was doing that, Harry, who was staying in Mestia, arranged parking for a month and agreed to settle on the actual fees when they returned from Russia.

While the others loaded their duffle bags and themselves, and waited for Joe and Charlie, Jack told the Georgian driver of the first vehicle that they wanted to get to the border.

"You no go into Russia," the driver said. He looked back at Jack and added, "No go! Not allow!"

Jack held up a roll of twenty dollar bills. "Five hundred dollars," he said, "American."

"We go border, I know secret crossing," the suddenly smiling driver said as he turned and waited for the last two Americans.

"I love your reasonable personality," Jack commented with a wry grin, "Homo flexibilis, that is to say, flexible man."

Once loaded, they drove around a large lake where the scenery was spectacular and the water was the blue of the clear sky. The mountains piled higher and higher as they drove north. They entered a small canyon with high cliffs on either side. The canyon floor was covered with grass and occasional flowers of various colors. The cliffs were very rocky. There were several small farms scattered around the canyon. The driver stopped his SUV and the second cab stopped as well. While the team unloaded their gear, Jack gave the driver five hundred dollars.

"Good luck with Rus," the driver said. "What's a Russ?" Billy asked.

"Probably he meant the Russian border guards," Tucson offered.

The team loaded their backpacks and started hiking. Five minutes later, they turned a corner in the canyon and saw a wooden shack up ahead. Two men were standing on each side of the shack aiming AK 47s at the team.

"The jerk tricked us!" Charlie exclaimed. "He set us up!"

Jack advanced with outstretched hands. When he got to the armed men, he said. "We want to climb Elbrus. Is it permitted?"

"Visas?" One of the men asked. "No, Sir." Jack responded.

The man lowered his rifle. "No problem," he said. "We welcome climbers. You have cash for penalty fees?"

Relieved, Jack smiled and said, "Of course. We are happy to pay. How much?"

"American dollars?" The man asked. "Yes, Sir."

The man assessed the team and said, "Five hundred each. Three thousand five hundred American dollars."

"Thank you," Jack walked back to the team, stepped behind Billy and opened his money belt that was wrapped around his waist under his sweatshirt and extracted thirty-five one hundred dollar bills. He carried the wad of bills in his hand and walked back to the Russians. He looked at the men, one had short blond hair and the other who had short but darker hair. They looked to be in their twenties and both were very lean and about five and a half feet tall. The blonde guy set his rifle down and the other held his rifle with a casual pose. The blonde went into the hut and now came out holding some papers.

"There are several teams ahead of you," the Russian said. "An English team of five men, an American team of two men and two women, and another American team of five men and two Georgian guides on skis, and a Chinese team of 12 men. Busy mountain!" The Russian concluded. "Climbers try to beat end of the climbing season."

"Sounds good," Jack enthused. "And I think the weather will be good for a week." He returned to the team and passed out the plastic cards filled with Russian lettering. "We're good to go," he said'

"That was pretty easy," Charlie commented.

"If you call thirty five hundred dollars easy," Jack responded. "From what I hear, that is a lot cheaper than Everest," Joe said.

"You are right and by the way, there is a Chinese team ahead of us," Jack said.

"They are a long way from home, Jack," Tucson remarked.

"Yeah, I wonder what they are doing here," BIlly remarked. "But I guess the Chinese climb all over."

"Who cares," Joe interjected.

CHAPTER 34

$\mathbf{T}$igger stopped and sniffed the air. He could not smell the man, but he had a feeling that the man was growing closer and with an excited feeling coursing through his body, he quickened his pace as he moved north along the shores of the Caspian Sea.

After hiking up all day, the first night found Jack's team still below the snowline. They huddled together and rolled out their sleeping bags. Then they ate their dinner, which were cold MREs consisting of chicken burritos, beans and tortilla chips.

Anakan and Dakota pushed together some dry twigs and made hot tea with a small kettle. It took two fill ups to serve all.

The team slept soundly after the hard day's climb. At sunrise, they shared more black tea and heated oatmeal. Jack halted their progress by instituting combat exercises for the team.

"Any invasion of a building will start by checking loads and safeties on the weapons. Then one team member going in straight, one going in left and the next team member going in right. Two will provide rear security and two will provide flank security." He traced the outline of a simple hut and walked the team through the movement over and over and practiced it until it became second nature.

They then filled their canteens from a rushing small stream and Jack made sure all added purifying additives to the water.

After two hours of steady climbing they were on snow covered ground at a depth of two feet. They were hiking up a long valley with steep slopes flanking the line of March. They hiked in the path of several previous climbers.

In another hour they spotted two pitched tents at the point where the valley ended.

"Hello, the camp," Jack called as he saw no one outside the tents. There was no answer. When the entire team joined him, he called out again and received no response. Dakota went to a tent and pulled the flap open to look inside. He uttered an oath of "What the hell?" and stepped back.

Billy went to the second tent, looked inside and said--"Dead!"

Jack and Charlie looked in the first tent and saw two bodies sprawled on top of each other. They turned and joined Tucson and Billy at the second tent and saw two more bodies. There were blood splatters all over the inside walls of the tents. Large pools of blood had flowed from the victims.

Jack dropped his backpack, opened it and pulled out his assault rifle. He stood and glanced around but saw no strangers or climbers nearby or up the slope.

After they left the tents filled with bodies. Billy said, "Jack, there's something I gotta tell you. I think Zhang may have ratted us out to the Chinese government."

Jack asked, "Why do you think so? She's your girl!"

"She was really pissed that I left her. She said don't bother coming back. Then she started crying and kissed me. But she must forgiven me cause she gave me a packet of meth."

CHAPTER 35

Bruno Utecht, a Kapitan in the Russian Army, temporarily assigned to the FSB, entered the offices of the Reserve Minister for Internal Affairs. He saluted the receptionist and smiled when he realized the man was also a Kapitan and a friend. Bruno shook hands and hugged husky but shorter Igor Kloptan.

"Old friend!" Igor exclaimed.

"How are you, Kapitan?" Bruno replied. "It has been since when?"

Igor looked up at the six foot tall Russian carrying a green beret under his left arm and replied, "Crimea. We were both lieutenants."

"Of course," Bruno said. He looked at the new gold, red and green ribbon on Igor's chest and rubbed his short, blonde hair. "I heard you got the Distinguished Military Service medal. Congratulations."

"Thank you," Igor replied. "Go right in, the Reserve Minister expects you."

Bruno stepped to the door of the Minister's office and knocked briskly. "Enter," the command rang out.

The Reserve Minister was a former General in the Russian Army and was wearing the distinctive pale blue uniform of his former rank. He still wore the epaulets on his shoulders adorned with a star and wreath.

"Kapitan Utecht, thank you for reporting so promptly." "Of course, Minister General, how can I serve?"

"We have a situation in Min Vody." The minister, a white haired man, was very handsome for his age which looked to be about 65. "You are probably not aware," the Minister continued, "But The People's Republic of China was granted permission to establish a secret entity that had a mission preparing to be ready to utilize ransomware versus the United States if needed in a future conflict. China has an abundance of people skilled in computer sciences that exceed our country's level of sophistication. In that arena by a huge margin and they have now shared that expertise with an attachment of Russians."

"I am surprised and was not aware of such a secret entity," Bruno responded.

"No reason why you should," The Minister added. "Very little is known of computer warfare, but it will be a very powerful tool in future wars. Communications, fuel, operations, and every aspect of combat will be attacked and affected."

Bruno thought of the most important element of combat and added, "The infantry man with a rifle and bayonet will still work, as always."

The Minister, who looked like he had always been an admin officer, waved a hand in dismissal. "But the facility in Min Vody which is being organized and utilized as a temporary ransomware entity has been deemed unnecessary by our government. One of their elements, mistakenly or not, attacked a Russian oligarch and denied the man's thirty meter yacht. It was anchored in a harbor in Crete and it lost the ability to refuel.

As a result the yacht was marooned in the harbor in Crete and an alert Italian bank had the time to have the boat seized as the oligarch had not paid a fuel bill in Venice.

The oligarch complained to our wonderful leader, Vladimir Putin, and as a result, the Ransomware gang will soon be history. I want you to go to Min Vody and assess the best way to shut it down and kick them out of Russia."

Bruno responded, "With a terminal action?"

The Minister regarded Bruno. "There may be no need for that hostile an action. The Red Chinese are after all our largest ally in the world. The whole gang could just be sent back to China." The Minister added, "Luckily, the Chinese gang had time to train an entity of ours which is now based in Moscow and easier to control than the Chinks." He looked up at Bruno. "Another complication is that the woman who spearheaded the Chinese op has powerful friends in Moscow, so tread carefully."

"Who is this woman?" Bruno asked.

The Minister smiled. It was a ghastly grimace. "I believe you already know her. She is a Pakistani spy who works for the Second Department of China. Mara Bhutto. I want you to go and make me a full report. As you know, Min Vody is a long way from Moscow and the local authorities have a pattern of independence. I will send an operational unit to back you up if it is deemed essential. I want an accurate report at once. Kapitan Kloptan will take care of the details of this mission."

"Yes, Minister, but there is a lot of sentiment in Russia against the Reds, at least the Chinese version. What if I find a reason or need to eliminate with terminal action, the ransomware gang? And, yes, I know her, but only slightly."

"As I said, the Chinese are our ally. Just send them back to China." The Minister swept away the issue with a large gesture then looked at the Kapitan. "But I might add, off the record, the oligarch who lost his yacht in Crete might look very favorably if the stupid Chink Reds suffered for their action." The Minister looked out a window on the side of his office. "And there is one more complication."

"What is that, Minister?"

"The Chinese have received intelligence that there may be a foreign group that is going to try and destroy the facility in question."

"Americans?"

"There is no clear intelligence but the leader, I am told, has a Nipponese name."

"So the Japs are circling," Bruno surmised.

"Hard to say, but you get the reaction force I am sending ready to roll when you get to Min Vody."

"Maybe the Japs will solve the problem for us," Bruno added.

"Be ready and tread lightly," the Minister ordered. "If the Japs destroy the unit, so be it. But make sure the Jappos do not survive the action."

Bruno saluted, about faced and left the Minister's office. In Igor's office, he stopped and said, "Why me?"

Igor stood and smiled. "You are a well-known alpinist. You have climbed our biggest mountain in that neck of the Caucasus a number of times. And you were temp attached to the United Nations. In Pakistan., where you worked closely with the Americans."

"Yes, I did. So what?" Bruno admitted. I speak English, I speak German, and some French, as well."

"Why so many languages?" Igor asked. "Is that why you have a German name?"

"I was the son of a Lebersborn."

Igor had a confused look on his face. "A lebor–whatever. What is that?" "During Hitler's reign, the Nazi's had a practice of kidnapping blonde, white women and impregnating them so as to expand the Master Race that Hitler wanted to create. My father, a Lebersborn, was such a person. After he was born, he was given to a German family, and then his adopted German parents and he were kidnapped and taken to Russia after the war.

Because my quasi adoptive grandfather. was a German rocket scientist. The Soviets kidnapped and took many German rocket scientists after the war as did America. LIke the famous Wernher Von Braun.

Actually, my grandfather was a spy for America so when my father–his adopted Lebesborn son– learned the truth, he turned him into the Soviets."

"That was cold. His own father?"

"Remember, my dad was a Lebersborn. So his supposed German parents were not really his."

Igor laughed. "You've got my head spinning. Anyway, now I know why you have so many languages, I guess. You were really a German immigrant. And numerous languages got you sent to the United Nations in Pakistan."

Bruno sat down in the chair in front of Igor's desk. "But I have to say, I detest the Chinese and I wish we could just send their bodies back to China."

"Who gives a shit about Chinks?"

"I served in Pakistan and the Chinks drove me crazy. I share no love for the slopes!"

"Well, stick to the guidelines, Bruno, or you might face blowback."

Bruno smiled. "Well, I am guessing my familiarity with Min Vody is getting me stuck with this weird assignment."

"You got that right on the ruble!" Igor sat back down at his desk. "Probably your familiarity is another reason you are being sent to find out what is going on."

CHAPTER 36

$\mathbf{M}$ara Bhutto looked at each Chinaman on the ten man force team. She no longer wondered how effective they were. She had been impressed with the way they coldly killed the four American climbers in the first encounter. And they had listened to her and willingly set up the second scenario after killing the next group they had overtaken, which proved to be the English team of climbers. In neither group had she found Jack Flashhardt after intently and hopefully gazing into each victim's face.

The ruse she had suggested would slow down any pursuers. But as a woman she was always on the lookout for doubt by her fellow soldiers. She still had self-doubts and she could not afford to look weak in any way around her fellow soldiers. She had noticed that three of the Chinamen were using ski poles as they hiked up the slope. She suggested to the leader that they cut six inches off the ends of the poles.

"Why do you want to do that?" He asked.

"If we make the poles look like guns, we could slow up any pursuers." "Excellent idea."

The result was the hollow ski poles looked like gunbarrels from a distance. Then they had set the poles up to look like they were aimed down the mountain by hidden ambushers.

And she was so excited to have another chance to match wits with the American. He had bested her every time, the last being when she and Mo Poo had unsuccessfully attacked his ranch in Montana.

There was the earlier time she had failed to kill him when she stabbed him with a knife in her apartment in Islamabad. Now she had a chance to redeem herself. She was so thankful Zhang Poon T'ang had tipped her off as to the American gang and their plan to strike the Ransomware outfit in Min Vody, Russia. She was glad she had spared Zhang's life in their last encounter in Afghanland. Now, she thought that Zhang could replace her and take over supervision of the fentanyl operation. Now she had the opportunity to defend the Ransomware gang she had created six months earlier.

She tried to tamp down her eagerness. She wanted Jack Flashhard so badly. To look down at a fallen Jack and smile as she killed him. She wished she had a black orchid to put on his corpse. In Pakistan she had been known as The Black Orchid when she was a Chinese operative working there. She had left the signature flower on every victim. To do so to Jack would be so great, so wonderful! Especially if she could be able to do it before his termination.

She looked at the slopes in front of them. There were numerous crevasses visible. She signaled the leader and he ordered the team to rope up as two groups of individuals on a rope and the two teams started up the slope.

CHAPTER 37

Billy's team was leading and when he spotted strange things on the slope above near a small ridge of bare rocks, he halted everyone and he and Charlie and Jack huddled. "It looks like prone shooters on that ridge. I see rifle barrels," Billy announced.

"Then why aren't they shooting at us?" Jack asked. "Maybe they are waiting for us to get closer," Charlie said.

"We'll have to wait for it to get dark before we move up. This time of day, they'll pick us off at their leisure," Billy concluded.

You would be right if there were no crevasses." Jack agreed. "Let's hunker down and send one guy up to check it out. We'll cover it from here." The two teams scooped holes in the slope and sat down. Billy advanced as the rest of the team got ready to lay down fire. When he got to the ridge, he

called out, "It's all a fake! There's nobody here!"

The team converged on his voice and saw the fake rifle barrels. "Somebody succeeded in slowing us up, the bastards!" Joe exclaimed.

Billy suddenly remembered his call to Zhang. He had pleaded one more time to get back in her graces after his mission. He had told her they were leaving on the 13th and should be back in a couple of weeks. Her response

had been noncommittal and cold. They had not left until the 17th. And the border guys had mentioned a Chinese team.

"Jack, I'm telling you, Zhang might have told her Chink spy guys about us. But why would they care?"

Jack looked closely at Billy. He saw that Billy was on meth. 'You can't take that shit up here!" Jack said. "Where did you get it anyway?"

"Zhang," Billy mumbled.

CHAPTER 38

Mara Bhutto hung back when her Chinese team entered the Quonset hut on the top of the saddle between the North and south peaks of Mt. Elbrus. Wu Ting had determined that the second hut was empty. The Chinese team knocked on the other hut's door and when they were invited in by the resident climbers, Mara joined them and watched as they spread out and with a command shout from Wu Ting they all calmly pulled pistols and shot all of the five climbers and then the two astonished guides in the hut.

It was so unexpected from who the climbers thought were just fellow climbers, that they offered no resistance and they fell dead to the floor. The two guides held up their hands in an attempt to surrender but were mercilously killed as well.

Mara first looked for Jack but saw he was not among the fallen. She noticed that one of the men, a black man, was not dead so she calmly walked to his side and sunk her ice ax in his skull. His body trembled, then lay still. His dying throes reminded her of the time she killed the Pakistani general with a one shot Russian pistol that was disguised as a lipstick container. She had shot him through the mouth as he playfully puckered his lips to receive bright red lipstick from what he thought was a common prostitute. His body had jerked just like this black man. She went outside and scraped the climber's blood and brains off her ax in the snow.

Mara was joined by Wu Ting. He said, "These were Americans. But not the ones we are looking for."

"Too bad," Mara retorted. "We will have to continue on until we find them."

"If only we could identify climbers first."

"It would be too dangerous. We cannot let them know what we are about." She looked up . "We are very close to Min Vody. We must hurry. I want to catch the Americans before they get into the city, Wu."

"We can't hurry at this altitude," he said.

"It's all downhill from here," Mara pointed out. "Let's get started," Wu Ting replied.

CHAPTER 39

Before first light, the three person team composed of Billy, Tucson, and Jack were roped together and set off with the four man team of Joe, Charlie, Dakota and Anahan roped together and following in trace. They were soon crossing a large glacial ice flow coming off the mountain. The four man team had a problem when Dakota realized his right foot was numb from the cold. His team stopped while he repeatedly swung his foot to force blood into the foot to recover circulation. Finally, he had to sit down, take his boot off and massage his foot. Without radios, and because it was still dark, the three man team did not notice the second team's hold up.

Catastrophe struck ten minutes later after Billy walked over a snow bridge spanning a large crevasse. Tucson was second on the rope connecting the three climbers. When she crossed the snow bridge over the crevasse, it collapsed and she fell into the open trench in the glacier. Her fall yanked Billy back and before he could react he was pulled backwards by the connecting rope into the crevasse. Jack was pulled forward by the same rope towards the crevasse and he stabbed the ice with his ice ax to stop his slide. But his self-arrest did not work as his axe hit a crack in the ice and he tumbled into the crevasse as well when the weight of the first two on the rope pulled him down. It felt like he fell about thirty feet before he hit the bottom.

Tucson and Jack pulled themselves together and only saw the rope connecting to Billy was disappearing over the ledge they had landed on. Jack realized that Billy had bounced and fallen deeper into the crevasse.

He peered over the edge and saw BIlly's crumpled form wedged in a narrowing of the crevasse. He was not moving.

Jack called, "BIlly are you alright?" There was no answer.

They pulled themselves together and took stock. Luckily, Tucson and Jack were not injured beyond pain and bruises. But Billy looked stuck and unmoving below them.

They looked up for the other team and saw nothing, not even the sky. The crevasse was deep but luckily had a navigable base. They yelled but there was no answer.

"Are you okay?" Jack asked.

"If you call bouncing down an icy rathole okay!" Billy shouted from below. "My rear end is damned sore!"

"How do we get out of here?" Tucson asked. She was terrified when she looked up at the icy walls looming over them, but she tried to swallow her fear.

"I don't see the other team, so we have to climb up the sides of the crevasse or walk to where the crevasse daylights,'' Jack said.

Tucson looked up at the vertical ice and said, "I'd rather walk."

Jack yanked on the rope that connected Tucson and Billy. "We'll pull you up to us," he called.

Billy yelled okay and Jack and Tucson began pulling. Together they soon got Billy up to their level. He stood, turned and started limping downslope in the open crack in the glacier. He quickly grunted and stopped,

"What's the matter?" Jack asked.

"Dead guy! I think," Billy said. Jack and Tucson caught up and eyed the crushed together clothing. The clothes looked ragged and torn. If the remains were a human there was no way to tell by looking at them.

"Now you know what you'll look like if you stay here awhile," Jack said with a very flat tone. "These crevasse splits in the glacier open and close like refrig doors."

"Please let's just get out of here before they do that!" Tucson pleaded. She turned back to Jack and when he stepped forward, she hugged him and buried her face in his chest. "I'm scared!" she exclaimed.

"Don't worry, we are making it out of here," he reassured her.

They continued to walk along the crevasse, slowed by Billy's injury, sometimes having to turn sideways to negotiate a path whenever the crevasse narrowed. Billy stopped again. Some kind of carcass was at his feet.

Jack looked and said, "It's a Red deer's remains. See the broken antlers?"

The body looked completely crushed. They stepped over it and continued slowly.

Suddenly, Jack stopped and looked up at the blue sky. "I just had an idea.

Billy," he asked, "Do you have a lighter?"

"Yeah, sure," Billy answered. "How do you think I start fires to melt snow for tea?"

"Great idea!" Tucson exclaimed.

Jack looked at the FBI agent. "You get it."

"Yes! We light the animal on fire and the team will see the smoke."
"Gotcha!" Billy limped back to the deer remains, bent over and started the animal on fire.

The three watched as the smoke from the fire started to curl up the crevasse.

Billy stood and slowly moved back along the crevasse to the human remains. He returned with an armful of clothing, which he threw on the fire.

Soon they heard a human shout.

"Down here!" Jack and Tucson both responded. "Quiet!" Jack said. "We don't know who it is." "Who else knows we are done here?" Tucson asked.

"Billy, what's wrong?" Jack asked when he saw Billy on his knees. As he waited for an answer, he saw Billy fall face forward in the crevasse.

"Over here!" Someone shouted. "Smoke! I've found them!"

Jack hurried to Billy, turned him over and brushed icy snow out of his brother's face. Suddenly, green foam oozed out of Billy's open mouth as he gasped for air.

Tucson immediately recognized the symptoms. "He must've taken fentanyl!" She exclaimed.

Jack saw the foam as the same foam that Jose had vomited as he died from fentanyl poisoning.

"Billy! Did you take a drug?" Jack shouted. "Just meth for the pain" Billy whispered. "Zhang gave me … capsules when I left."

"They spiked your meth! Why would they do that?"

"Zhang… said it was… a good lock…I guess she really was trying to tell me… that she still loves me…" Billy gasped and more green foam spouted out of his mouth and he quit breathing.

"Billy!" Jack hugged his brother. "Don't leave us! Billy!"

Tucson checked Billy's pulse. She could not feel it. "He's gone!" Jack hugged Billy's body.

A few minutes later, an uncoiled rope cascaded down the crevasse as voices from above shouted "Hello!"

"What are we going to do with his body?" Tucson asked.

"We will leave it here in the crevasse. It is a fitting… burial… site for my… brother," Jack said. He brushed remaining ice crystals off his brother's face. He leaned over and kissed Billy's forehead.

Tucson tied the rope to her belt, and was lifted up and out of sight. In fifteen minutes, they both were rescued and Tucson told the others what had happened.

Jack sat on the snow and held his head in his hands, then he rose and kicked snow into the crevasse.

"What happened to you guys?" Tucson asked.

"We got held up by a minor problem." Charlie remarked. "Where's Billy?" Joe asked.

"He …is…dead!" Jack responded.

"What the hell happened down there?" Charlie asked. Tucson said, "Billy took a drug. It killed him."

"That is so weird!" Anakan exclaimed.

The six climbers reassembled after a water break and headed up the slope. The sun was very bright on the snow and during the next rest break, Tucson took her glasses off and rubbed her eyes. She opened her eyes and was immediately blinded. She put her dark glasses on and could see again. She was feeling the altitude now and it looked like they were about halfway up the saddle. Each step was becoming difficult and she wondered if the others were having the same trouble she was.

Each time they came to a snow bridge over a crevasse, she held her breath until she made it across. Many of them she could just step over without using a bridge.

When it looked like there was about two hours left of daylight, they spotted two huts several hundred meters up ahead. They looked like aluminum metal quonset huts. The teams held up and huddled for a conference.

Jack said with a defeated, lifeless tone, "We'll have to send a team to scout the huts."

Anakan and Dakota looked at each other and Dakota said, "We'll go."

The group sat down behind a small ridge of drifted snow and boiled some snow to make tea while they waited.

Just before sunset, the Indians rejoined them. They were curiously silent as they sat down and accepted some hot tea.

"So tell us, what did you find?" Jack asked.

"The guard mentioned a climbing team with five members and two guides," Anakan said.

"We found them in one of the huts," Dakota added. "All shot dead! Like the ones below!"

"Were they the Chinese?" Tucson asked.

"According to the border guards, one of the groups of climbers was Chinese," Jack said.

"No, they were not Chinese,'' Dakota said. "They were mostly white guys."

"What the hell is going on?" Charlie asked no one.

"Bellum internecinum!" Jack said. Tucson gave him a look of irritation but said nothing. "A war of extermination!" Jack interpreted. "Either there are some real crazies running loose or someone has heard about us and is hellbent on stopping us! And the only people left are the Chinese. They must be the killers!" His voice was more animated now.

"But why?" Tucson asked.

"Somehow the Chinese have heard about our mission. And they are involved."

"To what end?" Charlie asked. "The Ransome guys have nothing to do with the Chinks."

"You think they are looking for us?" Tucson asked.

"I don't know but mountaineers normally don't shoot their competition," Jack responded as he glanced at her. "They just try to out climb them."

"Quite a few people know about what we are attempting," Joe said.

Jack glanced at the others,"The bad guys might be looking for us and got here before we did and are killing everyone on the climb thinking we are up somewhere above them."

BIlly's eyes fluttered and finally he was able to focus. His body felt like a dead log. He slowly swiveled his head and looked for his brother and the babe. He saw neither. He rose on one elbow, then to his knees. He was dizzy and confused..He knew not where he was or who he was. He shook his head and slowly stood. He glanced right and left, then staggered down the descending cleft in the forbidding ice.

CHAPTER 40

$\mathbf{M}$ick Nakamura looked at his strike team sitting in the Falconex jet. The three engined jet could carry 12 passengers but it only held him and his team of six soldiers, He glanced back at the pilot and co-pilot. He ached to fly himself. With traffic and collision avoidance, modular avionics, and a Honeywell autothrottle, the jet practically flew itself. They had left Moscow airspace four hours ago.. Mick could not believe how easy it was to get into Russia. Evidently their jet was owned by a Russian billionaire capitalist and because of that, his jet was treated like it had golden wings whenever it was rented by Americans and flown to Russia. Agent Hermosa had arranged the rental.

With all their weapons stowed in an uninspected hold, they were home free to go to Min Vody and conduct their mission. They even had visas delivered at the Moscow airport by a nervous, young Russian woman.

The only issue was the weapons. They were all Russian AK-74s. He decided to tell the team to break down the weapons so they would be familiar with them.

After a while, Mick went to the galley and helped himself to a bottle of Baltika lager. It was cold and had a wheaty aftertaste. His strike team members were now all asleep except for the sergeant, Jake Anderson. He was the son of an Iowa farming family. He had blonde hair and blue eyes like Jack Flashhardt, but he was a little shorter. He had climbed a couple of fourteeners in Colorado and had trained with Mick in Alaska. He was also a seasoned combat veteran and Mick knew he could count on Anderson, but the rest of the team were mountain trained but not truly combat ready.

Hermosa had dismissed Mick's concerns by pointing out that they were not going against a hardened target. And they had gone through bootcamp and advanced infantry training. So it was unlikely they would shoot themselves. The only issue was the weapons were all Russian AK-74s.

He sensed the jet's change in pitch as it started the descent to Min Vody. He checked his notebook in order to remember the Min Vody contact's name: it was Valdmir Pushkin. He pulled out his Iridium satellite cell phone and dialed Pushkin's number in Min Vody. A man answered and he asked for Pushkin.

"It is I, Pushkin."

"This is A Bird," Mick used his designated call sign. "Where are you?"

"About twenty minutes out of Min Vody airport. There are seven of us." "I will pick you up in front of the terminal. A green bus."

"Good," Mick hung up.

When the jet landed and taxied to the terminal, Mick and his team unloaded their duffle bags containing their Russian AK 74s and a lot of 9mm ammo and spare clothes.

CHAPTER 41

$\mathbf{M}$ara Bhutto saw the SUV parked next to a sheepherder hut in the distance. She called a halt and motioned for Wu Ting to join her. The other members of the team sprawled and relaxed, drinking water and smoking cigarettes, as they all did.

"I am guessing that the SUV next to the hut is there to pick up Jack and his team," Mara said.

"What do you want to do? Go around and continue on?" Ting asked. The driver might have a cell."

"True," he said. "Probably the sheepherders are too poor to own cell phones, but if the driver does, he could spot us and call down the mountain. We would lose the element of surprise."

"We had better take precautions," Mara concluded. "Everybody, right?"

"Of course," Mara agreed. "And we will take the truck."

Ting motioned the team to rise and move out. With little communication that Mara could observe, the Chinese advanced to the hut, and proceeded to kill the Russian driver and the sheepherder and his presumed wife and a toddler. They executed the hit without firing a shot. They used their ice axes.

Mara, standing outside, saw a second child come around the hut and observe the slaughter. Standing, petrified by the horror of the scene, he did not notice Mara approach and ax him in the back of the head.

She was relieved again that she had not lost the killing trait that she had exercised in Pakistan and Afghanistan where she held the horrific title of The Black Orchid Assassin.

Ting stepped outside and inspected the SUV after a glance at the fallen child. "The driver did not have a key on him for the vehicle," he relayed to Mara.

"Do any of your men know how to get it started?" Mara asked.

"Bunch of rice farmers," Ting snorted. "None of them own a vehicle. And I am not mechanical. We will have to walk until we can take a drivable vehicle."

CHAPTER 42

"**W**e can't move on the two huts until just before sunrise," Jack instructed the team members. "So let's eat and get some sleep. Charlie, you set up a watch rotation. I'll take first watch."

After standing his watch, he woke Charlie, then went to lie down next to Tucson. She stirred and then slid over until she could put her arms around Jack. She hugged him tight and she wished that he would make love to her. But she knew she could not endure the act.

Jack woke at 0400. All were asleep around him except for Joe who was sitting up and keeping watch.

"Reveille," he announced. "Time to get up."

Tucson awoke and looked around. The two huts looked like they were on top of the saddle. The split peaks of Elbrus loomed over them. She idly wondered where Zeus had chained Prometheus to the mountain.

After gulping oatmeal and tea heated over a small gas stove, the teams set out in a long line, perpendicular to the line of advance towards the huts. All had their weapons ready. As they grew closer. One team would hunch over in the snow and the other team would advance about fifty meters. Then they would sink down as the second team moved up to them. They continued to hop forward one team at a time until they reached the huts. Jack kicked open a metal door and saw two dead men sprawled on the snow covered floor. The blood pools around the bodies stained the snow red. He motioned the two Indians to check out the other hut. He looked closely and saw three more bodies of men lying in a pile.

The Indians shouted that the other hut was empty.

They all moved into the body free hut. It was a metal Quonset with curving walls and one door in the end and a door in the middle that slid up to open. There were no windows, and like the first hut, the floor was snow.

Jack motioned Charlie to stand outside guard while the teams met.

"I wish we knew what is really happening on this mountain. But we are at the top of the saddle and it is all downhill from here. Now when I was climbing Elbrus from the Russian side, our guides armed us with rifles. They said we had to worry about Muslin bandits. I don't know if that is still the case, but at least we are already armed. If attacked, we'll use the same tactics as when we approached the huts.

Main thing is, we will counterattack instantly. Nothing works as well as aggression."

"The question still remains-- who did all this?" Tucson wondered out loud. "And why?"

"Obviously, we don't know but if somebody is hunting us and killing all these climbers--it really pisses me off!" Dakota exclaimed.

"Let's eat and head out. It is all downhill from here," Jack said.

The team consumed oatmeal bars and water, then gathered their gear, roped up and headed down the saddle. After about one hour, they were off the glacier and they no longer had to encounter crevasses, so they undid the ropes that joined them together and continued on their way. Everybody noted a spectacular waterfall shooting out of a sheer cliff that was draining the glacier. It was coming straight out of an opening in the side of the cliff. It turned into a rushing river that roared down the mountain.

In another hour, they encountered a very finished trail and Jack announced, "Last time along this trail I saw a monument stating that we are on The Marco Polo Trail. He came through here in the thirteenth century. Hard to believe!"

The terrain turned to grasslands between mountains and soon they encountered herds of sheep eating the lush grass.

"When do we catch the ride to the city?" Charlie asked. "How will he know when we get there?" Tucson added.

"I called my guy on my Iridium Satellite Phone," Jack responded. He stopped, shrugged off his pack and pulled out and showed the phone. It looked twice as big as a normal cell phone. "He is waiting for us at the end of the highway. We should reach it tomorrow."

He laughed and added, "When I was climbing this was the only road in this area but now they have a paved road and our guide should be waiting for us at the end of it, tomorrow."

At sunset, they halted near an abandoned sheep herder's hut, ate a meal of canned beef stew and hot tea. Then all thankfully went to sleep outside the empty hut except Jack, who took the first watch again. He watched as a couple of hundred sheep, with nothing as interesting as humans around their fields. Gathered around the team in a huge circle of spectators and just watched as the team went to sleep. Finally, the bored sheep wandered away.

Jack's mind turned to his brother. They had never been close in their youth but had bonded in Afghanistan.

Billy had everything going for him except for the drug addiction and that had been his fatal flaw. Jack flushed those thoughts and thought of playing with his son. After his watch, he quickly fell asleep.

The next morning, after oatmeal and tea, the team saddled up and headed down a herder's trail.

Jack stopped after an hour, shucked his backpack, got out his satellite phone and called his Russian guide, Nikita Pavel. When the Russian answered, Jack asked, "Do you have comm with the guy you sent up the mountain to pick us up?"

Nikita said that he did not have telephone service outside of the city. By noon, they saw a hut in the distance with a SUV parked next to it.

As they grew close, Jack hailed the hut but nobody came out to greet them. With growing apprehension, they reached the hut and SUV. Then they saw a small body next to the door and they noticed that all four wheels on the vehicle were flat. They circled the hut as Anakan stepped over the boy's body and pushed through the doorway.

"All dead!" He shouted.

The team crowded into the one room hut. The bodies of a man, a woman, one more very young boy and a differently dressed young man were lying side by side on a plank bed that stretched from one side of the hut to the other side.

Jack went outside to check the SUV. In addition to the flat tires, he noticed bullet holes in the ignition.

The others joined him, muttering to themselves and others. Jack started cursing out loud and knowing that this catastrophe had happened to all the victims on the mountain and that it was their fault in part. The immediate question was, had the Chinese learned anything new or were they just housecleaning everything in their way?

CHAPTER 43

Mara Bhutto and Wu Ting climbed out of the truck they had stolen and had driven down the mountains after coldly ending the life of another sheepherder who owned the truck. Ting walked to a bush and relieved himself. He soon was followed by the rest of the team.

Ting joined Mara and said, "We are going to be in Min Vody in about a half hour. Your friend may have gotten there before us."

"Jack? My friend? Hardly," Mara exclaimed. "I know him well but after I stabbed him in the back in Islamabad last year, I am sure he does not count me as a friend."

"And you had another go around with him in America if I recall your history."

"Yes, he bested me there but this time things will be different," Mara said firmly.

"Maybe he is behind us," Ting speculated. "We should check. It would be a lot easier than trying to find him and his crowd in the city."

"Send two of your best men back to check out behind us," Mara agreed. "I will send my number two and I will go as well," Ting responded. "My

Russian contact tells me there is a monument in the center of the city and it is on the main highway so you cannot miss it. It is a Russian soldier statue. Our man will meet you there and take you to our safe house. I have described this truck. And he will identify himself as Sergi and will ask for you, Mara."

"And you will take the backtrack team how far?" Mara asked.

"As far as the top of the Saddle," Ting retorted. He picked up his back pack from the vehicle and a rifle. "We will go to Ransomware headquarters. They are expecting us," Mara stated.

CHAPTER 44

Jack called Nikita Pavel back and said, "Your driver is dead. It looks like robbers or vandals killed him. They also slashed all four tires on the SUV. Can you send someone else up here to pick us up?"

Nikita was astonished by what Jack had told him. He agreed to send a truck up to get them. And he said he would drive it and meet them the next morning,

"One thing," Jack cautioned. "Just in case there is something funny going on, why don't you send the truck up the old German road. We'll get to that road and follow until we meet you."

"What do you mean by funny?" Nikita asked.

"I don't know," Jack responded, "We have encountered murdered climbers up here. Might be some crazy natives. But just to make sure, take the old road. Nobody knows about that old road except locals. So if anybody is looking for climbers, they probably won't look on the German road."

After Jack hung up, the others who were standing around him, just stared.

Finally, Tucson asked, "What's the deal with the German road?"

Jack announced, "This is a road built by the German Army when they invaded Russia in WWII." He added, "When I was climbing it was the only road in this area but now of course, the Russians have built this paved road for climbers of Elbrus."

"Let's get out of here," Charlie cautioned.

The team picked up their packs and followed Jack as he swung to the west and started up a long slope. When they crested the hill, they entered a large valley with scattered flocks of sheep. There were no huts visible. At the bottom of the valley, they could see a dirt road that looked like it had been cut clean and had a smooth surface.

The team followed Jack single file across the grass covered, treeless meadows and skirted around flocks of sheep. In two hours of steady progress they reached the German road. The sun was making everything much warmer than it had been on the snowy saddle and soon all had shed their parkas, gloves and caps.

At the German road, they set up camp stoves and heated their beef strip MREs and boiled water from a small stream that ran alongside the road. Their activity attracted crows that circled and watched for abandoned food.

The German road was in remarkably good shape considering that it was over seventy five years old.

The Germans built it to last. They must have had big plans for Russia when they invaded in 1939 or 1940, Tucson thought as she looked at the road.

After their meal, Jack had them practice the team tactics again.

He reminded them, "We start by checking safeties, then one team member goes in right, one goes in left and the next team member goes in straight. Two for rear security and two for flank security."

After running through the maneuvers for a half dozen times, they settled into their sleeping bags then instituted the same watch routine.

Tucson woke several times, and gazed at the brilliant stars for a while as the canopy crossed the heavens. She thought of Jack and wished she could overcome her emotions, her painful past. Finally she fell asleep again. At five AM she and the others woke to find Anakan and Dakota boiling water for tea.

BY six AM, all had finished their morning libations as an old, weathered military SUV ground to a stop. A slender, short man who appeared to be about forty years old got out accompanied by a teenage boy. The man grinned and hugged Jack.

Jack introduced Nikita Pavel to the team members. He noticed Nikita, while he was welcoming the team to Russia, quickly sized up each member and then his gaze lingered on Tucson.

Jack took Nikita by the arm and said, "Tucson is a trained and experienced member of our national police agency, the FBI."

With awakened respect, the Russian nodded to Tucson.

Jack immediately realized that he should not have singled out Tucson as an FBI agent but he could not deny his words. *Not easy to be a criminal,* he thought.

CHAPTER 45

After the team loaded in the Russian truck's three rows of seating and an open bed in back, Nikita turned around and introduced the teenager as Nikolai, his son. Jack and Tucson sat in the front row with Nikita.

The group then headed down the mountains towards Min Vody. After an hour, NIkita said, "I sent two men up to tow my other vehicle back to the city. I wonder who killed the driver, Josef."

"Have you heard about other news of violence on Elbrus?" Tucson asked. "No," Nikita said. "Did you see anything unusual?"

Jack looked at Tucson, then Charlie before he answered, then he said, "Some climbers were killed by someone. We don't know who nor did we see anything except dead bodies."

Nkita stared at Jack. "There have always been bandits but not on the mountain. Probably they are too lazy to climb up high."

"There were bodies in the hut that is on the top of the saddle," Tucson said.

Just then, the truck's progress ended and they coasted to a stop. The engine was still running.

Nikita exclaimed something in Russian. Charlie said, "What the hell!"

Other members of the team exclaimed surprise. Jack asked Nikita, "What do you think is wrong?"

Nikita got out of the truck and lifted the hood. He then went to the bed in the rear of the truck and found a hammer, which he carried as he returned to the engine area. Soon they heard him pounding on something metallic.

Everybody looked around and realized how desolate the terrain and vegetation was. There were no gas stations or garages to be had. There were only scattered groups of sheep wandering about on treeless, grass covered meadows and hills.

As they continued to hear pounding and cursing from under the hood, they maintained vigilant observation and soon saw a man come over a rise and approach the vehicle.

The man appeared to be unarmed and was dressed like a peasant but Jack ordered the team to quietly deploy behind the vehicle and then ordered Tucson, the only team member with a handgun to go on alert.

"He doesn't have a weapon," Tucson protested.

"He might have something, even an explosive," Jack insisted. "We have to be extra careful."

"He looks like a sheepherder," Tucson insisted.

"Look, Tucson, you are not experienced with combat in other countries.

This is not America. Be on alert, please," Jack commanded.

As the man grew to within ten paces, Nikita stepped away from the truck and confronted the man. They spoke in Russian and Nikita then said, "He is what he appears to be, a sheepherder. He's just curious."

He pointed at the engine compartment and added, "I got the differential banged back into working order. We can go. The man has invited us to a cup of tea. When I told him you were Americans, he said that he loved America. I think we should go for tea."

"How long?" Jack asked.

"Maybe a half hour delay. We might find out who killed my driver. And it is getting late. We can spend the night."

"You're right, " Jack agreed. They climbed into the truck and slowly followed the Russian until they crested a hill and saw a small hut. They parked and followed the Russian into the one room hut that looked like it had been built out of leftover scraps from a jobsite. The only furniture was a table with several chairs. A large barrel sat in one corner. The back half of the hut was a bed built out of planks that created a platform that stretched from one side of the hut to the other, There were no pillows, no blankets, just the wood plank bed that was about two feet above the floor which was also made of rough planks.

The Russian went outside and left the Americans in the hut, there were only four chairs, so Tucson and three others sat down. The others remained standing. A young, very plain looking woman entered with a large teapot, took cups off a shelf and poured tea for all. It was hot and sweet. The Russian re-entered and NIkita introduced the Sheepherder as a young man named Boris. Nikita remembered Jack's name but no one else. Boris had a large ceramic mug in his hands. He lifted the lid on the barrel, scooped out a mug full of yogurt and offered it to the closest American, Charlie. He said with a vigorous tone as held out the mug, "Yogurt, goot for you!"

Charlie drank half the cup and handed the rest to Dakota. Soon all had drank except Jack. He refused the drink when offered and rubbed his stomach saying, "I have an upset stomach."

"So, Nikita," Jack asked, "has your son climbed Elbrus yet?"

NIkita glanced at his son and smiled. "We have tried twice but have been turned back by storms. Now it is getting too late in the season, we will climb in the spring." He clapped his son on the back and smiled again.

"How many times have you climbed Elbrus?" Dakota asked.

"Too many times to count," Nikita answered. "I have guided climbers for fifteen years."'

"And you have never heard of climbers being killed on the mountain?" Charlie asked.

"No," Nikita responded, "There have been bandits in the foothills but never on the mountain. This is a new development."

The sheepherder, Boris, took a large bottle of vodka off a shelf and poured two small stemmed glasses. He offered one to Tucson and one to himself.

"I know the drill," Jack said. "This is a contest. You bend your arm and put the glass on top of your elbow. Then you drink it without spilling."

NIkita and Tucson tried. Nikita was successful and Tucson spilled her glass. Everybody laughed as Jack, expecting a failure, caught her glass in midair.

Soon, everyone had tried the contest with Boris and Nikita. Only Charlie had been able to tie them. After a half hour, the team broke out MREs, heated and ate their meals while the Russians ate some cheese and bread the young woman supplied. After dinner, Jack set up a watch program and everyone including the host and his wife stretched out on the long plank bed and went to sleep lying side by side. Tucson made sure she was lying next to Jack. When she woke in the early morning, she was happy to discover his arm was around her and she was especially happy that she was not horrified by his embrace. She wondered if she could consummate a union with him without reliving the Serbian horrors of the California Mountains.

The next morning, Anakan, the last to serve as sentry, woke everyone up at sunrise. The Russian wife made tea and oatmeal for all. After breakfast, Jack gave the sheepherder ten twenty dollar American bills after Nikita told him the American cash was very desirable in Russia. Everyone loaded in the truck and Nikita began driving down the German made road. It was sunny and soon the sun's rays warmed all up. Finally, the German road merged with the new Russian road and the drive got even better than it had been traveling on the eighty year old Nazi German road.

They descended to a lower part of the Caucasus Mountains where the slopes were covered with pine trees. At about lunch time, they encountered the first vehicle coming up the mountains at them. Nikita stopped and the other vehicle stopped as well about fifty meters away.

It was a small SUV that had a high clearance. A man got out of the vehicle and stood in front of it. No one could see any features on the man as he had sunglasses and a brimmed cap.

Nikita said to his son, Nikolai, "Go ask him what is the problem?"

"Wait," Jack cautioned. "Maybe you had better go." He motioned to Charlie to get out and take cover, flanking the vehicle.

Nikolai jumped out and walked up to the man. They spoke for a couple of minutes, then the man pulled a pistol out and shot Nikolai several times until the boy fell to the ground.

NIkita groaned in horror and jumped out of the truck and ran to his fallen son, shooting as he ran.

Another man, hiding behind the SUV door, shot at Nikita who dived into bushes next to the road. As the man redirected his aim and shot their vehicle, the others returned fire as well.

Slowly they advanced towards the enemy vehicle, firing as they advanced. Quickly, the first man was struck by multiple bullets and sank to the road's surface. A second man jumped out and ran into the brush and quickly disappeared.

Nikita sprawled on the ground next to his son's body and wrapped his arms around the dead boy and sobbed. When Tucson pulled the goggles off the dead man, they realized he was Asian.

Soon most of the others gathered around the father and the dead boy. Dakota and Anakan continued down the road, searching for the escaped killer. One covered while the other searched hard to see spots in the brush along the road. Suddenly, Dakota shouted and fired his rifle. A man jumped up and raised his arms in the air above his head. Like the first killer, the man wore goggles and a cap. Anakan ran forward and stripped the eyewear off revealing another Asian who was very tall.

Dakota prodded the man in the back with his rifle and the Asian moved back to the team's position. Nikita drew his pistol and was going to kill the Asian but Jack stepped forward and prevented Nikita from shooting.

"They must be part of the Chinese kill team!" Tucson announced. "This is one of the guys that were killing all the climbers!" Jack agreed.

"So they were backtracking," Tucson said. "That means they're already in Min Vody."

"Let's go get 'em!" Charlie exclaimed.

Everyone jumped back in the truck after putting the fallen Nikolai in the truck bed.

"How far to Min Vody?" Tucson asked.

"Less than a half hour," Nikita responded between broken sobs.

Charlie started the truck and began driving. After about fifteen minutes, Jack noticed that the Asian prisoner sat up straight and began to look ahead.

"Hold up for a minute," Jack said. Charlie stopped the truck.

About fifty meters to their front, a pine tree grove was growing on one side of the road. The fields were covered with flowers and the scene looked peaceful. The sky was cloudless, nevertheless; Jack felt uneasy.

"Charlie." Jack instructed, "Put a grenade in the grove up ahead."

Picking up his M320, Charlie shot a 40mm grenade into the heart of the grove. Multiple screams were heard by the team,

"I thought our prisoner looked too optimistic," Jack said. Charlie whirled and shot the man with a pistol he drew.

"Damn! Good thing you were very aware," Tucson commented.

Half of the team got out of the truck and advanced on the grove while the others deployed to cover them.

They discovered that Charlie's lucky grenade shot had killed two more Chinese attackers.

Joe spun around and put his rifle under the prisoner's jaw and asked, "How many more?"

The man blanched but did not respond. "He doesn't speak English," Jack surmised.

Suddenly, an all-white giant tiger leapt from the brush it was hiding in and mauled the Chinaman just as he was about to stab Jack with a hidden knife. The tiger and the man rolled on the ground. The man immediately dropped the knife as the tiger engulfed the guy's head with this giant mouth,

The tiger rose from the motionless man and Joe raised his rifle again. "NO!" Jack shouted. He ran forward and threw his arms around the tiger's neck. "It's Tigger! He saved me again!"

"Holy shit!" Anarkan exclaimed. " The animal. He saved Jack! How–?"!"

Tucson remembered the stories that Jack had told her about the amazing tiger that had saved Jack when he was sick, and when he was being chased by Mo Poo,

"Too late now," Jack said as he looked at the man's head laid open by the bullet. "Let's get on down to the city." He looked into the tiger's vibrant blue eyes. "Tigger, I don't know how you got here, but thanks!" He tousled the cat's head and added, "Unfortunately, you can't come with me into the city. So… go forward and take care ... you are loved. And I hope we cross paths again."

CHAPTER 46

One by one, Mick's team climbed over the perimeter block wall and dropped to the ground inside the estate. When all had made it, Vladimir patted Mick's shoulder and whispered "Go now we must, rapid."

"Let's go, Guys, single file." Mick whispered to the team.

The stars were bright in the Russian sky but luckily there was no moon as it was early evening. The mansion on the hill, with its steeples blocking out the city's evening glow, loomed darkly in front of them. There was no underbrush, just knee high grass until they drew near the building where head high bushes surrounded the structure. Vladimir stopped in front of a large window, about five feet by five feet on the east side of the building. He removed masking tape from his coat and applied long strips to the window in a large X shape. Then he applied more strips to the window and when Vladamir was satisfied, he pulled a small knife from his coat pocket and softly tapped the window until large cracks spread across the pane without making a sound. He grabbed a small piece and pulled the shattered window out of its frame.

Then, with Mick's helping hand, he climbed over the sill and silently entered the mansion.

After careful surveillance, he assisted Mick and the others into the building.

"Wake!" Wu Ting shook Mara's shoulder. "The Americans have arrived," he said as she looked up at the tall Chinese man.

"Where…" Mara began.

"No time. Follow me," he ordered.

Mara stood and followed the Chinaman to the security entry room to the main computer center. She saw the team readying their weapons as they filed behind the five foot barricade wall that spanned the room with gates at each end.

She went through the entry and into the main Data Center computer room. There were many computer screens of various sizes on the long wall. At the base of the computer wall, a long desk seated half a dozen men. Three armed guards stood against the far wall and stood in front of a large screen that displayed the entry room.

Now, all the Chinese team men were concealed in the entry room. Moments passed and after about five minutes, a single American opened the entry room door and looked at the room. Seeing nothing suspicious, he withdrew his head and said, "Come on, it's clear."

As Mara watched, seven men, all carrying Russian AK-74M assault rifles, entered the room. The first man she had seen, started to cross to the main computer room's door.

Suddenly, her Chinese team stood and opened fire with a hail of automatic fires. The Americans returned fire even as they fell to the floor.

The outbursts of gunfire were deafening. Then as every American fell to the floor, The Chinese team members strode forward and put a bullet into every American's head.

Unseen by the Chinese, Sergi, the American's guide, who had not gone into the entry room, quickly retreated and left by the front door to the mansion.

Mara entered the death room and checked every face. None of the bodies was Jack's. The last man was lying on the front of his body so his face was not visible. He looked too heavy to be Jack but this was the last man so she hoped as she turned him over.

His face was covered in blood from a gunshot that had been meant to kill but had only creased his forehead. He also had a wound just below the rib cage. The man was hiccuping, proving he was alive. Mara realized he had been shot in the diaphragm. She started to rub the blood off his face and immediately discovered the features were Asian.

She wiped the blood off her hands on his jacket, then approached a member of her team who was treating a wounded man. She quickly ran to the man and grabbed a Quikclot package out of his medical bag and returned to the wounded American. She put a piece of the Quikclot on his frontal wound and pushed it into the wound with a finger. Then she heaved and pushed the man back on his stomach and with another piece of Quikclot she shoved it into the posterior exit wound.

"Why do you administer aid to the enemy?" Wu Ting demanded with a harsh tone.

Mara looked up at the Chinaman towering over her. "I want to question him," she responded. "Then I will eliminate him."

"See that you do," he turned and left.

CHAPTER 47

$\mathbf{A}$s Charlie drove the truck into the city, Jack said, "Min Vody, which means mineral water in Russian, is named so because of all the mineral water springs in this part of the Caucasus Mountains. It also has a large mineral water bottling plant that ships water all over Europe. It is about seventy-five thousand in population and has a lot of Russian looking cathedrals and public buildings with typical Russian spires and towers. Also newer Muslim temples as Islam has grown now that the Soviet Union has gone away.

It has an international airport which we may use to make our getaway. And it is about one thousand miles from Moscow although it felt farther when I came here by train to climb Elbrus."

Jack pointed at Nikita, who was still suffering from his loss with his face buried in his hands. "He is going to lead us to the computer crowd."

"What's our base of operations?" Charlie asked. "Where now?" Jack asked Nikita.

The Russian raised his head, then said, "Let me drive." He switched places with Charlie and headed into a neighborhood peppered with one story concrete buildings that all were similar in architectural style with flat roofs and windowless walls. Nikita stopped in front of one of the buildings and said, "Here is our base of operations. Let us enter.".

Large patches of siding had flaked off the building. The parking lot surface was packed with dirt.

The team got out of the truck, picked up their gear and entered the single door behind Nikita. Inside was a large room. Nikita grabbed Dakota and asked him to help unload his son's body. They retrieved the boy and carefully laid him on the wood plank floor next to the front wall. NIkita took off his jacket and put it under the boy's head and put a sleeve over the boy's face. He knelt down and embraced the boy's body for long moments then he stood and said, "I will go recon the Ransomware crowd."

Jack said, "Let me go with you."

Nikita looked at Jack and siad, "Alright. All of you get out of your mountain garb so you will more fit in. You would look strange in your present clothing. I will pick up Natasha, my assistant, and bring her here after I show Jack our objective. If any of you do not have proper garb, she will get some apparel for you." He turned and they left the team in the warehouse. An hour later he dropped off Jack and left again to pick up his assistant.

Jack assembled the group and said, "We are in incredible luck!" "How so?" Tucson asked.

"When, that is, after I climbed Elbrus a few years ago, I stayed in a huge mansion on a hill here. It was owned by the former owner of the local mineral water factory. After the Soviet Union collapsed, the manager of the water company seized ownership and took possession of the water company's twenty room mansion. He was renting part of it out to Nikita for climbers of Elbrus. So I know a big part of the place. Now the mansion, where the ransomware outfit is, is the same place and is now owned by the Chinese that set up the Ransomware outfit." He took out a pen and began drawing a sketch of the facility.

An hour later Nikita returned with a very attractive young blonde woman who spotted Jack and immediately walked up to him and with a big smile, embraced him and kissed him on the lips. Her hair was cut short but everything else about her screamed, *Beautiful babe!* She wore skin tight jeans and a light blue sweater. Her blonde hair just barely frosted her collar. Jack smiled and said, "Natasha! It is good to see you again." He turned to the team and said, "This is Natasha. She was Nikita's assistant guide when we climbed Elbrus years ago." He patted her on her very well shaped rear and added, "She's a helluva climber!" Everyone said, "Hello."

Natasha went to Nikita's son's body and knelt and touched the boy's face. "So young to die," she said sadly.

Jack immediately thought of Billy and unconsciously nodded his head in agreement, as he mentally swore payback for his brother's death.

"Huba, Hubba," Dakota said quietly to his brother. Anakan nodded in agreement.

Natasha took out a notebook and checked out each of the team member's clothing. She made a couple of notes, then said, "I will be back shortly. "Jack, can you come with me and pay for the purchases?"

He nodded in agreement and the two left after going outside and climbing in a light blue, four door, Hyundai Creta, which looked just like a typical small American car.

As they drove away, Tucson frowned with a dejected air and sat down on the floor.

"Lucky Jack," Charlie said.

"I don't think his mind is on pretty Russian girls," Tucson commented. "He is grieving over his brother."

"Billy was a good kid," Charlie added. "Too bad about his Meth addiction."

Tucson struck her knee with her fist. "It wasn't Meth that killed him, it was fentanyl!"

The group lapsed into silence and everybody fell asleep except Tucson. Jack and Natasha drove into the city through light traffic as it was Sunday, not a normal work day in Russia.

"Where are we going?" Jack asked, after Natasha pulled into a parking lot next to an average looking three story apartment house. It had a stucco exterior and was light brown in color. "We are going to my apartment to have a cup of tea and talk over old times."

Old times? Jack thought. *We only spent two weeks together with my father, who was my climbing partner, and two guides and you…* but he said nothing.

They climbed out of the Hyundai and as he followed her into the apartment house, he could not fail to notice her extraordinary rounded rear end.

I guess I should refer to it as her wonderful derriere, he thought. *Or maybe a fine patootie.*

She unlocked a plain slab plywood door and he followed her into the apartment. The furniture looked like it had escaped from a cheap hotel, but the place was neat and clean.

The kitchen was just a part of the living room and was created by a cabinet topped by a plastic counter top. She motioned for him to sit on the sofa and she went into the kitchen to make tea.

"How has your expedition gone?" Natasha asked.

"Pretty much a disaster," Jack responded. "My Brother, Billy–he is three years younger than me– was with us but he died of an accidental drug overdose on the mountain. We buried him in a crevasse."

Jack thought of when Billy had joined him in Pakistan when Jack was assigned to the United Nations service. He had been so cocky. Ready to fight anything and anybody.

"I am sorry for your loss, Jack." Natasha delivered two cups of hot tea she had poured from a kettle on the stove. "Events should be smoother because of me."

"Why so?" Jack asked.

"It never came up during your expedition, but the man who took over the water company was my father, and he took over the имущество, or castle that we lived in that came with the water holdings. I know the security system in the estate and how to gain easy entrance."

"That's great!" Jack exclaimed

She sat on the sofa next to him, put her hand on his upper leg and wrapped her other arm around his neck then kissed him passionately.

"Whoa!" Jack exclaimed as he spilled his tea on the glass coffee table and pulled back.

Natasha leaned forward and kept her one hand on his upper thigh and the other on his neck. "Jack, I have thought about this kiss ever since we spent that night in the sheepherder's hut. And you said it was my mission to keep everybody else in the bed–I think there were nine of us sleeping in a row in that slab bed– away from you.

I wanted you so much. But it was impossible in that bed with all those people...now, years later, it is not crowded." She kissed him again.

"I thought we were going for-"

"We have plenty of time, Jack. We cannot attack before it is dark in a few hours." Natasha leaned back. "Am I not desirable to you?"

"Natasha," Jack began, "You are a gorgeous Russian woman. The first time I saw you when you met us at the train station when I came from Moscow to climb Elbrus, I thought you were a vision of beauty. But..."

"Jack, please stop objecting. I want you." She kissed him again and it was a fantastic, encompassing kiss.

Jack looked at Natasha as she leaned into him, kissed him again and stroked his leg. He could only make one response.

"Well..."

CHAPTER 48

Two hours later, Jack and Natasha walked into the warehouse carrying a bundle of clothing.

As the group gathered and received clothing from Natasha, NIkita entered the building.

"Your target was attacked!" he announced. "I had a man working for the defenders of the transsite. He said an American team attacked, killed two transsite fellows before a Chinese force came out of nowhere and set upon the Americans.

The Americans managed to kill two of the Chinese. But the Chinese killed all but one Asian American that at first was spared. They must've thought he was one of the transites. But when they figured out he was an American; now he is a prisoner of the Chinese gang."

Nikita walked up to Jack. "Did you know about these Americans? Or the Chinese attackers?"

Jack, with an astonished look on his face said, "Hell, no! I had no idea there was another American team sent after the Ransomware guys." He looked at the rest of his team. "The Chinese guys musta been the ones who killed all the climbers on Elbrus. They were looking for us."

"Or the other American team," Charlie opined.

"The Chinese government must have a very close connection to the Ransomware crowd. Otherwise, why would they care? Why would they go through all this trouble?" Jack looked at everyone but no one answered. "The question is— who were the Americans? Who sent them? And who is the lone prisoner?"

Again, no one had an answer. Finally, Tucson said, "We must rescue this American."

"That's not our mission!" Jack exclaimed. "We came here to take out the ransomware crowd."

"But it sounds like these Americans had the same mission!" Charlie said. "And they failed," Anahan added.

"Let's save him when we take out the R-gang," Dakota offered. "Everybody check your weapons. "We'll attack after dark," Jack ordered.

CHAPTER 49

T ing pointed at the American. "We thought he was one of your original people from when you set this up because at first glance he was an Asian. He was shot in the head and is still alive because you helped him. But all his equipment is identical to the dead Americans. When he regains consciousness, we can interrogate him."

"Thank Mao he survived!" Mara exclaimed.

The unconscious man was still lying on the floor in a front hallway. His face was covered with blood.

Mara leaned over, wiped his face more and was shocked to recognize Mick Nakamura's bloodied but recognizable face. "Where is Jack?" She demanded as she shook his shoulder.

He did not respond. She wiped his bloodied scalp and saw that the bullet had just creased his head and he should wake up. The wound did not look fatal.

"You were right," Mara said.. "He is an American soldier. An officer. He was probably the leader of these troops sent to destroy the *Open Pockets Operation I* set up last year here in Min Vody. This man must be interrogated. We must contact Russian authorities and tell them there has been a gun incident but that everything is under control. I will text you Moscow authorities and local law enforcement contacts and my I. D."

"Can you take care of it?" Wu asked.

"I must interrogate this American," she responded. "Have one of your men clean him up and bandage his wound and tie him to a chair."

"Why bother?" Wu nudged Mick's body with the toe of his boot. "Just kill him."

"Please comply," Mara directed. "I will kill him after interrogation, But I want him fully conscious when I end him," she said with a slow smile.

When he looked at her, he felt a chill as he remembered her Pakistani moniker– *The Black Orchid.*

"My men want to celebrate our victory. They discovered a cooler filled with French champagne, Don Per something, and heaps of beluga caviar to boot. The men are tired of the hardships of climbing the mountain. And I want to reward them for their success." He raised a fist in victory. "We have killed them all!"

"No!" Mara exclaimed. "One man, their leader has escaped. But I am sure he is not coming back to take us all on. He will be alone. Tell your men well done. They have successfully done all we asked," Mara said. 'They deserve a huge treat." She grabbed Wu's arm and added. "But leave a couple of men on guard."

"Why bother? All the Americans are dead. "No one will want to be left out of the celebration."

CHAPTER 50

"**K**apitan, you were right!" The Serzhant (sergeant) uttered with an excited voice.. The Data Center has been attacked!"

"All of them? Destroyed? By whom? The Nipponese?" Bruno exclaimed. He picked up his cell and called Igor Kloptan. When Igor answered,

Bruno said, "Tell the Reserve Minister that the Ransomware unit has been attacked. I will confirm what happened shortly."

"Call as soon as you know more," Igor said. "I will inform the Minister.

CHAPTER 51

Tucson finished cleaning and reloading her pistol. The other members of the team were still working on their rifles.

Jack stood and announced, "We'll hit them tonight. As soon as it is dark."

He knelt down next to Tucson. "I'll be glad when this is over," he said. "I want to get back to the States and get major payback for Billy's death. He died because he was helping me. I feel so guilty!"

Tucson put her hand on his shoulder. "No, Jack. He died because he is a drug addict."

He looked at her with sad eyes, "I know you are right but the suppliers are the only ones I can strike back at. And I want them to pay. I have heard that China supplies fentanyl. They are going to pay."

The team loaded in Nikita's truck and they drove through the city until they came over a rise and saw a large, sprawling estate on a solitary hill, back lit by the faded sunset. The roof had multiple Russian domes that made the mansion look exotic and strange against the darkening sky. NIkita proclaimed, "It is a имущество– an estate." They disembarked and hiked single file towards the hilltop estate.

It was completely dark as they began climbing the side of the low grassy plain covering the hill, next to the bricklain entry.

CHAPTER 52

Mick Nakamura slowly regained consciousness. He lifted his head and felt a shooting pain go through his skull. He opened his eyes and foggily realized that a woman was standing in front of him in an empty room. He tried to move and slowly discovered he was tied to a chair. The woman had a very angry voice and her eyes were hatefully glaring at him.

"Mick– whatever, do you recognize me?"

She looked a little familiar but it was hard to concentrate because of the pain in his head. "No, I don't," he muttered. His mouth and throat were so dry his words sounded like croaks.

He cleared his throat and said, "No!"

"I'm Mara! We met at the Marriot when you and your friends celebrated Jack Flashhardt's escape from the Taliban." She raised her voice and shouted "Remember? In Islamabad! Now tell me where he is."

His head hurt so much, he murmured, "Escaped." "That bastard!" Mara shouted. "How did he escape?" Mick dropped his chin to his chest,

"Wake up!" Mara shouted as she slapped his face. The utter pain made him instantly pass out.

"He is of no use to us, Finish him." Wu Ting exclaimed as he left the room. "I am going to relax with the others. We got all the Americans except this one is still alive."

"I'm not giving up. The one I want has escaped. Their leader."

"One coward on the run. Who cares? He's probably halfway to Moscow by now." He pointed at Mick and added, "Anyway, how do we know he is telling the truth. I don't see how anyone could have gotten by us during the attack."

Mick slowly opened his eyes. They were unfocused but open.

Mara grabbed his chin and raised it. "How did Flashhardt get away?"

MIck tried to form words, and tried to think. He thought of Mara. She had tried to kill Jack with a knife in Islamabad. "He… escaped you. He… ran… away."

"Bastard!" Mara screamed as hatred bubbled out of her when she mistakenly realized Jack had slipped through her grasp once again.

CHAPTER 53

Jack's team stopped at the wall next to the entry gate. Jack tried it but it was closed and locked. Jack got a boost from Charlie and he hooked a rope ladder to the top of the three meter high block wall. Nikita had placed the ladder earlier. He climbed up and dropped over the wall. The rest of the team followed and when all were over, they moved single file across a high cut lawn. It was very dark but they found the driveway and followed it to the giant building and the huge wooden entry door.

It was partly open. Jack slowly pushed it completely open and discovered the large entry was vacant. It was illuminated by a huge electric lighted chandelier. The team entered and heard the noise of a celebration–a lot of laughter and yelling– somewhere in the building. They quietly crossed to a closed door opposite the entry. The walls were decorated with large pictures of solemn men dressed in old fashioned attire.

The painted faces were not angry but looked uniformly stern as their eyes seemed to follow the intruder's progress across the entry.

Jack opened the door. It squeaked horribly. At the noise he jumped through the doorway into a room and saw Mick Nakamura tied to a chair, A woman and a man whose backs were to Jack, wheeled around at the noise. It was Mara Bhutto! Without hesitation, Jack leaped forward and slammed her in the jaw with his rifle butt, knocking her to the floor. He leaned over Mike, and the other man pulled a large knife and raised it. Tucson, ran up and shot the man before he could stab Jack in the back.

Jack glanced at the fallen Chinaman and said, "Thanks!"

Then he turned and with Tucson at his side, led the rest of the team to a far double door. Charlie and Joe hit the doors with their shoulders, knocking them open. The entire team burst into the large room.

What followed was a thunderous roar of gunfire and explosions from grenades as the team encountered drunks scrambling for their weapons. Screams rang out. The entire team passed through the door. Finally gunfire stopped and all Jack and the team heard was moaning and cries of pain. All the enemy were on the floor. Bottles of champagne littered the scene, most empty, some bubbling wine onto the floor..

"Into the next room!" Jack shouted. He and the team ran through an opposing door and began firing. Jack led and saw a room covered with dozens of computer screens. There were also free standing computers built into large cabinets. Anakan and Dakota started shooting every screen while Charlie was checking for survivors. He shot several wounded men.

Seeing there was no more trouble, Jack and Tucson returned to Mick and the woman lying at his feet.

He stood over Mara and realized she was still unconscious. He turned to Mick. "What the hell are you doing here, Mick?"

MIck looked at Jack, still confused by the head wound's effect on his mind. "You escaped!"

"What the hell you talking about? I didn't escape. I just got here. But I never heard about another American team attacking. Who sent you?"

"Your old nemesis. General Farley. But he never said word one about another team. Thank God you are here, Jack. We got wiped out by some Asians!"

"How did you survive?"

"I have no idea. I guess I got shot. My head is splitting. I woke up and Mara what's her name–that babe from Pakistan who had the hots for you and then tried to kill you, was questioning me. What the hell is she doing here? Am I totally fucked up?"

CHAPTER 54

$\mathbf{T}$ucson cut the ropes tying Mick to the chair. "Can you walk, Mick?" Jack asked. "We have to get out of here." He turned and yelled, "Charlie, throw a couple of grenades in the Data Center and let's skedaddle." He could not believe how relatively easy it had gone down as all the enemy were drunk..

When Charlie and Joe and the Indians re-emerged from the data center, Charlie pulled the pin on a M26 grenade and then on a second and threw them into the data center, shut the door and they cowered as two grenades exploded.

"We took no injuries," Charlie said. "It was like shooting a gang of drunk ducks! They were all drunk on Dom Pérignon of all things. At least they had expensive tastes! And the computer guys were just Chinese hackers and just as drunk!. We're done here! All the crooks are dead! All the computers are destroyed!"

"Let's get the hell outta here!" Jack repeated. He asked Mick again, "Can you walk?"

MIck slowly nodded his head but he swayed as he stood. Joe grabbed one arm and Charlie grabbed the other.

Jack looked down at the unconscious woman, Mara Bhutto, and thought about the time she tried to kill him in Islamabad. Why did she hate him? He had really never done anything to earn that hate. He decided to leave her in place.

He carefully stepped over her and walked through the huge entry with its staring portraits and stepped out onto the wide entry steps. The rest of the team followed. Suddenly two spotlights illuminated them. The huge lights were about fifty feet apart and were blinding.

"Holy shit!" Joe and Charlie both exclaimed.

Jack held up his rifle to shade his eyes and saw about thirty men standing next to each other in a row. Each was aiming an assault rifle at the Americans. At their feet kneeled at least twenty more men aiming their weapons as well. It was obviously hopeless. The huge group of men was ready to cut down the Americans.

Jack dropped his weapon and stepped forward with his hands above his head, "Drop your weapons or we'll be massacred!" He shouted at his team.

Four Russian soldiers advanced and roughly searched the team. Another four Russians advanced and collected their weapons.

Then the team was pushed and shoved into a covered truck that was parked in the driveway behind the troops.

Two Russians with leveled rifles stood at the end of the truck and covered the Americans. The truck pulled away from the estate, through the entry gate, and soon was driving through the bumpy roads of Min Vody.

The team was in shock but little was said, One of their guards, a kaprol, equivalent to a corporal, took a facial photo of each member of the team, then returned to guard duty.

After about a half hour drive, the truck pulled into a parking lot and when it stopped, one guard got out and the other motioned for the Americanas to disembark.

The team slowly climbed down and two men were waiting with zip ties which they used to fasten the team's wrists behind their backs,

They were led into a windowless concrete block building with no signage. Once inside, the leading guard pointed to a door and opened it as the team filed in and stood against the wall. The room was about fifteen feet by twenty and had no furniture of any kind. The floor was bare concrete and the walls were concrete blocks. There was little ventilation and the air soon got stuffy.

A Russian Kaprol said in English, ""Who is your leader?" Jack stepped forward as the others looked at him.

"Come with me," the kaprol prodded Jack with his AK74 assault rifle.

The Russian who had taken the pictures of the team's faces, re-entered the prisoner's room and prodded Jack again with the end of his rifle barrel. Jack noted it was an AK-74. He hoped the weapon's safety was on as he left the room. They walked across a hall and into an office with one window, with no curtains, and a desk behind which a Russian officer sat. There were no other chairs and Jack positioned himself in front of the desk. The officer had a shaved head and angry black eyes.

"You are American invaders! What the blazes are you doing in my country?"

Jack did not know what to say so he kept quiet. "Well, speak up!" The officer demanded.

"We were sent to destroy the Ransomware crowd that has been invading my country on the worldwide internet," Jack blurted out.

"You will be shot! Executed!" The officer made an angry gesture. "Take him away!"

The Russian kaprol shoved Jack towards the door. Jack walked through the door and his fear measurably increased as he was escorted to another room.

The Russian kaprol in charge of the men guarding the prisoners left Jack and went to another officer's temp office and handed the cell containing the photos of the invading terrorists.

The officer, Kapitan Bruno Utecht, who had arrived from Moscow and had announced that he was in charge of the affair and conflict, scanned the pics carefully to see if any of the terrorists were recognizable. He was shocked to see the familiar face of Jack Flashhardt on a pic. And on another he recognized Mick, as well.

What in the name of Tolstoy is Jack Flashhardt doing here? Bruno wondered. *Last time I saw him was in Islamabad.*

The American had been attached to the UN Station in Pakistan just as Bruno had, Bruno remembered Jack was a great kidder and had climbed Elbrus prior to his military service as Bruno had climbed it many times as well while in boarding school in Min Vody as a teenager.

He showed Jack's picture to the kaprol and ordered him to fetch Jack. Bruno picked up a landline and gave several instructions to a man in the maintenance yard.

When the kaprol returned with Jack, he led him to a room that contained a bare wooden desk, and two metal chairs, and a woman who was holding her face in her hands. She looked up when Jack entered the room and he immediately recognized the now conscious Mara Bhutto. He felt his heart pounding in his chest. She gave him a hateful look but said nothing as she covered her face with her hands again.

Jack wondered what was going to happen, the Russians knew he was the leader of the team. But Mara's presence explained a lot. The guard left them in the room,

A man entered with his face buried in a file of papers. He had a short blonde beard and was wearing a beret that shaded his face. When the man looked up Jack was astonished when he slowly recognized his friend, the Russian officer, Bruno Utecht. Jack noted the square jaw and hawk nose and could not believe his eyes. He exclaimed, "Bruno Utecht!"

Bruno laughed out loud and shouted, "Jack, you old trickster! What in blazes are you doing invading my country? But half your team is dead. Killed by the now dead Chinese that you so ably cut down with the other half of your team! And somehow you brought Mick and Mara as well. But where in the hell is your brother? We must make a complete team!"

Jack felt a momentary wave of grief at the mention of Billy.

"My brother died coming over Elbrus. Our old pal Zhang gave him fentanyl and it killed him, the bitch!."

Bruno shook his head. "Well, three out of four is not bad. I am sorry about your brother, but at least you were successful in invading my sovereign, must I say again, my sovereign country, Russia!"

Mara lifted her face, looked at Bruno and then at Jack. "Kill–no, let me kill him."

Bruno looked at Mara and burst out laughing. "Mara, sweet Mara, you must contain your emotions."

Mara looked at Jack and immediately thought of the hanging execution of her father by an American backed mob that she had witnessed as a young child. That act had started her on her ever growing hatred of everything American. She thought of the destruction of her Serbian terrorists that Jack had defeated in America. He was everything evil!

Mara spit out the words, "He destroyed my ransomware unit! He must be killed immediately!"

Jack felt a horrible clinch in his stomach when Mara uttered the words. He faked a smile and responded, "Mara, what happened? You were such a great kisser in Pakistan!"

"Mara, Mara, contain yourself!" Bruno said. "This is our pal, Jack. And though he has invaded my country–"

"Wait a minute," Jack protested. "We have entry visas we purchased on the border of Georgia!"

"And you just came here to climb, right?" Bruno's voice was loaded with sarcasm. He looked at Mara and added, "Mara. you must leave the room during this interrogation."

Mara rose and left the two men alone. She spit at Jack as she passed him.

Jack wiped his face as he looked at his friend and ally and asked Bruno as his apprehension rose to a high level, "So what's the deal, Bruno?"

Bruno Utecht smiled. "You must be very nervous, Jack. You invade my country with murderous ambitions and you destroy one of my government facilities." Bruno's smile broadened. "Congratulations, my friend. You have solved a difficult problem for me!"

Incredulous at Bruno;s statement, Jack asked, "What the hell do you mean?"

Bruno crossed to Jack and slapped him on the back, "I was sent to Min Vody to throw this Chinese gang out of my country. Now I don't have to. Thank you."

"Great!" Jack exclaimed. "But what about my team and I?"

"Well, you should be sent to prison for at least twenty years," Bruno said with a serious look on his face. "If not executed. He smiled again. "Or I could just turn you over to Mara."

"Holy shit, Bruno!" Jack stood up.

"I know, I kmow, it seems harsh considering what a good deed you've done for me." Bruno stepped back and added," I have a better solution. Does one of your men have helicopter training?"

"I used to fly a small helicopter on the ranch but one of my men has a rating to fly transport helicopters."

"Excellent!" Bruno exclaimed. "Let me tell you my idea. We will take your team to the airport, commandeer a chopper, fly it up to Elbrus, crash it and you can escape to Georgia."

"That sounds great!" But what about you? Won't you get in trouble?" Bruno slapped his thigh hard and growned. He said with a harsh voice,

"Jack, I am going to beat you for a while in order to amuse my Russian guard standing outside the door and then I am going to get you safely out of my country. Could I do anything less for a friend who has saved my life more than once?"

He clapped his hands together and pointed at Jack who caught on and emitted a short cry.

Bruno slapped his own arm and Jack groaned. They repeated the sound circus for half an hour with Bruno shouting in English and Russian and Jack continually saying "No, please!"

Finally, Bruno grabbed Jack's arm and pulled him out of the room. Jack tucked his chin into his throat and staggered as Bruno pulled him, slumping and limping as he walked. In the hallway, Bruno gave instructions to a guard.

When they got to the room where the rest of the team and Mick was, Bruno cuffed Jack in the head and shoved him into the room. Jack stumbled and fell over Tucson.

"Oh, Jack!" Tucson exclaimed. "Are you alright?"

"We're getting out of here," Jack said. All heads turned to Jack with shocked expressions.

"Just play along, guys. We.re going to be okay."

"What the hell you talking about?" Charlie asked in a low voice.

Bruno took an assault rifle from a guard and aimed it at the American. "Let's move!" He shouted. "в Москву!"

He poked Jack with the end of his rifle. "To Moscow!" he translated.

The team all rose and followed Jack. Bruno fell in behind them. "Straight down the hallway," Bruno directed. "We are going outside."

When the team got outside in the parking lot, Bruno pointed at an idling truck with a Georgian Moslem, who wore a cloth wrapped around his head, behind the wheel. The sun was just rising and starting to lighten the scene.

The team slowly climbed in the canvas covered back of the truck. Bruno spoke to the driver, then climbed in and sat next to Tucson. "What a lovely warrioress!" Bruno exclaimed. "I wish I had more time to become acquainted. Do you think you could stay awhile?" He smiled at Tucson who was still in shock. "Is he hitting on me, Jack?" She asked in a low voice.

"He stole a newsbabe from me in Pakistan so I'd say, Hell, yeah, if he only had the time."

"So you know him?" Joe asked.

"Yeah, we served together in raghead land," Jack said. He owes me, big time. That's why he's gonna get us out of here."

CHAPTER 55

After driving the city streets, they finally drove into the countryside and stopped at the guarded entrance to a small airfield at 0600 hours.

After the driver stopped the truck, Bruno jumped down and exchanged words with the guard who then motioned to another guard to open the gate to the airfield. The driver pulled forward as Bruno jumped back into the truck and directed the driver to pull into the aircraft parking area . They stopped next to a medium sized helicopter that Bruno identified as a Mil Mi-8.

Joe jumped out of the truck and said "It's a medium sized twin-turbine helicopter, should carry us all."

""Can you fly it?" Bruno asked.. "No sweat," Joe responded.

"Then, let's get out of here." Bruno said. "Load up, Jack."

He handed a key module to Joe as the others climbed aboard the twin- turbine helicopter.

It had wheels instead of skids. As Joe fired up the engines and the team started to climb aboard, Bruno looked around and saw no observers so he drew a pistol, the M17 9mm Sig Sauer, one of his guards had recovered from Tucson, and shot the truck driver to death. He dropped the pistol next to the dead body and climbed into the co-pilot's seat.

The team was shocked but Bruno motioned them to get in the chopper and they hustled aboard.

Bruno turned from the co-pilot seat and noted Tucson's shocked open mouthed expression.

"He was nothing but an off duty Georgian guard hired by the Chinese," Bruno explained. "Nothing but a rag head, and deserved to die for failing to defend his post," Bruno continued. He told Joe to head for Mt. Elbrus, then added, "The Georgian now is my alibi. I'll tell you where I want you to land," Bruno said to Joe. "I went to school in Min Vody. "I know every square meter of that mountain. It should take about a half hour to get to our landing spot."

"Tell me how you are going to get away with this," Jack asked.

Bruno smiled broadly. " I was going to take you to the main airport and load you in a jet transport for Moscow to hold a trial for your sin of invading Russia. You overpowered the driver and escaped holding me as a hostage.

Joe lifted off and headed towards Mt Elbrus on the city's horizon. "Why are you letting us go?" Charlie asked.

Bruno glanced at Jack and said, "Your leader saved my life during a roadside ambush in Afghanistan and again later when we rescued his friend, ya amerikanskiy negar– that is, an American black soldier." He smiled at Jack. "Now I got a chance to return the favor. For my rubles, it was lucky for you, Amerikantsky!"

Jack clapped his hands and said, "Thanks, Pal! I need to call my Russian guide."

Bruno Gave him one of the cells the Kaprol had earlier taken and Jack, after a couple of misdials, got Nikita's number correctly.

When Nikita answered. Jack greeted him and added, "Did you get the promised funds in your bank?"

"I will check, I cannot thank you enough." "I am so sorry about your son."

"You and I have both lost much," Nikita replied. "Is Natasha taken care of?" Jack asked.

"She will be rich beyond her wildest dreams."

"We'll talk when things settle down. We are getting out of here." "You resolved the local apprehension? That is wonderful news!" "We'll talk when I get back home." Jack disconnected.

CHAPTER 56

Bruno spent a while talking on his satellite cell phone on the flight up to Elbrus. Near the bottom of the huge glacier close to the saddle, Bruno pointed at a flat area on the glacier just above the sheer cliff that the huge waterfall was erupting from about 100 feet below the ledge. The water was gushing straight off the sheer cliff and shooting about twenty feet into the air before it began falling.

Joe slowly landed on the icy glacier with the front of the chopper facing the edge of the cliff as Bruno instructed him. He turned the engine off. Bruno climbed out and motioned for the team to follow. When they had all debarked, he instructed everybody to push the helicopter off the ledge and over the waterfall.

The team closed up and pushed until the chopper started rolling. In seconds it rolled off the cliff and smashed into the waterfall and then the water far below.

"In a mile or so, the helicopter will have disintegrated and all evidence of your team will disappear."

Just then, Bruno's satellite phone rang and he stepped away from the team and talked and listened for about ten minutes, then he motioned Jack to step away from the cliff and the team. "Everything has changed," he said. "My mission has changed. I have kept my superiors up to date and I am instructed to go with you. Will you let me? You guys are still free to leave and I was going to report that you let me go after your escape. Later the strewn wreckage will be found without any bodies and you will have presumably been eaten by wildlife after crashing in the river." Bruno added, "But as I said, I have been instructed to accompany you."

"Why, Bruno?" Jack, mystified by Bruno's request, stared at his Russian savior.

"The Bhutto bitch left Min Vody and the oligarch who has lost his one hundred million dollar megayacht is pissed and wants her back. I have been ordered to track her down if she goes to America. Others will search for her in Asia or the Middle East. It was determined that if I accompany you, I will get to America the fastest way possible. And our intelligence says she is going to America. So FSB wants me to catch up with her."

"Of course you can come with the team! You have saved us!" Jack hugged Bruno and the others lined up and slapped hands with the

Russian when Jack announced that Bruno was coming with them and maybe defecting. Then the team turned, and started hiking up the mountain.

Tucson realized they were not roped together since they had no climbing equipment. She thought about the crevasse she and Billy and Jack had fallen into. "Jack," she called, "How are we going to do this without being roped up?"

"Very carefully when not roped up as always," Jack responded. "Look carefully at every snowbridge you cross. It should take about two hours to get to the saddle huts. We can take the dead climber's ropes. "Jack paused and took several breaths. "And if I remember, the dead guys in the hut were on skis. That will make it very easy to go down the other side of the saddle. And if we use skis we won't even need to rope up."

"Why not?"

"We'll just haul ass over the snow bridges too fast to collapse them."

When the team finally got to the saddle huts at close to 1100 hours, they all collapsed after the hard climb. About fifteen minutes later, Anakan and Dakota went into the hut where the dead climbers were and removed the skis from the dead climbers and brought them outside.

The team and Bruno used their own boots and adjusted the bindings to fit. After a break for meals scavenged from the hut, the team strapped on the skis and took off. Tucson, a great skier, was soon in the lead. The others, except for Jack and Bruno who were also accomplished skiers, took many tumbles at first but soon they were doing alright.

Tucson felt like a great weight was lifting off her shoulders as they fled from Russian hands.

By sunset, they reached the snowline, kicked off their skis and headed for Georgia.

After an hour, they decided to stop as the light grew dim. It was quite chilly as the glacier affected the temp but there was dead brush scattered around so they made a good fire and everyone crowded as close as possible until they were warmed up.

They had nothing to eat but Dakota had a metal cup in his pocket and he repeatedly melted snow until everyone was hydrated.

All the members of the team were exhausted but they were exhilarated at the same time because of their good fortune at escaping Russia.

The next morning, at predawn, the team, with no food or liquids, started down the trail but Jack took a hard left after ten minutes so they would not enter the canyon where the Russian border guards' hut was sitting.

They stopped at several opportunities and drank untreated water from running streams. An hour later, they spotted small farms in the distance and they headed towards the first.

Tucson hailed a farmer walking to his barn and asked where they could get food and drinks. She had to make eating and drinking gestures as she knew no Georgian. She glanced at Bruno but he shook his head.

"I don't speak Georgian," he said.

The farmer looked at her antics and understood, and pointed at a nearby well. Dakota dropped a bucket on a rope down the stone circle well. He quickly pulled up water and everyone lined up to drink until their thirst was quenched.

The farmer made a gesture indicating they could not eat but Jack held up dollar bills and pointed at the farmer's truck. He nodded and in a couple minutes they were on their way to the Mestia airport.

Jack spotted what looked like a restaurant and grabbed the Georgian's arm and pointed at the structure. He gestured as though he was eating and the man nodded, then pulled over. Everyone unloaded and entered the one story concrete structure,

The driver ordered Khachapuri from the host, which turned out to be a combination of fluffy homemade bread shaped like a boat, multiple kinds of cheeses and scrambled eggs in the center when it finally came. The Georgian added an order of khinkali for all which was a pork/beef mix. made with cheese mixed with cottage cheese, mushrooms, and mashed potato.

Tucson gestured for drinks and the waiter brought two bottles of red wine which with he filled all their glasses

The team waited for the food and devoured it feverishly.

Then Tucson called for coffee and after a rich serving, Jack told the Georgian that they were ready to go to the airport. He gave the host a hundred dollars. The man smiled his thanks.

When they got there, Jack paid Gurgann two hundred dollars American and then thanked the non-English speaking Gurgan by giving him a hug.

Joe and Jack went to the airport office to pay for their parking of the jet they had arrived in when they came to Georgia. The bill was over three thousand dollars American and luckily, Jack could use a

Visa to pay the bill and also to pay for fuel that Joe had told the airport to supply when they first landed.

Within an hour, the Gulfstream C-20G jet lifted off whereupon the entire team and Bruno gave a sigh of relief.

Mick looked around and said, "A song: The Yellow Rose of Texas!" Charlie, Joe from the cockpit, and Jack joined Mick.

"There's a yellow whore in Karachi, That I am going to see. No other GI screws her, no other only me."

Tucson, semi-shocked, gasped as the four belted out the next verse.

"She cried so when I stiffed her, It like to broke my heart, And if I ever pay her, We never more will part!"

"One more verse!" Jack shouted. The others belted out more.

"You may talk about your Aghanlass, Or sing of Islamalee, But the yellow whore of Karachi is the only gal for me."

Jack added, "Apologies to Mrs Gross, who made us sing that song and other tunes in grade school. Not this version of course!"

CHAPTER 57

Colonel Weatherbee, burst into General Harmbruster's office and said, "General, Jack Flashhardt is on the line. They made it! Mission accomplished! They're coming home!"

"That's great news!" The General agreed. "Now, how do we get his deserter status relieved as I promised?"

"Easiest would be a Presidential pardon," Weatherbee stated. "I'm not sure that would scrub his record," the General said. "You are probably right."

"But it is worth a run at the problem. The President is going to be delighted. I'll call and let him know that we have solved a major problem!"

"I think the best and cleanest would be to say it was a misfile." Weatherbee said. "Let's try that angle first. But wait until he reports in to me."

"You are right. He has a history of taking his own path." "Any losses?" The General asked.

"He had no combat losses, but he reported that his brother died during the initial climb."

"What a shame!" The General commented. "It is strange. His brother was an accomplished alpinist."

"Hard to say until we get more details."

"See that they report directly to me," the General instructed. "Yes Sir," Weatherbee responded.

CHAPTER 58

Jack and Charlie huddled with Joe once they were clear of Georgia's airspace and Joe had turned on the autopilot.

"We're thinking we need a vacation, new clothes and long showers," Jack said. "I could make a pig in wallow look good."

Joe turned in his pilot's seat and looked at them. "What do you have in mind?" he asked.

"We're thinking of the French Riviera. Maybe Saint Tropez," Charlie said.

"I am pretty sure they don't have an airport. But Nice does. Great beaches and just down the coast."

"Sounds good to me," Jack said. "Let's make it there."

Joe turned and worked on the navigation gear for a while then said, "Next stop, Nice. Look out topless babes on the beach." He looked up from the controls and grinned. "But as I remember, there's a ferry to Saint Tropez. If you guys get tired of mugging the topless girls on the beaches of Nice, we can troop over to Saint Tropez and enjoy any more willing topless babes."

Dakota and Anakan both cheered and Jack yelled, "Hooray for Hollywood!"

"I wish we had some of that Dom the Chinese were drinkin' when we whacked them," Charlie commented.

"You shoulda grabbed a couple of bottles when we left," Jack laughed. "Oh, yeah, I'm sure the Ruskies woulda let us keep any bottles," Charlie laughed as well. He and Jack returned to the main cabin and settled into their seats.

The cockpit radio beeped and Joe answered.

A voice asked, "Do you have a satellite phone?" "Yes," Joe responded.

"Call 720-119-9191," the man's voice instructed.

Joe did as instructed and the same voice said, "You have changed your destination."

"We decided to take a side trip to Nice's beaches for a couple of wind down days."

"That is a negative. Continue to Lisbon, refuel, then the US. Bangor, then Denver. Then refuel and come to Cheyenne."

"Who is this?" Joe asked.

"I sit in the office next to Charlie in Cheyenne. Do not say my name."

Joe said, "Yes, Sir." Then he unbuckled his seat belt, and moved to the main cabin,"

"Alright, team, loosen up."

All looked at Joe except Bruno and Dakota who were asleep. Joe pointed at them and Anakan shook each until they awoke and sat up.

"We have been redirected to refuel in Lisbon. And then make our way back to Warren Base at Cheyenne Mountain."

Jack emitted a groan and said, "General Harmbruster is demanding a recall!" He guessed. "I had hoped he would let me off the hook and let me head back to the Flying Eagle Ranch." He glanced at Bruno. "I wonder if you are the reason."

"I hate to report in, dressed in this Russian garb," Tucson exclaimed. "And please. a shower or bathtub."

The rest of the team looked at their clothes and each other and chuckled.

Charlie went to the galley and found two screw top bottles of chablis wine. He came back to the cabin with armfuls of wine and plastic glasses. "May as well make our party here," he offered.

Bruno opened his pack and pulled out a bottle of vodka. "I brought this to fortify me in the land of bourbon."

After consuming beverages, they all fell asleep, still exhausted from their escape journey. Joe, who had not consumed any drinks, flew on to Lisbon. Once there, Joe was instructed by the same caller from Cheyenne, to taxi to a specific hanger and park inside. He was told a black VW van would escort him to the correct hanger, and sure enough, a VW stopped in front of the jet, turned around and slowly led Joe to a nondescript aluminum hanger about a half mile from the terminal.

Once he parked the jet inside the large hangar, Joe was told to have everybody deplane and transfer to another identical Gulfstream C-20G jet that was parked next to their jet.

He shook Charlie awake and all the others and told them what was up.

Everyone slowly stretched and then followed Joe to the new plane.

After all were settled, Joe was called and told he was cleared to take off with a destination of Bangor. Joe, after takeoff, told Charlie to take over for a couple of hours while he caught a nap as they started across the Atlantic Ocean to Bangor, Maine.

CHAPTER 59

When Joe began a descent into Bangor, Maine at just past 1200 hours, the group shook loose from their lethargy and brewed and drank coffee from the galley.

After finishing her second cup of black coffee, Tucson said, "You guys all smell! Let's stop in Bangor and clean up before we hit Cheyenne Mountain."

"I agree," Jack and Charlie both blurted out. Everyone else began laughing and by the time Joe had coasted to a stop at the parking area for Bangor International Airport, a joint civil-military public airport on the west side of the city of Bangor, in Penobscot County, Maine; they had ordered a van taxi from Alamo Rentals. While Joe, Dakota and Anakan chocked the wheels, Jack and Charlie had the van signed for and waiting to load up. First they drove into Bangor and stopped at a huge Walmart where they all outfitted in new clothes.

Tucson, like the men, opted for Levis, Denali hiking boots, and hooded sweaters. With an unconscious air of rebellion, she picked out a flaming pink bra, pink panties and pink sweater. They stopped at a Hardee's Restaurant next to the Walmart and all ordered double burgers and fries and large milk shakes.

After lunch, the group climbed in the van and drove a block to a Motel 6, where Jack and Tucson went in to rent four rooms. They all separated and agreed to meet at six PM to go eat dinner after they had all cleaned up.

Jack and Tucson went to their room and sprawled on the king bed. In minutes, Jack, comfortable with unavailable Tucson, fell asleep.

Tucson, though still exhausted from their expedition, with a very light touch, stroked his jawline, tried to think happy thoughts, failed, wished for a return to wonderful memories with Jack, failed, and then she rolled to the side and fell asleep as well.

CHAPTER 60

Colonel Weatherbee entered the General's office. "They changed planes in Lisbon and have arrived in Bangor," he announced excitedly. "They spent a night in a hotel to clean up and will arrive here early this afternoon." "Excellent!" General Harmbruster exclaimed. "Do we have the Deserter status taken care of? And the DD 214 issues?" The General leaned back in his chair. "And did you get that Naval Commendation done for Flashhardt,

Davis and Fresco?"

"Yes, General," Weatherbee stated. "All done."

"It is too bad I can't give Flashheart another Silver Star," the General said. "Yes, we would have to be too specific. The Commendation medal is just

for overall excellence. No specifics."

"Can't really say good work invading Russia while assigned to Eagle's Aerie," The General agreed. "So let's have all the paperwork ready and signed when they get here. You'd better get his back pay taken care of as well."

"Yes Sir, and here is the Navy Commendation Medals for Flashhardt and the others," Weatherbee handed a document and medals to the General;

The Secretary of the Navy takes pleasure in presenting the NAVY COMMENDATION MEDAL to
CAPTAIN JACK FLASHHARDT
For service set forth in the following:

For meritorious service while serving in various capacities with the Marine Corps Reserve in connection with operations against enemies of the United States. Captain Flashhardt performed his duties in an exemplary and highly courageous manner. He consistently performed his duties as a professional. By his leadership, and steadfast devotion to duty, he contributed to the excellent accomplishment of his mission.

FOR THE SECRETARY OF THE NAVY
B SURGER
LT. GENERAL A SVENSEN, USMC

"Looks good! You sure can't get more vague than this! Send a thank you note to Surger and Svensen. And do we have the DD 214 doc for his discharge?" Harmbruster handed the citation back to Weatherbee.

"All drawn up. All he has to do is sign and he is discharged honorably." The Colonel glanced at his watch. "They should be landing momentarily," he said.

A few minutes later, Joe flared and made a smooth landing known as a kiss on the landing strip at Cheyenne Mountain. All the team clapped in appreciation of a perfect landing.

When he rolled to a stop in front of a parking area, a marshaller stepped forward with raised arms holding red flashlights which guided him to a parking spot. Two other men moved forward with a temporary stair step so the team could unload. Two black SUVs parked and waited for the team to disembark. When they disembarked, they loaded in the SUVs and were driven to the same large concrete block building with parked helicopters sitting next to it, where they had met General Harmbruster last time.

One of the drivers escorted them into the building and to General Harmbrster's office.

The General and Colonel Weatherbee were standing in front of the General's desk with broad smiles of greeting.

With Jack in the lead, his cap in his hands, they strode forward and stopped in front of the two senior officers.

"We did it, Sir," he said.

"Congratulations, Captain. You did an amazing job!" The general responded. "You have struck an immensely significant blow for America!"

"Thank you, Sir. You previously met the members of the team," Jack said. "This is our new addition. The man who helped us escape. We could not have done it without his help!" Jack grabbed Bruno's arm and brought him forward.

Bruno, almost the same size as Jack, and with blonde hair like Jack, could have been a brother except Bruno had a hard face with a hawk shaped nose. "Good afternoon, General," Bruno said. "If you remember, I met you at the party for Jack's safe return after his escape from the Taliban, at the Marriott Hotel in Islamabad."

"I do remember, Kapitan. That was quite a party." "He would like to request asylum," Jack continued.

"You want to become an American?" Colonel Weatherbee asked.

"I am afraid I have burned my pathways in Mother Russia, when I helped your ransomware attackers escape." Bruno hugged Jack. "But this man has saved my life at least twice in Asia. I could do no less."

"Your bridges," Tucson corrected. "You have burned your bridges."

The General looked at Weatherbee. And said, "Take care of this man.

Whatever he needs."

Weatherbee looked at Bruno who said, "I have significant funds paid to my father from your country, General. They sit in a bank in Switzerland. For his service to the US after WW Two."

Jack added, "His stepdad was a rocket scientist, kidnapped by the Russiians after the war and taken to Russia. But he made them pay for the deed by spying for the US."

"And your country was very generous," Bruno added.

"Good, good!" The General exclaimed. "We will be so again. Please everyone, thank you all for your wonderful service to our country. Davis and you others, go with the Colonel and please step across the hall so I can speak with the Captain alone."

Everyone left with Weatherbee and the General then handed the Navy Commendation document to Jack.

Jack read it and said, "Thank you, General."

The general then handed Jack the DD214 and said, "Sign this and you are a civilian."

Jack took the one page discharge document that showed his rank, medals, and term of service.

"If you want to think about it, tell Weatherbee you need thirty days medical leave which can stretch to sixty if need be," The general said.

"Maybe that is a good idea, General. Thank you."

"You are a good, an excellent Marine. A little loose, too loose, but excellent service," the General added. "And you could have an outstanding Marine Corps career if you tightened up. But I think you could serve the government better right now with more service attached to Eagles Aerie." The General smiled broadly. "And we want you in the unit. You should know that we have a special dispensation from Posse Comitatus, so we can operate freely in the U.S."

"I do tend to get reckless with orders and the Chain of Command," Jack admitted.

"Well, I must say, It works for you. You have done excellent service. And we want you to continue to do so."

"Thanks again, I'll think about it," Jack about faced and left the General's office. He walked outside and waited for the others by the two black SUVs. In about ten minutes, the team joined him, loaded in the vehicles and were driven back to the jet. Minutes later, Joe took off in the refueled aircraft and headed for Billings.

A while after take off, Dakota ad and Anakan sat down behind Jack. Dakota leaned forward and said, the $100,000 the Colonel gave each of us is wonderful. Thank you for the opportunity to earn such a huge sum."

"We are going together and improving a small ranch that the Reservation had agreed to give us, before we left," Anakan said.

"You guys earned it. You were great!"

"It was a super time, as well!" Dakota said. The two Indians got up and moved to the back of the cabin.

Jack took a nap until Tucson sat next to him and shook his shoulder. When he looked up she said, "Joe is taking me back to Denver where I will report to FBI offices there."

Jack regarded the beautiful redhead. "Is it out of line for me to suggest you get treatment?"

"No," Tucson responded, 'but you know what will happen. I get counseling and I will be grounded and my FBI career will be zero from then on."

"Can you get private treatment?" "I can't afford private care."

"Do you want to stay in the FBI that bad?"

"I guess that is what I have to decide." Tucson;s mouth turned down. "The only way you will ever lead a normal life is if you get over what Happened in Big Bear. What those animals did to you."

Tears began sliding down Tucson's cheeks. Jack hugged her and did not know what to say.

After the landing in Billings, the team decided to rent rooms at a Motel Six in town. They all went to their rooms and collapsed.

CHAPTER 61

The next morning at five am, they all went separate ways and Jack caught an Uber to the ranch. His dad was out on the South forty and did not know Jack had arrived.

Jack was still exhausted and went to bed.

After he fell asleep, the cook came and woke him for a call. It was an overseas operator with a connection to a General Hammar calling from Singapore.

The call disconnected before the two could speak. Jack went back to bed and thought about his time spent with the general.

They had met in a Pakistani prison camp. Jack had been thrown in prison without a trial, by elements of the Pakistani government when he tried to warn the Pakistani President about an attempted assanation plot against the man. At the prison he met the Pakistani General Hammar who was in Bharakan Prison for unknown political reasons.

They had decided to escape together and had successfully done so by a very unusual method: they and other prisoners had built a catapult out of hut construction timbers and the two were vaulted over the fence into an adjoining river. Jack's friends had by prior arrangement picked them out of the water.

The General had later assisted Jack and his team in stealing a Pakistani aircraft which was used to haul weapons and munitions needed to a fight with Taliban forces.

Jack thought about how the General had retired to Malaysia to escape the political turmoil in Pakistan and was now living on a large riverboat above Singapore. He had successfully removed himself from the twists and turns of war and intrigue. He wondered why the General was calling him in Montana, where Jack had also escaped the turmoil of war. He finally fell asleep.

He was just setting out for a morning romp with Bullet when the maid, Gertrude, called him back to the house for a call from Malaysia.. He looked at the clear sky and spotted an eagle soaring overhead. He patted Bullet and went back in the house.

The General was on the line, "Hello, Jack?." "This is Jack Flashhardt." He answered.

"I have heard a rumor that you went on a mission to Russia. Is that true?" "How in hell did you hear that?"

"I still have solid connections back home," The General responded. "I just wanted to congratulate you."

"Thank you, General," Jack responded

"Look me up next time you are in Singapore, Good travels."

Jack, numbed by Hammar's call, felt an additional tug of remorse as he thought about the jet that had carried Tucson Luvabrest away from Billings Airport.

He sighed, turned and walked towards his dad's Jeep Wagoneer. He saw Bullet sitting in the back seat with his head hanging out the window and Bill in the front. As he got to the Jeep, he patted Bullet on the head and sat in the front with his dad.

The big dog panted with happiness and leaped onto the back rest to lick Jack.

"Congrats, son, you pulled it off," Bill said. "Yeah, except for Billy."

"So sad!" Bill exclaimed.

"His girlfriend gave him the fentanyl."

"It is a nationwide epidemic," Bill said as he pulled out of the airport parking lot. "And It's getting worse."

"Should we get something to eat before we hike?" Jack asked. "No, the cook, Martha, will have breakfast ready."

Jack looked around at the ranch buildings. The familiar sight of the structures always gave Jack a warm feeling of coming home. But then he thought of last years' experience when the Serbian terrorists and Mara Bhutto had attacked the ranch. He glanced at the grainery where he had snuck up on the first terrorist and then the hayloft where Billy had commandeered the machine gun and shot up the ranch house to distract the terrorists.

To placate himself, he thought of the fun times he had romped around the ranch on his first pony, Junket.

"I'm so hungry I could eat a dead rotten bear," his dad said.

Jack groaned and said, "I'd settle for a flank steak or a hunk of roast chicken."

"Wouldn't it be great if your son, Willy could play in our yard?"

"General Harmbruster gave me a Naval Commendation Letter and said that blew away my deserter status. He also gave me a DD214. If I sign it I have served satisfactorily in the Marines and I will be a civilian."

Bill glanced at his son. "What do you want to do?"

"I don't know, Dad." Jack shook his head. I'm not good at anything. I can no way go back to law school. It seems silly and irrelevant. I'm not trained to do anything except wipe out bad guys. But that seems like a dead end job."

"Relax," Bill said. "You don't have to decide anything right now. Get involved in the ranch operations. See how it goes."

Bullet whined to get out of the stopped car so Jack got out and opened the back door and patted the dog's back as it leaped to the ground.

Jack and his dad walked to the kitchen door and Bill introduced Jack to his new cook, Matilda. She appeared to be about forty five, was slightly overweight and had rosy cheeks and graying hair. She smiled a hello and began serving dinner.

They sat down at the kitchen table and helped themselves to a golden roast chicken, pancakes and grapefruit.

The next day, after a morning run with Bullet, he called the FBI offices in Denver to talk to Tucson. He was told she had been transferred at her request back to Seattle. The receptionist gave him the Seattle office contact information. When he called, the person who answered said that Tucson Luvarest had not arrived yet. When Jack said he was a friend of Tucson and had worked with her in the past, the agent said he would tell Tucson Jack had called. That afternoon, Tucson called him back.

"How are you?" Jack asked.

"I can't go back to work right now," she responded. "I'm just hanging at my house in Port Ludlow. The one you saw last year."

"I remember. You have a great view of the harbor." Jack thought, then added, "I understand. Do you want me to come visit you?"

"That would be nice, but I want to clear my head first," Tucson said with a sad tone In her voice..

"Call me if I can do anything." "I will, I promise."

Jack spent the next two weeks hiking with Bullet, riding the horse, Blaze, and watching news channels. He thought about his son and Penelope often, wondering. He ached to play and tussle with his beautiful son, Willy. He wanted to put the boy on a pony and teach him how to ride.,

He found that with his conservative bias, he could only watch Fox News or a local Billings news channel.

After two weeks, Jack was going crazy with the good life. He even mucked out the barn's gutters a couple of times. But one night, the evening news electrified him when he heard a father bemoaning his fifteen year old daughter's death from an overdose of drugs containing Fentanyl.

Jack went to his dad's office and googled the man and discovered he was a wealthy Silicon Valley entrepreneur. Jess Thormond was forty one years old and his company had been bought out by a large tech company, making Jess an instant multimillionaire.

But Jack realized that no amount of money could bring the girl back to the heartbroken father. Jack discovered that Thormond was a mountain climber like himself and lived in Palo Alto, California.

Jack decided to look the guy up. He told Bill what he was planning and Bill was not overly encouraging, but wished Jack luck when he determined that his son was adamant.

After a restless night of little sleep, Jack unplugged the ranch ev SUV from the solar shed charger and took off for Palo Alto. He headed south to Salt Lake City after tuning in a map of superchargers from Billings to Salt Lake. He only had to stop once to recharge for forty five minutes while eating lunch at a nearby Burger King as the car had a 333 mile range.

In Salt Lake, he got a room in a hotel that had EV chargers. At the hotel, he recharged the car overnight, then hit the road and drove the next day to Reno, Nevada. Again he only had to stop once to recharge during a leisurely lunch and after a long drive, he repeated the last night's performance and also avoided the casinos as he was exhausted from the long drive. The next morning, he drove up to Donner Pass on Highway 80. As he drove up the highway towards San Francisco, he wondered what it must have been like for the Donner Party to be stuck in the Sierra Mountains and so hungry they would eat fellow travelers. He shook his head and could not imagine the Donner Party's plight. He shifted to a happier thought train and smiled as he thought about the zero dollars he had spent on fueling the Tesla during the trip. He smiled even more when he remembered that BIll had invested the three million dollars China had given to BIlly and him as a reward for returning the Concubine Emeralds eighteen months ago – in Tesla stock and had cashed it out when the stock price doubled in six months.

Jack crossed the Bay Bridge from Oakland to San Francisco and took the 101 down to Palo Alto where he got a room in The Stanford Park Hotel on El Camino Real. He had to smile at the unusual combination, except in California, of palm trees and pine trees towering over the street.

His days at Stanford University law school flooded back to him but he had no desire to check out the campus. He was already shocked to see that his favorite bar, the Oasis, was permanently closed, another victim of China's sneak COVID attack on America.

After dropping his bag in the room, he went to the business center and paid twenty five dollars on the internet to get a phone number for Thormond. He called and got a voicemail saying, "Leave a number."

In the room, he put on hiking shoes and went outside to run along the tiny stream that ran under El Camino Real and bordered the Stanford campus as it flowed westward. Huge, bark shredding eucalyptus trees shaded his run. When he reached Stanford University's golf course, he ran alongside a couple of holes until he reached a point where the creek crossed Sandhill Road. There he turned around and headed back to his hotel.

At the hotel, he checked and saw a message from an unknown woman. When he called her back, she identified herself as Jess, Thormond's assistant. When he asked for an appointment, he was told that Thormond was not available.

Stymied, Jack took a shower and decided to go out for a spell of relief from his cares and worries.

He remembered a Starbucks a couple of miles to the south on El Camino so he decided to start with a cup of coffee. He walked there. Jack entered and looked for old acquaintances but saw no one he knew so he ordered a large cup of dark roast and sat at a small table on the side of the cafe to wait for his drink. When he observed a lot of customers looking at their laptops, he thought of the Chinese hackers he and the team had destroyed. He shivered at the memory of firing his weapon on auto at the hacker defenders and then the protectors.

Just then, as his coffee was called out, he tried to dump the memory and luckily he saw a familiar face enter.

It was Carol Steinway, an old classmate from law school. She looked over her shoulder at what turned out to be another old friend, Cos Warner. She encircled his waist as the couple walked to the order counter. After they ordered, Jack called out a greeting.

Carol looked and smiled when she recognized Jack.

"Hey, blue eyes," she called. Long time!" She pulled Cos and they walked to Jack's table. He rose and hugged Carol, then bumped fists with Cos.

"You guys still at Stanford?" Jack asked.

"No," Carol responded with a laugh. She was tall, had long blonde hair and had a great bust over a slender body. She wore black slacks and a blue top. "Cos is just finishing an internship with a Superior Court judge in San Jose, and I am working for a law firm here in Menlo Park." She leaned back and looked at Jack. "We heard you got activated from Marine Corps Reserves and then got in some trouble in Asia."

"More than once," Jack agreed, "but I'm on the right side of the law now." He slipped his hot coffee. "And I am debating whether to sign a DD- 214 and become a civilian."

"Wow!" Cos acclaimed. "Big change. I had heard you got a couple of medals in Afghanistan." He glanced at Carol and added, "And then…"

Jack regarded Cos. The man wore bifocal rimless glasses, was balding and had a scholarly thick waist. He wore a gray suit, with a white shirt and rose colored tie. "Yeah," Jack replied, "I got in some trouble over too aggressively chasing some bad guys but that has been straightened out and like I said, I've been issued a DD-214 which will give me an honorable discharge if I sign it."

"Why wouldn't you?" Carol asked.

Jack took a big breath then said,, "Leaving the Marine Corps is not as easy as it sounds." He took a sip of coffee and added, "The Corps has been pretty exciting. Now I have been trying to get used to ranch life in Montana but…"

"That's right," Carol said. Your family has a big ranch." She grabbed Jack's wrist and added, "Say, has some Montana cowgirl – how do you say it? Hogtied you?"

A server brought two coffees to the couple. Carol took the lid off her latte and sipped it, then asked, "So what are you doing here, Jack? There are no lost steers or lost Asian babes in the Palo Alto hills."

Jack sighed and asked, "I'm sure you've heard about the fentanyl drug epidemic in the US. Well, my brother died after taking fentanyl."

"Oh, Jack! I am so sorry!" Carol exclaimed.

"Yeah, well it was his own damn fault for taking drugs but he did not intend to take fentanyl. So, anyway, I heard about this Silicon Valley jillionaire who lost his daughter to the same drug. So, I thought maybe we could join forces. Jess Thormond."

"He lives here in Palo Alto! Mucho Arribe Ranch." Cos exclaimed. "Right. So I tried to contact him but I've gotten nowhere."

"And you'll never get past his protectors. But guess what? My firm works for him," Carol said with a smile.

Jack looked at her and said, "So you could introduce me."

"Not that easy. But I could at least get you in contact with him. He would decide if he wants to meet you."

"Outstanding!" Jack exclaimed.

"What is it you intend to do?" Cos asked.

"I know one of the ringleaders involved in smuggling the Chinese fentanyl into the US. A Chinese spy and mayhem spreader. She hates

America." Jack slammed his coffee down on the table, the coffee splashed and all three jumped back.

"She is a lot responsible for my brother's death. I'm going to make her and her ilk pay, big time."

"I don't think Thormond would want to get involved in something illegal," Cos protested.

"Since when is it illegal to stop drug smugglers?" Jack asked.

"What you are talking about is a matter for law enforcement," Cos added. "Hey! I've been US law and order for a long time. It's time for a little personal justice for my brother."

Carol looked at Cos and added, "I don't think this is such a good idea." She and Cos rose from the table, and headed towards the front door.

Jack watched his former sometimes work together and more, law student partner walk away.

He threw away his empty cup and left the Starbucks and walked back to the hotel. When he got to his room he collapsed on the bed and called Tucson. Luckily she answered with a happy hello.

"Are you still on leave?" He asked.

"Yes, I am taking two more weeks, then I'll have to report to my office in Seattle."

"Can you come to Palo Alto? I need help." "With what?"

Remembering how his frankness had spooked Cos and Carol he said, "It is regarding Billy's death."

"Well, luckily I have time off so I could come and help you," Tucson paused, then said, "But you understand that my personal issues are still a huge mountain in the way of my behavior."

"I understand and I would not do anything to complicate your life." Jack paused and thought to himself, *but Ms Luvabrest, I do love your breasts and I would love to put my face against them and then continue more heavenly pursuits.*

"Alright," Tucson said, I'll book a flight to San Francisco. You pick me up, so I'll give you arrival time after I get the flight. I will leave tomorrow as early as possible. I will get there by late afternoon.".

"Come on down," Jack said happily, then thought, *Come on down!* "And by the way, I need a weapon."

He tried to watch TV but quickly got bored so he went downstairs to the hotel bar and after two 1800 tequilas chased by a Corona beer, he returned to his room and immediately fell asleep in front of theTV

The next day, he took a long hike along the creek. Across the Stanford golf course, and up into the oak covered hills above Palo Alto. He got a text telling him Tucson would arrive at 2 pm and would wait on the curb outside the luggage area. Jack fell asleep in front of the TV again and was awakened by the lobby attendant at 1:00. He was soon on the 101 freeway heading north. In 45 minutes he spotted Tucson on the sidewalk outside the terminal. He honked and she waved.

"You made it! Come on up and jump in."

A moment later, she opened his door and he got out and threw her baggage in the back seat.

Tucson wore a very form fitting pair of green slacks and a white halter top. She looked sensational!

"I'll bet you are not feeling as good as you look," Jack said.

"I am kinda toast," she responded. She hugged him and kissed him on the cheek.

"Do you have a swimsuit? My hotel pool has a jacuzzi." "Yes, and that sounds perfect!""

"You brought me a weapon?"

"You'll have a Beretta, I've got in my suitcase." "Perfect," he responded.

Jack retraced to the Palo Alto hotel and they went up to his room.

Minutes later, she emerged from the bathroom wearing a one piece blue swimsuit. It showed off her fantastic figure perfectly. Jack was already wearing baggy red swimsuit. The two walked down to the pool area and stepped into the spa.

"Oh! That feels heavenly," Tucson exclaimed. Then she looked at Jack and asked, "What is it you want me to help you with? Another mountain to climb? Another invasion by an FBI-Eagle's Aerie joint operation?"

"You are very responsive to my request for help without supplying any details." Jack responded.

"Are you kidding me?" Tucson asked. "You saved my life in Big Bear! I would do anything for you. Not to mention what bliss we had…before Big Bear."

"No mountains to climb or countries to invade, I am going to strike back at the gang that is sending fentanyl to the US. As I said before, on average three hundred Americans died every day last year from the China supplied drug."

"The US government won't touch it except for physical intervention, because of China," Tucson opined.

"We should be declaring war on the pricks!" Jack slapped the water.

It's China. They're too big," Tucson declared

"So, anyway, there is this guy, a very rich Silicon Valley type who lost his daughter to fentanyl. I have tried to contact him but I can't get through his protectors."

"Why do you want him?"

"He has money and influence."

"Have you forgotten?" Tucson asked. "Because of that China reward last year, you are rich. What do you need him for?"

"I guess you are right. But I don't want to go it alone."

"You have me. You could call Charlie. How about Eagle's Aerie?" Tucson paused and looked at Jack. "Look at what you've just accomplished. You put together a team at a moment's notice. You went to Asia. You destroyed the hackers. You got the team out safely. You were amazing!"

Jack thought for a minute, then concluded, "You're right. I'll call Charlie when we get back to the room."

Tucson climbed out of the pool and retrieved a cell from her purse. "Here, call him now."

"No," Jack said. "Let me think about it." He was distracted by the sight of her beauty as she stood next to the spa in her one piece suit.

She caught his admiring glance and said, "Let's go to the room and see if we can clear your mind."

"Do you mean…?"

Tucson smiled and said, "Are you going to stand there all day?"

CHAPTER 62

Jack kicked his legs in the air and levered himself to a sitting position. "I'm sorry, Jack," Tucson spoke through tears.

"That's OK. Tucson. I just feel so bad for you," Jack responded. "Don't you think you should…"

"Get help? I can't afford private treatment," Tucson swiped the tears from her cheeks with the back of her hand.

"I'll help," Jack interrupted. "It costs too much!"

"I don't care. Let's try it." He stood and looked down at her. "You've been there for me. I want to help."

"Oh, Jack!! Thank you. Maybe I will try. There's a private treatment center in Malibu. With your help, I'll go."

Jack raised Tucson up and hugged her.

"Before I go, let me help you set up a team. I think you will be wasting time trying to get a civilian to join your team. Use your tried and true compadres." Tucson rose out of the bed and hugged Jack. "Give your friends the opportunity to help attack and destroy this fentanyl gang?" She laughed and added, "You didn't mind hauling me in."

"You're right, but there were extenuating circumstances." He couldn't help but glance at her beautiful breasts.

She hit him with a pillow as she laughed. "Call the General," she ordered. "I'm not sure this is a National Security issue," Jack responded. "And you

call the treatment center."

"If what I have heard, over 100,000 Americans are dying every year from fentanyl, it certainly sounds serious to me." Tucson concluded. "And if China is behind it, what if they sent a battalion of soldiers to our shores and killed 100,000 citizens? Would that be serious enough?"

"You're right. I'll talk to the General first." He hugged Tucson. " Call that clinic and see what their opening cost is."

CHAPTER 63

"Charlie," Jack began when his friend answered the phone. Are you rested up enough to take on a new mission?"

"Whoa! Who are you invading now?" Charlie exclaimed with a laugh. "No invasion. I want to stop an invasion by China."

"You talking about the drug stuff we discussed? I saw in the paper yesterday about a college boy here in Denver is dead from fentanyl."

"Right. Fentanyl. The stuff that killed Billy." "What do you want to do?" Charlie asked.

"Well, I've discovered that the Chinese are sending fentanyl to the US as part of their plans to defeat us."

"You had told me about more Chinese Crap. Spare me the details. I'm in." Charlie said.

Jack gave Tucson a thumbs up. She smiled and clapped her hands.

The next morning, Jack and Tucson drove to the Malibu clinic where she had made a reservation for treatment. They took the 101 freeway all the way and the scenery was great: massive vineyards that sprawled on both sides of the road and huge hills covered with massive oak trees. They spent the night in a Motel 6 in Santa Barbara and left early the next morning for Malibu. The drive south on the 101 along the Pacific Ocean was gorgeous. It reminded Jack of his last run in Baja when he met wonderful Margarita. He glanced at his beautiful companion, Tucson, and wished she could rise above her pained past.

The Malibu facility was gorgeous as well. All white, modern one story buildings surrounded by green lawns and palm trees overlooking a cliff that loomed over the ocean.

An older, gray-haired man met them in the parking lot and Jack carried Tucson's bag as they went inside. Jack dropped the bag in the entry, kissed Tucson briefly and waved goodbye. He drove south to the 405, turned south to the Hilton nearest LAX Airport and after he parked, he called Charlie in Denver. He said, "I'm heading your way. Can you set up a meeting with the General?"

"Earliest possible will be in two days. He's in D.C. right now. But I will bring a jet to pick you up.

"A jet! Why the special treatment?"

"Are you kidding? You are a superhero around here! Our operation, which you ran, is still knocking the phones off the desks."

Jack took a big breath, "Good to hear."

Charlie added, "I can be at Santa Monica Airport day after tomorrow around noon. Will that work?"

"Sure," Jack responded. "That will be great! See you then."

With an open evening ahead, Jack called Zhang and when she answered, he asked, "I have some free time, can I swing by and pick up Billy's stuff?"

Zhang felt a thrill shoot through her body, "What time would you come?" Jack glanced at his watch. "It is too late for lunch. How about around

1800 hours."

"No, come earlier," Zhang said. She held her breath then said, "Say around four."

He glanced at his watch. He had an hour and a half to get there. "You still at the same address you and Billy had?"

"Yes. I'll text it to you." "I'll see you at four."

Zhang hung up and felt another thrill of anticipation run through her body. She immediately called Mara Bhutto. When Mara answered, Zhang informed her, after seconds of calculation that Jack would be coming to her home the next night.

"This is Tuesday. He will be there on Wednesday night?"

"Yes,." Zhang falsely confirmed. She hung up and reveled in the anticipation of a free night with Jack Flashhardt.

After Jack hung up with Zhang, he thought of the last time he had been alone with Zhang: what she had said in that hotel room last year, "I won't shoot you, but I must secure you so I can question you. Now do it or I will shoot you!" After he tied himself up, she uttered, "Now perform, Jack, if you want to live. Big white man, Lord of the mountains, get it up!"

"Whooh!" Jack muttered to himself, trying to get the memories out of his head. He wondered what he would do if she tried to repeat her past antics. After all, he thought, she was the agent that had killed BIlly.

He walked to a bar next door to his hotel. It was empty except for a lone bald headed bartender who looked bored. Jack ordered an 1800 tequila shot and a Corona beer chaser. When the bartender put the drink and the bottle of beer down, he pounded the tequila and chased it with half the beer.

It worked! Jack felt better. He put down a $20 dollar bill, found his key fob, then walked out of the bar and over to the hotel parking lot.

In the Tesla, he entered the address that Zhang had texted in the GPS and followed directions that took him to the Beverly Hills address.

Parking his car on the street, Jack felt a pang of anxiety as he walked and then climbed the exterior steps to Zhang's third floor front door. He wondered for a moment whether he should turn and leave. But the thought of cowardly bugging out was immediately more repulsive than anything he could endure with Zhang. A moment after he rang the doorbell, Zhang opened the door, turned and said, "Come in." as she walked into the living room. Her walk away movement revealed that the t-shirt she was wearing only covered the topmost part of her naked hinder. Her delicious rear end flashed at Jack.

"Am I early?" Jack said stupidly as he stared.

"No," Zhang smiled. "Your timing is perfect." She pointed at a khaki canvas bag lying next to the door. "Billy's stuff," she said. Jack stopped but Zhang walked to a leather sofa in front of a white brick fireplace.

"Sit here," she said. She turned and walked into an open kitchen and returned with a tray carrying snacks and a bottle of wine and two long stemmed glasses.

Jack sampled a piece of cheese on a cracker. It was limburger and very tart. *Typical of Zhang,* he thought.

Zhang poured from the already open bottle of Chardonnay and offered a toast. "To life," she murmured. Jack sipped the wine after touching glasses with Zhang. She stood, left the room for a moment then reappeared. She was totally naked and was stunningly tall, slim and beautiful as she crossed the room.

Jack sighed, kicked his saddle shoes off, and unbuckled his belt as Zhang grabbed his pants legs and pulled.

CHAPTER 64

"Can you help me?" Zhang asked Jack as she ran her fingers across his chest.

"With what?" He asked.

"I am being sent back to China. I entered the US illegally and Immigration has caught up with me."

"So what? You're Chinese."

"I am in trouble back in China." "Why?"

"For starters, I am looked down upon because I am not pure Han." "You're part black. But what can I do?"

"I know about two huge shipments of fentanyl China is sending to the US."

Jack rose up on one elbow and asked, "Where and when?" "Will you help me stay in the U.S?"

"I think I can get you a green card." Jack offered. "Perfect!" Zhang exclaimed.

"Tell me what you know," Jack directed the naked beauty.

"I will tell you where and when, but you must leave at once," Zhang said as she rose and stood over Jack, who was still sprawled on the floor in front of the fireplace.

"What's the rush? Tell me the details first." He responded as he gazed at her fantastically flawless body.

They are delivering a 1000 kilogram shipment by drone. It will fly into Camp Pendleton and land next to the beach near a VOR, whatever that is. At the same time, a boat will land on a beach nearby and the second smuggled shipment, also carrying 1000 kilograms, will come from Mexico and as I said, land on the beach near the same VOR. What is that?" Zhang asked.

"Never mind," Jack said as his mind raced over the details. "Mara Bhutto is on her way here." Zhang cautioned.

"Mara! Why? Last time I saw her she was busy in Russia, plotting to kill me."

"She called earlier and I let something slip that made her suspicious. She asked me and I dared not lie." Zhang rubbed her brow with the back of her hand. "I told her you were coming."

"But she's in Russia."

"No! She is here to coordinate the fentanyl delivery. She is in charge of shipments from China. And she said the two huge shipments are due to be delivered next week to Southern California."

"Well, let's welcome her," Jack suggested. "No! She will kill you!"

"I think Mara is a lot of hot air." Jack opined.

Zhang gave Jack an exasperated look. "Do you want a list of the Black Orchid's victims?"

"I've reviewed the list. Very impressive. But Mara and I have a history." "A short ending to your history if you don't get out of here," Zhang concluded. "If you want to die, do it somewhere else."

The mood killed, Jack rose, pulled on his clothes, shook Zhang's hand and said, "Get me the details on the delivery. You said next week?"

"I will find out when she comes here."

Jack picked up Billy's bag and started to leave the apartment. It was dark outside and Jack glanced at his watch. It was just after 2000 hours. He heard voices when he looked down, he thought he recognized Mara and two men coming up the steps. He turned, pulled his pistol and when they entered the front door, Jack shot the two men and ran through the bedroom door. Then he vaulted over the bed, shoved Zhang aside, and ran through the open door to the patio. He leaped over the rail and sailed through the air until he crashed into a bushy pine tree. He felt jarring pain as he struck each tree bough. When he hit the ground, the tree had slowed his progress, but he felt a sharp pain in his lower back.

Ignoring the pain, he began running. Shouts from the stairs told him the pursuit was on. He ran onto and across the driveway and jerked the car door open when he reached it. He heard Mara yell with frustrated anger.

The Tesla started immediately and he floored the accelerator. The electric car shot forward just as a man ran up to the side of the car. He threw an arm out and was struck and knocked to the ground as the car shot away.

CHAPTER 65

Jack could feel a sharp pain in his back. He slowed and tried to steer carefully as he swept down towards the 405 freeway between LA and the San Fernando Valley. When he gained the freeway, he took the south onramp towards Long Beach. He thought about going to the VA hospital in Westwood but he was familiar with the more distant Long Beach facility.

By the time he passed LAX he had calmed down, so he called Charlie.

When his pal answered, Jack said, "Mara Bhutto and her thugs almost got me."

"You're kidding! We left her in Russia."

"She's here now. To handle a fentanyl drug arrival. From China."
"When?"

"All I know is sometime next week. At Camp Pendleton."

"They are smuggling drugs onto Camp Pendleton? That's crazy! The Marines will eat them up."

"From what I have heard so far, it sounds like they are using the VOR next to the beach."

"Very High Frequency Omnidirectional Range," Charlie concluded. "A lot of airplanes fly directly over, utilizing its signal. But it's only good for line of sight up to about one hundred miles."

"I'm pretty sure they know where they are going. I remember seeing the monument of it between the freeway and the beach. In an abandoned tomato field. Maybe they figure, the Marines will just think it is another wayward civilian flight, using it and looking for guidance, "Jack summarized.

"I'll call Mick and Joe Fresco and maybe you can call the Indians, see if they'll help." Charlie paused, then asked, "You said Mara almost got you."

"Long story, but they were arriving when I departed via a jump onto a landing in a pine tree. After I shot two Chinese guys."

"You're kidding! Are you alright?"

"Screwed up my back, but I'll survive. Talk to the guys and I'll see you tomorrow. But make it John Wayne Airport 'cuz I'm going to the

VA hospital in Long Beach to get checked out. My back is screwed up. From my fast exit."

"I'll see you tomorrow. John Wayne Airport. At the private aircraft parking lot. Call me if there is a problem."

"Thanks, Charlie. I'll see you manana."

By the time he hung up he was almost at the 7th Street exit in Long Beach. He turned off and drove to the VA hospital. By the time he found a parking spot, he realized his back had stiffened up so he exited the parking lot and drove to the valet in front of the hospital. He lowered his window and said to the valet, "I need a wheelchair from my car to Emergency."

The valet, a young Hispanic man nodded and said, "Go park your car." When Jack turned off the car, the valet was waiting with the wheelchair.

Jack had trouble and the boy helped him out of the car and into the wheelchair.

Jack settled back and was pushed into the emergency clinics. At the front desk, he told the reception nurse that he had hurt his back.

The valet left him in the waiting room and in about five minutes a nurse aid called his name and he raised his hand and said "Here.'' The female aide, a very cute Filipino young woman came to him, pushed his wheelchair to a desk with medical equipment on it and took his blood pressure and temperature.

"Pretty high blood pressure," she commented. "What do you expect, gorgeous," Jack responded.

The Asian girl giggled as she entered his info on a computer after asking for the last four digits of his Social Security number.

Then as she pushed him along the hallway to an x-ray room, she joked, "Well, I don't have to worry about you. There's not much harm you can do with an injured back."

Jack looked over his shoulder, and responded, "You look like you are beautiful enough to heal any injury."

The girl laughed as she handed the wheelchair over to two male orderlies who helped him lift onto a table and one of them took an x-ray of his back. The first Asian guy helped him back into the wheelchair and took him back to the waiting room and left him.

After a half hour wait, the cute nurse came to him and said, "You have a crack in the Number 5 Vertebrae. There is nothing we can do. It will heal itself. Here are some medical pads that will loosen you up and alleviate any pain. I will take you to the exit." She applied one of the pads to Jack's back, got behind the chair and pushed him to the building exit, then wistfully said goodbye.

Jack walked to his car and was amazed that the flexible pad the nurse had put on his back had immediately removed any pain he had suffered.

CHAPTER 66

<After determining that Jack had in fact escaped, Mara climbed back up to Zhang's front door and pounded on the door.

Zhang answered immediately. She was dressed in blue jeans and a military t-shirt.

Mara glanced at the bodies of her two men, snorted, and then said, "What was Flashhardt doing here? You said he would be here tomorrow!" Mara shouted.

"He came early. Unexpected." Zhang's face was white with fear. "Why did you not tell me?" Mara's voice was dripping with anger. Speechless with fear, Zhang said nothing.

"Why did you say he was coming tomorrow?"

"That–" Again, Zhang could not get words out. Mara looked hateful with anger.

"You are my friend…" Zhang began to plead. "I could not stop him. I tried to delay him but it was a no go."

Mara considered killing Zhang but she tempered her anger. She could still use Zhang. "Why is Jack here in California?"

"He said something about taking a team member to a hospital or some kind of treatment ward for mentally disturbed. Maybe someone from his Russian team." Zhang tried to think of something to say, then added again, "Maybe someone from his Russian team. And his brother died on the climb of Elbrus. He came here to pick up his brother's belongings."

"So did he mention anything about me or our China shipments next week?

Does he know anything about them?"

How could he?" Zhang concentrated on the prize– the American green card. She stared into Mara's eyes without blinking.

"You realize that you and I stand to make a pile of American greenbacks when this op goes through." Mara stared intently at Zhang.

"Good! I want to leave America. I think the Philippines might be my next stop," Zhang said.

"I'm with you," Mara agreed. "But me for Singapore." She looked closely at Zhang, then added, "You will call Wu Ting and arrange to have transport for the shipments when they land at the VOR. They will need to transport two 1000 kilogram loads from the VOR next to the freeway to a safe haven in San Diego.

They will need to cut an opening in the freeway barrier fence to reach the VOR. There will be a signal light where the trucks will exit the freeway. Have Wu Ting call me and coordinate. Ashe glanced at the two bodies." Have him pick them up and dispose of them."

"I will take care of that. What day are the shippers exactly arriving?

"The drone will arrive at midnight on next Wednesday and the sea delivery should be at the same time," Mara concluded. "And you will be wise to leave as soon as we get paid. This is going to cause a huge upheaval when 2000 kilograms of fentanyl hit the streets disguised as designer drugs."

CHAPTER 67

$\mathbf{J}$ack picked up a couple of tacos and a side of rice at a Rubio's near the Orange County Airport and then checked into an Econo Lodge Hotel. After eating the food, he went to bed and tossed and turned for at least a couple of hours before falling asleep.

He finally slept soundly and got a scheduled wake up call from the front desk at 0700 hours.

He called Charlie's cell who said, "I'll be landing in a little over an hour.

I'll go to the south end of the airport where the private jets park."

"I'll find you there," Jack said. He took a quick shower and put his dirty but bearable clothes on and went downstairs to the Tesla in the parking lot. There were a lot of cars but he spotted the white Model X after surveying the scene. The automatically locking, unlocking door popped open when he touched the door latch. After he started towards the nearby airport, he called Zhang to see if she knew any more about the arrival date.

"Zhang?" Jack asked.

"Yes, hello, Jack. I have news."

Jack took a deep breath then asked, "Tell me."

"A drone will fly from Mexico and land Wednesday at the navigation point. What is it called?"

"The VOR."

"Yes, that is it. And a truck will enter the area by cutting a hole in the freeway barrier fence to haul the drugs away."

"If this works out, as you have reported, I will make sure you get the green card."

I'll call you a day after the delivery. I am getting outta here. I don't want Mara to find me," Zhang said.

Mara Bhutto waved to answer the man hailing her from the docked boat in Ensenada. She had her three borrowed Mexican workers from the Trafficante headquarters ready. After she gestured for the men to load and unload the boat from China, she turned and entered the Baja headquarters for the Mexican Coast Guard. As she walked into the offices, built of white concrete blocks, she felt her heartbeat increase as she grew tense. And when she was accompanied to the Director's office, she handed, without ceremony, a brown canvas bag with $100,000 in American money to the Director, a small Mexican in a khaki uniform. He accepted the bag without comment or a display of gratitude. After covertly glancing at the contents, he made a dismissive gesture with one hand. She turned and walked back on the dock and watched her workers finish unloading fentanyl to be carried back to the Trafficante warehouse and then loaded into an American acquired transport drone and into a sea going vessel..

The last two overland shipments to America had been interdicted by the American border patrol so she was trying another approach by smuggling a load of drugs into California by drone and another by sea.

The losses of the overland attempts had been a bad reflection on Mara's ability. This shipment of 2,000 kilos would make a huge impact when added to crystal meth drugs in her newly acquired warehouse in Los Angeles..

CHAPTER 69

$\mathbf{J}$ack parked in guest parking at the south end of John Wayne Airport. He walked across the street to the private jet parking lot and fifteen minutes later, watched as Charlie parked a beautiful all white Gulfstream C-20G that he had told his pal about. Jack walked out into the parking area as either Charlie or somebody lowered a staircasing.

As he started up the steps, Charlie stood in the entry hatch and waved with a big smile on his face. At the top of the steps, Charlie said, "Say hello to the General."

He stepped aside and allowed Jack to proceed. General Harmbruster was sitting at a table midway into the lounge area. He had a big smile on his face as he watched Jack stop in front of the table. He gestured and Jack sat in the seat indicated.

"I have details on the Chinese drug shipment," Jack said.

"And I have confirmation," the General responded. He laughed to himself, then said, "We got confirmation of the drug shipments you have discovered."

"So Eagles Aerie is onboard with my plan to stop these Chinese crooks?" "We're way ahead of you." The General frowned. "Those Chinese pricks think they can walk onto our shores with impunity?"

"So you've already heard about the drug shipments onto Camp Pendleton? The ones my ex-Chinese spy told me about. She hopes to get a green card out of this:"

The General nodded. "She's got it! And we got confirmation of the smuggling attempt from a paid Mexican official. The Chinese are sending a drone and a ship loaded with fentanyl. We--that is- you and your team are going to stop them."

"Why not use the Marines? After all, it is going to take place on their base."

The General pounded the table with his fist. "We can't involve the military. Posse Comitatus rears its head and the press can't know about this. We can't risk a war with China. And if the Marines get involved, the Press will hear all about it. Your team is the one that can pull this off as smoothly as possible." The General looked at Jack who nodded in agreement. "When the attempt takes place, we will have the freeway interdicted in both directions." The General concluded. "Your team will be waiting for them. "Terminate the Chink pricks! Destroy their drugs!"

He nodded at Charlie who went back in the cabin and returned with Mick Nakamura. Jack's old college roommate who was now a Captain in the Army.

"Mick!" Jack exclaimed. "Hey, there's no mountains in that Camp Pendleton tomato field."

The General growled, "Captain Mick has trained troops with the M60 crew served machine gun. He will bring a M60 and a two man crew to back your team up."

Jack grinned at his old friend, "Should be fun, Chopstick!" He used the nickname Mick had gained when his college friends back at Stanford realized he did not like Asian food.

Mick slapped Jack's shoulder. "Jack, old buddy, this will be great! No one finds action like you. But a Chinese invasion of a tomato field?"

The General interjected, "When Camp Pendlton was purchased by the US way back when, it was mostly agricultural. Some of the farmers still grow crops on the base with grandfathered leases."

"So the shipment and the drone are scheduled to arrive next Wednesday," Jack concluded. "We'll have to be ready."

Charlie added, "I'll have Joe, the Indians, and myself geared up and ready to go tomorrow afternoon. And a weapon and ammo for you, Jack. I have access to the nuclear power plant gates at Onofre. It has been closed for years. We can rendezvous there onTuesday at 1000 hours, day after tomorrow and move on to Pendleton."

"I have rented a suite in Oceanside as a secondary base of operations," Jack said.

The friends raised their arms and clapped hands in celebration, then said "Thanks." to the General and left the jet.

Jack walked back to the Tesla and drove south on the 405 towards Oceanside and the hotel suite he had reserved online. As he settled onto the Diamond Lane, he called Margarita in Texas. She answered with a squealing "Hello!"

"How are things going?" Jack asked.

Oh, Jack! I can't wait to see you. My face has turned out so wonderful. I can't wait to show you. My scars are gone and the doctors tell me that when the redness disappears I will be whole. Thank you, thank you! Words cannot describe my feelings. I want to show you and I don't mean my face."

"That is great news, Margarita. I am so glad."

"Jack, are you at your ranch? Can I come visit? Can I bring my daughter?"

"No, I am on an operation for the government in California."

"That means you must have got your deserter problem solved." Margarita concluded.

"Yes, I feel lucky. But now they have their hooks into me and I will be tied up for a while. But I am so happy your doctors could fix you up."

"Take care, Jack. And let me know when I can see you again. As soon as possible."

Jack took a deep breath, then said, "I will Margarita. You take care."

He hung up and remembered her beauty for a moment, then concentrated on his driving as he was almost in Oceanside. He glanced to the right just in time to spot the white target VOR tower in the middle of a vacant field overgrown with knee high weeds.

He took the harbor off-ramp and soon parked outside his hotel. He had stayed there once when he was on active duty. It fronted on the ocean and had a large pool as well. It was about four stories high and his room was on the top floor. He checked in and went to his room. He stopped and gazed at the expansive ocean view. His other window had a view of the harbor and all its parked boats and yachts.

He wondered where the Chinese invaders, who were still at sea, were at this time. He sat down on the king sized bed and called Tucson.

When he got a recorded message saying she would call back, he left his number and hung up. She called back seconds later.

"I was walking to my bedroom and just missed your call," she said. "Hi, Tucson, how is it going at the rehab center?"

"It is no way fun," she responded. "What are you up to?"

"We're going to interdict Chinese smugglers at Camp Pendleton." "When?"

"They are due to land on Wednesday.""

Tucson said without thinking, "I want to come." "It will be dangerous. Relax and learn in Malibu.:

"Please, Jack."

He thought for a second, then agreed, "You would be a valuable addition. To our team, but I would rather you stay in Malibu."

"I'll be down tonight, Pick me up at LAX." "No, if you are sure, come to San Diego." "I'll call you when I have a flight."

"Great, Tucson! How will your arm up?" "I'll bring my M17 9mm Sig Sauer pistol." "They let you keep that in Malibu?"

"I am FBI. They would not dare search my stuff.." "Sounds good."

Jack was waiting when Tucson arrived at San Diego Airport. She had a big smile and looked very happy. Jack hugged her and as they walked to the parking lot, he asked her again how she was feeling. She frowned and said, nothing had changed but she was hoping for the best in her future.

Noting that implied warning, Jack took her to the Oceanside harbor hotel, wishing forlornly that they could return to past glories. Both being tired, they undressed and flopped into bed.

CHAPTER 70

Tuesday morning, Jack and Tucson dressed early and went for breakfast in the hotel Breakfast room. They each loaded platers with scrambled eggs, hash browns, muffins and red grapes.

As she sat down across from Jack, who had his back to the crashing surf, she could see through a large glass window, Tucson ate a seedless grape and said with a smile, "Great last meal?"

Jack chuckled and replied, "Hopefully Charlie threw some MREs in with our gear."

Neither spoke more as they downed their food. They each topped off their paper coffee cups as they left the hotel and climbed in Jack's Tesla. There were no clouds in the bright blue sky and the temp was a sea breeze-cooled sixty degrees.

In minutes they were on the Five North and driving towards San Clemente.

"What are you learning in Malibu?" Jack asked the question he had wanted to ask all night.

"It's all about dealing with personal tragedy and I don't want to talk about it."

Jack immediately thought about missing Penelope and his son Willy and clammed up. He vowed to head back to the Far East as soon as they solved the Chinese invasion problem. He had to find out if he could change Penelope's mind about America.

Tucson broke his train of thought moments later when she asked, "Do you feel it is right to kill these Chinamen without a trial?"

Jack thought, then said, "They are invaders. Should we have arrested the Japs when they attacked Pearl Harbor?"

"Of course not," Tucson responded. "This is no different."

Tucson thought, then agreed, "You are right."

"Termination to the max!" Jack exclaimed as he glanced at a freeway sign that said San Onofre and slowed to take the off-ramp.

They wound their way along an asphalt road until they reached an open chain link gate where Charlie and the rest of the guys were standing and sitting.

Jack and Tucson both felt their heart rates increase at the sight of the men.

Charlie was talking to Colonel Weather be, the General's tall assistant.

Jack drove through the open gate. They got out of the Tesla and approached the tall officer and Charlie and another young man who looked familiar. When the boy turned around and broke into a smile, Jack was astonished to see his dead brother, Billy!

"You–" Jack was speechless as he hugged Billy.

"Yeah, you abandoned me in a glacier but it did not take." Billy joshed as he hugged his brother.

"How–?"

Jack was speechless.

"I woke up alone in the glacier, made it out and headed south. I eventually got to Afghanistan and then caught a ride home with the Air Force. "When I got to the States, I called the Colonel here and he hooked me up with you guys."

Weather be looked and nodded at the two brothers and Tucson. "I was glad to help.. I have two set actions ready to go. One at the border checkpoint and the other at the north end of Oceanside. When you give the word we will shut down the freeway at both ends. It will take about twenty minutes to vacate the freeway." The Colonel visually assessed Jack and Tucson. "They are already in place but my understanding is that the action will take place tomorrow night."

"That's great news, Colonel," Jack said. "We are ready to close the bad guys down." Tucson and Jack accepted the flak jackets and M4s that Charlie handed them from a pile of gear on the ground. Then they took the ammo belts and small backpacks with sleeping bags lashed to them. They looked inside the packs and saw extra magazines, bayonets, MREs, and night vision goggles.

Billy grabbed Jack again. I have news about Shangri La and you're..." "Let's head out," Jack stopped Billy and then ordered the team of Charlie,

Joe, the Indians, and Tucson and Billy to move out. They rose and made their way away from the gate area and headed south in a single file. Charlie took the point position and Jack took the last position in line. Tucson fell in front of Jack. He could not help but notice that she was wearing skin-tight stretch pants and her rear was as perfect as he remembered. As they walked, he fantasized about walking through a patch of bushes that would lend privacy and then the removing of her tight shorts and all the bliss that would follow. But the events surrounding Billy's return drove everything else from his mind.

Charlie set a rapid pace and they trekked down the coast line but stayed off the beach and far enough from the freeway to their left to be unseen by drivers.

As they hiked, Jack reflected on all the crazy combat situations the General had gotten him involved in in Asia. He had always been very lucky and he hoped his luck would not pass.

Ne was still astonished by Billy's survival and he wondered how he did it.

And he wondered what Billy's news about Shnagr-ila was.

As they walked, they encountered eroded gullies that they trooped down into and then back to the bluffs along the beach. The crashing surf to their right was a constant thunder. It reminded Jack of his run from La Fonda along the Baja coast. As he looked to the ocean he saw the sun dropping. He wondered if there would be a green flash but the sun disappeared below the horizon with no flash.

His thoughts turned to Margarita and he wondered how Margarita looked now that her beauty was restored. That led his thoughts to Penelope and little Willie. *What was Billy's news?*

"I've got to get to Afghanland and find out," he said out loud. Tucson turned her head and asked. "What did you say?"

"Just thinking out loud. Never mind. How are you doing?"

"I'm okay. What are those buildings up ahead with outside lights?" "Marine Base structures. We should skirt them."

Just as he made the comment, Charlie motioned the team to lower their profiles and they crept through Coastal Sge until they passed the structures. No one was visible outside.

Then they encountered a freeway rest stop to their left which they also crept by until they finally got to their objective: a grove of Eucalyptus trees that had an overgrown and abandoned equipment storage park.

Once inside the grove of trees that towered about 100 feet above the fallow fields to the south, they dropped their packs and broke out water bottles. It was eight pm.

Jack, Billy, Charlie and Tucson walked to the south edge of the grove and peered at the empty field to the south.

"So, I guess that is where the drone is going to land," Charlie opined. "Then I guess that is where the Chinese will come from the beach to the drone," Jack said.

We could take a stand next to the drone, " Tucson added.

"I'd say we should set up in that bank of sand dunes and cliff banks overlooking the beach, " Jack concluded.

"Yeah, Boss, that looks good," Charlie agreed. "Let's put one of us out in the field and the rest will flake out here."

"Let's do it." Jack agreed.

When they rejoined the team it had grown by three as Mick and his machine gun crew had caught up with them. The new additions were already sprawled on the ground and sleeping.

Charlie went to the Indians and gave them instructions on where he wanted them to set up as lookouts.

When he returned, he saw Jack was asleep on the ground and Tucson was sitting on the ground about ten feet away. He sat down next to her and asked, "How are you holding up?"

Tucson looked at him and replied, "Okay, I guess. But it is so weird to be potential executioners."

"The General and me as a tagalong met with the President back in DC," Charlie said. "The President said he wants Eagle's Aerie to act alone. He doesn't trust the FBI or the CIA as they are too political. And the Marines can't act because of Posse Comitatus."

"But we've been ordered to kill, not apprehend!"

"Invaders," Charlie replied. "They are invading our country." "But to just kill them…"

"Maybe you should sit this one out." "I think you are right," Tucson said.

It was too dark to read the expression on her face but Charlie could hear the relief in her tone of voice. He rose and walked to the Indians and saw that they were already gone. He decided to wake everyone and have them recheck their weapons but he was interrupted by the two running Indians.

"The drone just landed!" Dakota exclaimed.

"Piece of shit almost ran me down!" Anakan added breathlessly.

"Show time!" Charlie ran to the team and shook them all awake "We gotta get moving. The drone came a day early!" He shouted.

Everyone leaped to their feet, grabbed their weapons and gear and followed Jack and Charlie. As Jack ran he called the Colonel and told him to shut down the freeway.

"We'll run to the drone and set up a line ambush!" Jack shouted. All ran except Tucson, but she slowly followed. The others pulled their flack jackets on as they ran. It was about two hundred meters to the drone. Jack glanced back at the freeway. It was almost empty. Billy drew alongside and said, "Penelope has been kidnapped!:"

Astonished, Jack stopped but two men crashed into him and he started running again.

As the team drew near to the drone, they found multiple men surrounding it. Two flashlights were shining on the drone.

Jack opened fire and the others did as well as they spread out in a line.

Astonished by their discovery, the Chinese whirled and started to fire back as their comrades began to drop.

Jack, leading the others, ran up to a man and hit him with the butt of his rifle. As the man fell, Jack shot him and leaped to the next man. The rest of the team crashed into the Chinese, firing as they swept into the mob around the drone.

Soon the merging groups were shooting, wrestling and dying.

A Chinese man crawled around Jack, scrambling over bodies and he raised a knife as he stood up behind Jack, and waited for a clear run. Jack was trading jabs with a large Chinese man who had a horrible grimace on his face. He did not see the man approaching his back. The Chinese raised his large knife, aiming it at Jack's back. Suddenly he dropped the large knife, threw up his arms and screamed as Tucson arrived on the scene and shot him in the back.

Groans rang out as wounded and dying men screamed with pain.

More Chinese men ran up to the fight as the last front leading men dropped.

As they all passed the drone, Charlie threw a flash grenade under the drone. The Americans whirled and rushed the approaching mob firing as they ran. Behind them, the drone blew up in a ball of fire as the grenade Charlie had thrown exploded. More automatic gunfire rang out and then individual shots as the Americans finished the wounded. Finally the groans stopped and the surviving team took stock.

Charlie shouted, "Tucson is down!"

Jack glanced and noted all of the team was up except Tucson and Billy.. He glanced around for more enemy as he ran to Charlie and the fallen woman. Stopping by the two, he dropped to his knees and looked for a wound or blood. He saw neither as Tucson opened her eyes. Then Jack saw that a spray of bullets had hit the front of her flack jacket.

"Are you okay?" He asked. "I… can't…, she gasped.

He realized that the force of the gunshots had knocked the wind out of her. He bent over and blew into her open mouth and as he noted her luscious lips on his, she coughed and kissed back.

Jack stood and looked at the others. Anakan was clutching a wounded arm and grimacing with pain. Joe was being helped by the other Indian as they struggled to put a tourniquet above a gunshot on his left leg.

Billy was not moving. Jack knelt next to his brother and checked the wounds. They did not look terrible. His gunshots were survivable. *What? Jack wished his brother had told him more.*

Then he noted that Chopstick Mick and his two men were standing in front of two enemies and one of Mick's team was pointing his machine gun at the two Chinamen.

Jack approached and stopped by the grouping of his men and the two Chinamen.

One of Mick's men shouted. "Kill them!"

Suddenly the machine gunner fired a string of shells and the two Chinamen dropped at his feet.

Jack glanced around and saw no other enemy. Tucson staggered to Jack and hugged him fiercely. The rest of the team ran up to Joe on the ground and were joined by Mick, his men, Jack and Tucson, cheering as they also ran and physically collided with the celebrating group and they all shouted and cheered their victory over the invading Chinese.

THE END

POSTSCRIPT

$\mathbf{J}$ack, deliriously happy, took Tucson's hand and said, "Let's walk back to the hotel. "It's only about a mile down the beach and we can Uber back to the car from the hotel later."

The two climbed over the sand dunes that marked the edge of the beach and immediately were confronted by an amazing sight: the waves coming towards the shore were brightly lit up by bioluminescent organisms.

"What in the world is that?" Tucson asked. "That is glowing plankton," Jack responded

As each wave crashed against the shallowing shore, it was transported into a wildly living maelstrom of light.

Stupefied by the scene, the two stood and stared for minutes.

Tucson glanced at Jack and asked, "What happened to the Chinmen's boat?"

"This is a US military beach, I doubt if they would hang around after dropping off their men,"

Finally, Tucson shivered and said, "Let's go to your hotel."

The two began walking south along the beach towards Oceanside and soon they started across the mouth of the glowing San Luis Rey River where it ended in the ocean.

Tucson stumbled when she first stepped in the water. She twisted and fell on her rear end and elbows. Jack lifted her up and they continued across the mouth of the river. They waded in waters that were only inches deep, but the glowing plankton were alive in the waters just like they were in the crashing waves to their right flank, and each step sprayed water that was alive with glowing plankton. The scene was almost magical as they waded across the river for about a half mile.

To make the situation even more spectacular for Jack, Tucson's rear end and elbows, now covered with flashing plankton, were lit up as she walked. The muscles in her shapely rump, covered by her very tight pants, were now flexing with glowing plankton as she crossed the river.

When they finally reached the dry side of the river, Jack leaped forward, wrapped his arms around Tucson and stripped her pants off as they crashed to the sandy bank.

Tucson shouted, "NO!" But after a long moment, she said breathlessly, "Yes. yes, OH, YES!"

194